the
brief

the
brief

simon michael

URBANE
Publications

urbanepublications.com

First published in Great Britain in 2015
by Urbane Publications Ltd
Suite 3, Brown Europe House, 33/34 Gleamingwood Drive,
Chatham, Kent ME5 8RZ

ISBN 978-1-910692-00-4
EPUB 978-1-910692-01-1
MOBI 978-1-910692-02-8

Design and Typeset by Julie Martin

Cover by Julie Martin

Printed and bound by 4edge Limited, UK

urbanepublications.com

"The first thing we do, let's kill all the lawyers"
— HENRY VI, PART 2

PART ONE

1960, LONDON

CHAPTER ONE

Still in his pyjamas, the unshaven man sprawled in an old armchair, one leg dangling over its worn arm. He'd kicked off a slipper and was absently picking at his toe nails with one hand as the other turned the sports pages of a tabloid newspaper on his lap.

The armchair sat in the centre of a bedsit. It was the only inessential piece of furniture and from its stained embrace the man could have stretched his arm to touch the bed behind him, the small table against the wall opposite, and the stove to his right.

Music crackled from a transistor radio sitting on a sticky plastic cloth covering the table and the smell of curried goat drifted through the open window from the kitchen one floor below.

The man hummed along with Adam Faith as he asked his baby what she wanted if she didn't want money. The man was in his 40s. He looked 50, perhaps older. Although quite tall, what little muscle he had once possessed had turned to slack, grey flab.

A telephone started ringing immediately outside the man's bedsit door. He ignored it for a long time but eventually stood, still reading his newspaper and opened his door. It was one of four opening onto a dusty landing. Half-in and half-out of his room, the man waited to see if any of the other tenants would claim the call. Eventually, when they didn't, he lifted the receiver.

'Yeh?' he said.

'Del?'

'Who is it?' he asked.

'Do you no' recognise the voice Del? It's Robbie.' Del's eyes widened and his stubbly jaw dropped. 'Are ye there, Plumber? It's Robbie Sands.' Sands's voice was hard, Glaswegian. Del Plumber reached back into his room, the paper falling to the floor, and turned the radio off.

'Yeh, yeh,' replied Del, 'you just took me by surprise, that's all. When d'ja get out?'

'Last week,' said Sands.

'Yeh?' Plumber paused, his jaw gradually closing as he forced his brain into activity. 'Well, I'm honoured, Robbie, that you should look me up so soon after your release,' he blustered in his fast Cockney. 'Very…wossname… thoughtful.' The forced humour failed to hide the palpable nervousness in his voice.

'Cut the crap Del. I need tae see you.'

'Yeah, that would be…fantastic. Sure. But I'm a bit tied up at present. P'raps I could give you a ring in a few –'

'Tonight.'

Plumber paused. His eyes darted around the tiny room, calculating how long it would take to clear it and disappear. 'Look, Robbie…see…well, things is different now, since you went inside…'

'Och, dinnae fret yoursel' Derek. I'm no' mad at you. I just wanna talk, right? Just talk. Tonight at The Frog.'

'I can't tonight, honest. I've got something on. Next week maybe?'

'What about now? I know where ye are. I could be there in an hour.'

'No, no, no! Blimey, I dunno. I suppose I could slip in a quick one this afternoon.'

'Five o'clock then.'

Plumber reached a decision. 'Alright, around five. Just a quick one, right?'

'I'll be there. Dinnae let me down now.' The line went dead.

Plumber put the handset down slowly. 'Fuck,' he said quietly.

•

The clerks' room was its usual, frenetic, five o'clock worst. Stanley was holding conversations with two solicitors on different telephones, Sally was fending off questions from two members of Chambers while scanning the Daily Cause List, and Robert, the junior, was optimistically trying to tie a brief with one hand while pouring a cup of coffee for the head of Chambers with the other. Sir Geoffrey Duchenne QC had returned from the Court of Appeal ten minutes before, muttering that Lord Bloody-Justice Bloody-Birkett was to the law of marine insurance what Bambi was to quantum physics, ejected another barrister's conference already in progress from his room, and then slammed the door. He could still be heard giving a post mortem of the day's defeat to the senior partner of the firm of solicitors that had instructed him. Superimposed on all this was the clatter of the two typists generating an apparently endless stream of fee notes to go out in the last post.

Charles Holborne poked his head into the clerks' room and wondered if he would be able to make himself heard. He watched with a smile as Sally – pert, cheeky Sally from Romford, two 'O' levels and a nice line in caustic sarcasm – politely told Mr Sebastian Campbell-Smythe, a senior barrister of fifteen years' call, to return to his room and not to disturb her. If he caused her to miss his case in the List, he would not be best pleased, would he? Sally, thought Charles, not for the first time, was ideally suited to life as a barristers' clerk. She was quick-witted and quick-tongued enough to keep twenty-six prima donna barristers in line (all her senior in years, supposed social status and intelligence) without actually crossing the line into rudeness. At the same time she was attractive enough to flatter the crusty solicitors who sent work to Chambers. Stanley, the senior clerk, had high hopes of her.

Sally turned towards the door and saw Charles. She smiled. She liked Mr Holborne. He was alright, one of the few members of Chambers who didn't talk down to her.

'Going to Mick's,' he mouthed, making saucer and cup-lifting motions with his hands.

'Hang on, sir,' she called as he disappeared. His head reappeared round the door. 'Don't forget you've got a con in half an hour,' she said. She reached over for the diary and looked for his initials. 'The buggery,' she said, as nonchalantly as if the case had been a vicar summonsed for careless driving, 'case of Petrovicj.'

Charles nodded, waved, and departed. He'd already read the case papers, and there was time for a cup of tea and a bite to eat at the café on Fleet Street before his client and the solicitor arrived for the conference.

Pulling his coat around him, Charles stepped out from Chancery Court into the rain. A gust of wind bowed the bare branches of the plane trees towards him and threatened to dislodge his hat. He jammed the hat more firmly on his head and walked quickly across the shiny cobbles towards the sound of traffic. He still loved the sensation of dislocation he experienced every time he walked through the archway from the Dickensian Temple onto twentieth century Fleet Street. The Temple had barely changed in three hundred years, and the sense that it was caught in an accidental fold in time was always strongest in the winter, when mist regularly drifted in off the Thames and the gas lamps were still lit at four o'clock each afternoon by a man armed with what appeared to be a six-foot matchstick. The Benchers responsible for running the Inn were debating the installation of electric lights and Charles knew it would only be a matter of time, but he would miss the hiss of the gas, the fluttering flames and the shifting shadows.

Charles turned onto Fleet Street and walked in the direction of St Paul's Cathedral, its dome barely visible in the murky light, and through a small steamy door. He was greeted by a hot exhalation of bacon fat and cigarette smoke.

Mick's offered cheap meals for fourteen hours a day and

was second home to both Fleet Street hacks and Temple barristers. Its all day breakfast, a heart-stopping pyramid of steaming cholesterol for only 1s 6d, was legendary. Charles loved the feel of the place, the easy conversations and ribald jokes about cases, clients and judges. The tension of a long court day – particularly the miseries of the unexpected conviction or swingeing sentence – could here be assuaged in a fog of smoke and chip fat. It was also a welcome change from the rarefied air of 2 Chancery Court, where most of Charles's chambers colleagues dealt in the bills of lading, the judicial review, and the leasehold enfranchisement of civil work. It was, Charles thought with a wry grin, exactly the sort of place Henrietta detested.

At this time of day, with courts adjourning for the night and Mick's being on the route to and from the Old Bailey, the clientele was more barristerial than journalistic, although Charles saw and waved to Percy Farrow, a hack and friend who'd covered several of his cases.

Charles negotiated his way through the narrow gap between the tables towards the formica counter and ordered tea and toast. He looked for somewhere to sit, but Percy was deeply engrossed with a colleague, so Charles squeezed his way to a stool at the end of the counter, picking up a discarded Daily Mirror from an adjacent table. He turned to the back to check the football pages. West Ham had had a decent start to the season but they were playing Spurs that weekend, and Spurs were flying – odds-on to do the double.

When he returned to Chambers twenty minutes later, Charles could hear an argument in progress before he even opened the door. A tall barrister in pinstriped trousers was shouting at Stanley from the door of the clerks' room. He whirled round to confront Charles as he entered.

'There you are! Now look here, Holborne,' he said, using the formality of Charles's surname to show his displeasure, 'this is positively the last time. I'm going to take it up at the next Chambers' meeting.'

Charles looked up at the man. His name was Laurence Corbett. He was six inches taller than Charles, blond and handsome. 'Is there a problem, Laurence?' asked Charles quietly, pointedly using the man's first name.

'Yes. That!' replied Corbett, jabbing his finger in the direction of the waiting room.

'Your con's arrived, sir,' explained Stanley.

'And?' asked Charles.

'And my fiancée has been sitting waiting for me in that room with that rapist of yours!'

'Yes?' inquired Charles.

'Don't act the fool, Holborne. I know for a fact that you've been asked by several members of Chambers to keep your smutty clientele out of Chambers during normal office hours.'

'Is Mr Petrovicj with the instructing solicitor?' Charles asked Stanley.

'Yes, sir, your client is sitting between Mr Cohen and his outdoor clerk. Mr Smith's conference is waiting in there too, sir.'

'Well,' continued Charles, turning to Corbett and quickly stepping backwards to allow Robert to scurry past with an armful of briefs, 'I would have thought it unlikely that your betrothed would be ravaged in front of five witnesses, even assuming that my client was interested in her, which I doubt. Irresistible though you no doubt find her, Mr Petrovicj is charged with buggering another male. He's not, if you'll excuse the pun, into women.' Charles smiled.

'That makes no difference at all, Charles – '

'I thought it was "Holborne",' corrected Charles.

' – as you well know.'

'I would have thought it made quite a deal of difference, particularly to Mr Petrovicj. However, if you'll let me go and start my con,' said Charles, turning his back on Corbett, 'I can remove the evil influence from the room.'

Charles opened the door to leave, and then paused. 'By the way, Laurence, I know you don't do crime, but I'd've thought even you knew that a man is innocent until proven guilty. Mr Petrovicj isn't a rapist, or a bugger for that matter, till the jury says he is.'

•

'Over here, Del!'

Robbie Sands waited for Plumber at a table in the corner of the bar, two empty spirit glasses before him. The Frog and Nightgown was the boozer most frequented by south London's professional villains. Here you could buy or sell anything, recruit for any criminal enterprise, and get yourself killed if you bumped into the wrong man at the wrong time. It was reckoned to be one of the toughest pubs in London, but at this early hour Sands's was the only occupied table. Plumber's eyes flicked around the bar for possible danger and made his way over and sat down opposite the other man. Sands's lean face had acquired a couple more scars since Plumber had last seen him at HM Prison Durham. The Scotsman assessed Plumber, his hard blue eyes narrowing, and shook his head sadly.

'My God, you've got soft,' he concluded. Plumber smiled and shrugged. 'You must ha' put on two stones since I last saw you.'

'I suppose so. I'm older,' said Plumber. 'How you been?'

'Och, no' bad, all things considered.'

'Had a bit of trouble?' asked Plumber, nodding towards Sands's face.

'What, this?' replied Sands, fingering a long scar on his left cheekbone. It was healed, but still pink, relatively recent. 'You know what they say: you should'a seen the other guy. He was in the hospital wing for a month. Well,' he said, after a pause, 'are you gonna buy me a drink or no?'

'Sure, sure Robbie. What'll you have?'

'I'll have another large Bells thank you very much.'

Plumber bought the drinks and returned to the table.

'So, what have *you* been doing for the last four years?' asked Sands.

'Nothing. That's what I was trying to tell you on the blower. I ain't done a single job since that one. I reckoned it was a warning, with what happened an' all that, and I gave it up.'

'So?'

'So nothing. I do a bit of decorating when me cousin can get me the work, and I'm drawing wossname, dole, you know.'

'How's Mary?'

'Dunno. She left two years ago. Ain't heard a word since. My eldest, Maureen, she had a postcard from… wossname… Ireland once, about a year ago. That's it.'

'You must be happy,' said Sands with heavy irony.

'Me? Oh, I get by,' replied Plumber disconsolately. 'Anyway, Robbie,' he said, knocking back his drink, 'I've got a lot on this evening, and I really – '

'Patience,' said Sands, putting his hand firmly on Plumber's arm, 'is a great virtue.' Plumber sat back in his seat reluctantly. Sands took a small sip from his whisky, looked about him, and lowered his voice as he spoke. 'There are two things I want from you Derek, and the first is the whereabouts of a certain Connor Millar.'

Plumber looked surprised. 'Didn't you 'ear?'

'Hear what? Do you no' remember where I've been for the last four year?'

'Yeh, well… he's dead.'

'What?'

'Yeh. Heart attack. He was in the laundrette doing his smalls or whatever, and keeled over. Dead as a… wossname.'

'Bastard,' said Sands, with venom.

'Yeah, well, I get how you feel Robbie, given the circumstances, but the bloke's dead, so what's it matter now?'

'Dead? He's not half as dead as he would ha' been if I'd got hold of him! That fat slob always was lucky.' There was a long pause while Sands nursed his drink.

'What was the other thing, Robbie?' asked Plumber.

'Eh?'

'The second thing you wanted from me.'

'Och, aye. What'd you say to a hundred grand for two hours work?'

Plumber shook his head. 'No, sorry Robbie,' he replied, getting quickly to his feet, 'I knew it was gonna be something like that, and I just ain't interested. Like I said on the blower – '

Sand reached up and grabbed Plumber's wrist in a vice-like grip.

'You sit down!' he hissed dangerously, pulling the other man back to his seat. 'You owe me, you lanky Cockney weasel.'

'I told ya, it weren't me – '

'I know it wasnae you, Derek,' he replied, putting a nasty emphasis on his companion's name, 'or we'd not be having this nice wee chat. And you know I'm not joking, don't you?'

Plumber knew. Only the year before their job together Sands had been acquitted of the murder of a hapless East End cabbie who'd had the misfortune to see Sands emerging from the back of a bullion van as he pulled off his balaclava, and the recklessness to pick Sands out of a line-up.

'But let's not forget: I did four years, four years which you spent free as a bird. Do you no' think they asked me

21

who the driver was, eh?'

Plumber looked down.

'Oh yes they did, and I remained silent, didn't I, my mouth tighter than a carp's arse.' Sands's voice lost some of its edge, but he retained his hold on the other man's wrist. 'I'm just making the point that you owe me, Derek, for four years of silence.'

Plumber looked away unhappily.

'Two hours' work, Derek. 30 minutes for each year inside I saved you. And at the end you'll be a rich man. You could retire, buy yoursel' a wee place in… where was it your Maureen lived? Bournemouth?'

'Hove.'

'There y'are then.'

'I really ain't sure – '

'Oh, but I *am* sure. I'm sure you're the man for the job. I'm sure this one's a winner. And I'm sure no one else's on to it.'

'How can you be sure of that?'

'Cos the bloke whose idea it was got involved in a fight just as he was about tae get parole.' Robbie drew his finger slowly down the pink scar on his face and smiled.

'But – ' started Plumber, but Robbie held up a warning finger to let him finish.

'And most of all, Derek, my friend, I'm *sure* that Detective Sergeant Donegan would love to hear who *did* drive the getaway car four years and eight days ago on a certain robbery.'

'You wouldn't!'

'Aye, I would. This job's perfect. We could both retire forever. And I need you to be able to pull it off. You'd better believe me, Derek: there's nothing I wouldnae do to persuade you.'

Plumber stared hard at him, and then sighed. 'I'll get us another drink,' he said wearily. Sands released him.

•

'Thank you Mr Holborne,' said the alleged buggerer as they shook hands.

'Glad to help, Mr Petrovicj. I'll show you the way out. I think the clerks will have gone by now.'

Charles showed him to the door and pointed down the stairs. 'Are you going to the tube?'

Petrovicj nodded. 'If I can find it. I got lost on the way up.'

'Yes, it's a bit of a maze in the Temple if you don't know it. Go down the stairs and turn right. Turn right under the arch, go diagonally across the courtyard, and down the steps in the far right corner. Follow your nose, and you'll come out on the Embankment. If you get lost, just keep heading towards the river.'

'Okay. Thanks again.'

Charles returned to his room where Mr Cohen, his instructing solicitor, waited.

'Well, what do you think, Charles?'

Cohen and Partners had been instructing Charles loyally since he had been in pupillage, and Charles didn't mind Cohen using his first name. It was an informality that most of his colleagues wouldn't have tolerated.

'I don't know, Ralph. It's certainly helped, seeing him in conference, and I think he'll make a reasonable witness. He has a chance, but much depends on what we can make of Mr Thompson, the complainant, in cross-examination.'

'You're going to have a field day, Charles! Thompson's got half a dozen convictions for dishonesty.'

'Agreed – but nothing serious, and certainly not for blackmail. If Petrovicj is telling the truth, Mr Thompson's moving up a long way from shoplifting.'

Cohen packed his files into his briefcase. 'You haven't had a chance to read the Aaronberg papers I sent down, have you?'

'I'm afraid I haven't yet: things have been a bit hectic for the last week.'

'There's no hurry, but I would appreciate it if you could give them your special attention. The client's *meshpuchah*,' said Cohen, lapsing into Yiddish.

Ralph Cohen, a greying man in his early sixties, had been a solicitor since just after the Great War. He practised in criminal and matrimonial cases, with a sprinkling of business-related disputes, largely in the East End of London where having a Jewish surname had been a positive advantage. Charles on the other hand (né Charles Horowitz) had realised that too-Jewish a surname was going to be a disadvantage at the Bar. Anti-Semitism had been a daily nuisance – sometimes worse – at Charles's school, and his father had prompted him to take up boxing. He'd been good, too, representing the RAF for the year he was in before the war was over and then obtaining a Blue when he picked up his education again at Cambridge. His proficiency at fighting meant that he was never physically challenged there, where the anti-Semitism had been more subtle, but by the time Charles was called to the Bar in 1950 he had been known as Charles Holborne for two years. There was nothing he could do about the dark curly hair and deep brown, almost black, eyes.

Charles never referred to his background professionally and would have preferred others to do the same. Nonetheless, somehow, despite the camouflage of the false surname, someone had known someone; that someone had known Charles's father, and so shortly after Charles finished his pupillage, a drunk driving brief landed on his desk with his name on it – the first ever that was not a "return" from another barrister. It wasn't a case of a "Jewish mafia" as some of Charles's colleagues whispered – had he been no good, he'd never have received a second brief – but as long as he was as good as the next man (or better) there was nothing wrong, as old Mr Cohen used to say, with instructing a nice Jewish boy, even if he pretended he wasn't. A man's got to live, right?

'Family?' asked Charles, slightly embarrassed at not being sure of the exact meaning of the Yiddish word, and slightly irritated at the assumption that he would know.

'In-laws,' replied Cohen. 'Not that close, but close enough that my Sadie's giving me a hard time.'

'What's the charge?'

'Tax fraud. He's in the *schmutter* business – garments – in Mile End'.

'I'll look at it tonight if I can.'

'No rush. It was only committed from the Magistrates' Court two weeks ago; next week will do.'

'O.K.' said Charles, rising. 'I'll see you on Tuesday in any event at The Assizes.'

The two men shook hands, and Charles showed the solicitor out.

•

The pub on the Old Kent Road was getting quite crowded as the evening trade came in. Sands had pulled on a flat cap and was hunched over his drink. He didn't want to be recognised.

'Well, Derek, what do you think?' he asked, leaning forward and raising his voice just enough to be heard over Lonnie Donegan blaring from the jukebox.

'It sounds alright. That is, assuming you've done your homework – '

'I've done ma homework Derek, believe me. I've spent the last week checkin' it out – '

' – but I'm worried about the shooters. We never needed 'em before, and I don't see why we do now.'

'You've never done a job like this before. I'm telling you, we need them. Like I said, they're no' real anyway, just good imitations; just enough to put the fear of God into the bastards.'

'I still don't know,' said Plumber, shaking his head. 'You're talking a lot of time if we're caught. I'm older'n you. I'd be drawing me pension before I was out.'

'But we won't be caught, not if you do everything exactly as I told you.'

Plumber didn't answer at first. 'But I'm just a driver. Can't you get someone else to cross the pavement?'

'It does nae need three people; it needs two. You'n me. Why split it three ways when there's no need?'

'I dunno…. I'm not happy with it.'

'You'll be plenty happy with a hundred grand. Come on, smile you miserable bugger. You're gonna be very, very rich.'

•

Charles wrestled with the key in the lock of his front door, unable to get the thing to turn. His grip on the cloth bag containing his robes and the huge briefcase, both in his left hand, began to slip, and the set of papers clamped between his head and shoulder slid to the floor. He threw everything to the porch floor in exasperation, reached again for the keyhole, and the door opened. A pretty blonde girl of about twenty stood on the threshold, her hair tied in a ponytail. She had some sheets over her arm, as if she had been in the middle of making up a bed.

'Yes?' she asked. 'Oh, it's you Charles,' she said, opening the door to him. Her pretence of not knowing Charles raised his ire one degree further. Fiona, the au pair, had joined the household against Charles's wishes three months previously. Her older sister had been at school with Henrietta, and Henrietta had been prevailed upon to give Fiona a temporary job while she looked around London for something more permanent. Within a fortnight of her arrival Henrietta had warmed to the arrangement and Charles had cooled to it. With no children and a cleaner who came twice a week, Charles had protested that there was no earthly reason to pay the girl good money to sit around drinking coffee all day, but by now she and Henrietta were the best of friends and Fiona's stay had become indefinite. Charles was sure that her insolence, to which Henrietta seemed oblivious and which grew more offensive daily, was learned at her mistress's shoulder.

Charles scooped up his papers and other burdens and brushed past her. 'Where is – ' he began, but Fiona had closed the door and disappeared towards the rear of the house. Charles dropped his things onto the Italian tiled floor and went upstairs to Henrietta's dressing room. That was another innovation he had not liked. When they had moved into the house, a house he had thought far too expensive and ostentatiously large for the two of them, it had at least had the advantage of two spare bedrooms. Henrietta however had decided that she required a "dressing room", which had now become her own bedroom with an en suite bathroom. At least half the week her "bad head" or the demands of his late-night working meant that she slept there.

'Oh, there you are. You're late.' Henrietta was standing at her dressing table, trying to fasten a necklace. 'Here, do this for me, will you?' she said.

She was in evening dress, her long chestnut hair piled in a complicated way on top of her head. The dress was cut very low at the back, and Charles knew she was not wearing a bra. As she approached Charles and handed him the necklace, Charles could smell the perfume he had bought her for Christmas with the proceeds of the indecency plea he had done at Bedford Assizes. Almost everything they owned, with the exception of gifts from her family, was associated with the payment for a particular case, and it amused him, and irritated Henrietta, to identify their belongings by reference to the crime that had paid for them. Thus, last year's holiday had been the fraud at the Old Bailey; Henrietta's dress, the one she was wearing, was the armed robbery at Middlesex Sessions, and so on. Who said crime didn't pay?

'You smell good,' he said.

'Thank you.'

He finished fastening the necklace and kissed the nape of her neck. She moved away without response.

'You, on the other hand, look dreadful,' she said, looking at him in the mirror of her dressing table, and inserting her earrings. 'Late con?' she asked.

'Yes. The buggery I told you about.'

Henrietta shook her head. 'I bet half the Temple covets your practice, Charles.' She disappeared into the bathroom.

'Look,' he replied, calling after her, 'I've had a hard day. Can we save the shabbiness of my practice for the next row? We've the whole weekend free, if it's important to you.'

'I really can't see why you don't move completely into

civil,' she said from the bathroom, ignoring his plea. 'You'd earn more and you'd be able to keep up with the paperwork without working every night. Daddy says you've the mind for it.'

'How nice of Daddy,' replied Charles under his breath, as he followed her into the bathroom where she stood in front of the full-length mirror, straightening her stocking seams.

'And I just don't believe all this social conscience nonsense,' she said. 'I think if you examined your motives, you'd find you just hanker after the gutter.'

Charles put his arms round her from behind and cupped her breasts. 'So? We both like a bit of rough.'

She sighed. 'I may have liked it once, Charles. But now…' She shrugged. 'Take your hands away please. You'll mark the silk.'

'"Had a hard day dear? Sit down and have a drink, and I'll massage your shoulders. Dinner will only be a few minutes",' said Charles, with heavy irony, but he removed his hands as requested.

'Fuck off, Charles,' said Henrietta, walking past him out of the bathroom and beginning to search through her wardrobe. The words somehow carried added venom when spoken so eloquently, and by such a beautiful woman. Charles followed her out and sat on her bed, watching her bare back and slim hips, hating her and wanting her. She found what she was looking for: a fur coat, a gift from her father for her last birthday.

'Etta,' he said more softly, using what had once been his

pet name for her, 'can we stop fighting long enough for you to tell me where we're supposed to be going?'

She turned to him, her face a picture of scorn. '*We* aren't going anywhere. *I'm* going to Peter Ripley's do with Daddy. It's been in the diary for weeks.'

'What?'

'Charles, for God's sake, don't pretend you didn't know about it. I asked you over a month ago if you wanted to come, and you made it plain in your usual charming way that you wouldn't – and I quote – "*voluntarily spend an evening with that bunch of pompous farts*" – close quote. So I made an excuse to Daddy as usual, and agreed to go with him. Mummy's away till next week. Ring any bells?'

Charles nodded. He didn't remember the exact words he had used to decline the invitation, but he'd have to plead guilty to the gist. This particular 'do' was the dinner to mark the end of Mr Justice Ripley's last tour on the Western Circuit before retirement. All the judges and barristers practising on the circuit had been invited and of course Charles's father-in-law, the erstwhile head of his Chambers and now also a judge on the same circuit, would be present. In the absence of Martha, Henrietta's mother, who was visiting her sick sister in Derbyshire, Charles and Henrietta had rather unexpectedly received an invitation.

Charles had often attempted to explain to Henrietta why he hated these dinners. It wasn't that he didn't know which fork to use or how to address a waiter. The Judges, the Benchers, their wives, the High Sheriff – they all shared a common background. They had gone to the same schools, same universities, played cricket in the same teams, attended the same balls, knew the same people. Charles could "busk it" – be convivial, pretend to know what, or who, they were talking about – but it was an act. The sons of Jewish furriers from Minsk by way of Mile End did not mix well with the sons and grandsons of the British Empire. He may have cast off his Jewishness while at University, but he knew he'd never be one of them. When he did attend such events he often came home hating everyone there and, for some reason he couldn't explain, himself.

Henrietta must have read his mind. 'Tell me something Charles: what made you choose a profession where you'd feel such an outsider? And why, if you wanted to do criminal work, did you accept Daddy's invitation to join a mainly civil set of chambers? You talk about "tribes" – which you know I think is complete rubbish, but anyway – and then deliberately join tribes where you know you're going to feel uncomfortable. And then you complain!'

'You don't understand. If you'd grown up – '

'Oh dear,' she interrupted. 'Frying again tonight?' she asked acidly, referring to the chip she alleged Charles carried on his shoulder. 'If you mention the Jewish thing once more Charles, I'll puke. Your father may have grown up in Bow or wherever it was, but it's hardly the Warsaw ghetto. And not everybody's an anti-Semite. I'm not Jewish, and I married you, remember? The only person who's conscious of your religion is you.'

'What? Do you suppose for one minute I'd have got into

Chambers had you not committed the dreadful *faux pas* of marrying me? Half the members of Chambers can't stand me.'

'That may be so. But it's nothing to do with your religion. Every time you upset someone, it's never your fault – it's theirs because they're anti-Semitic. It's a perfect self-defence mechanism.'

Charles stood up wearily, pulling off his tie. 'Can we please leave this one for now Henrietta? I've had a particularly difficult day.'

'Yes, we can leave it for now, Charles, because I'm off. I believe Fiona has made something for you to eat, but if not I suggest you walk to the pub in the village.'

She swept past him, checked, and returned to plant a kiss on his cheek. She was about to move off again, but Charles grabbed her forearms. He looked hard at her, shaking his head slightly, a puzzled and pained expression on his face. Henrietta looked reluctantly up to his eyes and held their gaze for a second. Then the armour of her anger cracked, she bit her lip, and looked away, but not resisting his hold on her.

'I don't know, Charlie,' she said softly, in answer to his unspoken question. 'I wish I did.'

He pulled her gently towards him, wanting to put his arms round her, but she resisted, shrugging her shoulders and shaking her head. She ran from the room. Charles listened to the rustle of her dress and the sound of her feet flying down the stairs, and then the slam of the front door. He didn't hear her crying as she drove away.

CHAPTER TWO

'Three…two…one…GO!' screamed Sands.

Plumber's foot stamped on the accelerator and the two of them were pressed back into their seats as the Rover surged forward down the narrow path.

'Faster!' bellowed Sands.

'I can't control it any faster than this,' shouted Plumber. 'It's the surface.'

The vehicle bounced and shuddered as it hit another pothole and Plumber braked hard. The wheels locked, but he controlled the skid, the car sliding to a halt in a cloud of dust and pebbles, knocking a dustbin flying. He rammed it into reverse, and they shot backwards for a few feet and then, with the tyres screaming, he turned sharp right. Garden gates, wooden sheds and dustbins flew past them in a blur. They emerged after a few seconds into a garage area behind a block of flats, shot across its face, and out onto the road. Plumber slowed the car to a normal speed.

'This'll never do Derek.'

'Look, Robbie, you got me in on this 'cos I'm a driver. I'm telling you, there ain't a fucking police driver in Britain that can take that alley quicker. We've only got about six inches clearance on each side in any event – why do you think I took off the wing mirrors? Any faster, and when we hit a wossname we'll go straight into the side. How long was it anyway?'

Sands checked his watch. 'Thirty-five seconds.'

'Then what are you complaining about? You asked for thirty. That ain't bad for the first go.'

'Aye, first and last go. We daren't risk another. One'll be put down to kids on a joyride. More'n one equals practice, and I don't want the local constabulary wondering what for.'

'That's fine with me. I'll get five seconds off on the day anyway. Always do; it's the nerves. Nice car. I always go for the 3 litre; where d'ya get it?'

'Outside Deptford station.'

Plumber turned to look at Sands in astonishment. 'Ain't that a bit close to home?'

'Look, it was the right car, and it was left unlocked. Well, more or less unlocked. It was asking to be nicked.'

'But it's only a hundred yards from your front door!'

'I know, but then half a dozen cars go from my street in one night. One more won't be noticed.'

'Robbie, this is a P5 Rover. It's a luxury car! Ain't the Prime Minister got one? You should'a nicked something less conspicuous. The Old Bill aren't fools. Even with false plates, they'll work out where it was nicked, and then start wondering who lives nearby.'

'You dinnae think I gave ma real name now, do you? I'm Jock Stein to my landlady.'

'Oh, you gotta be jokin!'

Sands smiled. 'She's no heard of him. She doesnae follow football.'

Plumber shrugged. 'Well, for God's sake keep it in the lock-up till the job. Where to now then?

Sands looked at his watch again. 'Wembley Station.'

'Why?'

'We're gonna see a man about a dog. A gundog, you might say.' Sands's thin face screwed up in a grin of appreciation at his joke. His pale blue eyes almost disappeared behind slitted lids, and the scar pulled taut across his cheek.

'What, already?' asked Plumber, looking concerned. 'The longer you keep those things, the more risk you're in. You want to pick them up on the day of the job and dump them straight after.'

'I know.'

'Well, then?'

'We're picking them up tonight, 'cos the job's tomorrow.'

'Tomorrow? You're joking! Why so soon?'

'Cos it's to our advantage Derek. There's a new Tesco's opened up ten days ago, and they've not paid their milk bill for all that time. There'll be at least fifteen grand more'n usual tomorrow.'

Plumber thought about that. 'How is it you know all about this Robbie? You got a wossname? Inside man?'

'Never you mind your wee head about that. Your share won't be affected. Straight over the roundabout.'

'I know where Wembley Station is.'

They continued in silence. Plumber stopped opposite the underground station, and Sands got out.

'Wait here,' he said. 'I'll only be a sec.'

He walked away from the station towards a small parade of shops and entered a laundrette. Two minutes later he emerged carrying a plastic supermarket bag. He strode quickly towards the car, opened the rear door, put the bag on the floor well, and returned to the front passenger seat.

'Home James,' he said. 'We need an early night.'

•

It was sometimes said of Simon Ellison by his masters at school that he had been rather too conspicuously blessed. He was tall and fair, with a "Boy's Own" hero's rugged good looks, and he was a brilliant sportsman – cricket, rugby, athletics, he excelled in them all. He was, however, rather less clever than he thought he was, and he was certainly not as bright as his two older brothers. Nonetheless, he went to Buckingham where he scraped a third in English Literature, again excelling on the sports field rather than in the examination hall. He had hoped that one of his father's friends might be able to get him something in the City, but somehow that never had materialised. Instead he had resurrected the former family tradition and had joined the Guards, where he spent four happy years. He had then been injured in a riding accident. His left knee was damaged so severely that even six operations could not restore it. His excellence in sports and his army career were ended. He was changed too. The one aspect of his life in which he excelled had been taken from him.

He had decided to go to the Bar. Two years of cramming for exams, and he was called by the Inner Temple at the relatively late age of 29. Once in Chambers his family connections, relaxed style and abundance of charm combined to ensure a satisfactory practice, but he was still not the man he had been. 'The one thing about Scruffy' – his mother would say of him – 'is his temper. Ever since he left the Guards, he has had a deuce of a temper.' And as Stanley, the senior clerk at 2 Chancery Court, was appreciating, "Scruffy" Ellison was in a deuce of a temper at that moment.

'Just look at that!' commanded Ellison, throwing down the court diary on the desk before Stanley.

'What about it sir?' asked Stanley. He had been summoned to Ellison's room and told to sit down at one of the busiest times of the day, and he was anxious not to prolong the interview. The telephones would be ringing constantly back in the clerks' room and although Sally and Robert were competent, he would be needed to fix fees and sort out the diary.

'What am I doing tomorrow?' demanded Ellison.

'Well, nothing at the moment, sir. It's been a bit quiet the last few – '

'But what *was* I doing?' Ellison pointed to an entry against his initials which had been scored through. It had read "*R. v. Mousof*".

'That was a case for Richters –' began the clerk.

'Not "was" a case, Stanley. It *is* a case. It's just that I'm not doing it anymore. What's that?' He pointed to the initials "C.H." further down the page. His finger traced a line across the page. The words "*R. v. Mousof*" had been inserted against Charles's name. 'That suggests that Mr Holborne's now doing the case.'

'Yes, that's right.'

'And I want to know why.'

'When the brief came in I assumed it was for you, as Richters are your clients. So it went in the diary with your initials against it. But then they telephoned and asked to speak to Mr Holborne about it, and I checked. They intended it for him. So I altered the entry in the diary.'

'Do you realise what this case is? It will probably be the best-paid case Mr Holborne does all year! Mousof is stinking rich. He'll pay £750 on the brief, and the case will last a week. It's worth a fortune!'

'I'm sorry, sir. I did check with the solicitors to make sure there hadn't been a mistake, but Mr Holborne acted for them on the double-hander two weeks back while you were in Wales and they were very happy with him. He does have more experience than you at crime,' Stanley suggested gently. It was not a wise comment.

'Of course he fucking does! He does all mine!'

'I'd appreciate it if you didn't swear at me, sir, please. And as for the brief, I don't know what I can do about it when the solicitors actually ask for someone else by name.'

'I'm going to tell you exactly what you can do about it, Stanley. You're bloody well going to ring Richters again and see if you can switch the brief back to me.'

Disputes of this nature over work were not uncommon in any set of chambers, and it was the clerk's job to ensure that ill-feeling was kept to a minimum. On one hand all the members were part of a team, able to offer solicitors a range of experience and expertise on a particular subject, from the head of chambers to the junior tenant. On the

39

other hand each set of chambers was a microcosm of the Bar at large; every member was in competition with every other, and the rules of the marketplace applied. Touting for work was absolutely prohibited, but there was no preventing solicitors from expressing a preference for a particular barrister if he did a better job than his room-mate. Ellison did mainly licensing work for the large West End clubs, but that increasingly threw up criminal cases and, if he was not available, Charles Holborne was the obvious choice. Stanley had realised over the years that Mr Ellison was rather more sensitive about his "returns" than most, and he required gentle handling. So Stanley ignored his aggressive tone and replied as reasonably as he could.

'I can't do that sir, and you know it. If you consider that Mr Holborne has done anything improper to obtain the brief you had better speak to Sir Geoffrey about it,' he said, referring to the Head of Chambers. 'But, honestly sir, as far as I know, Mr Holborne had no hand at all in obtaining the instructions.'

Stanley had never before found himself in the position of defending Mr Holborne. Holborne's practice did not fit well with those of the rest of Stanley's "guvnors" and, frankly, he was happier clerking civil work where he knew what he was doing. He had nothing against Holborne personally but he wished he'd go to some set where they did nothing but crime, and they would both feel easier. But on this occasion Holborne had just done a good job, and had been rewarded for it by the delivery of this brief.

'Now I really must get back,' he said to Ellison as he stood to leave. He held out his hand for the diary, but Ellison did not move. Stanley picked the book up from the desk, and left the room.

CHAPTER THREE

Both sides of the suburban road were lined with semi-detached houses. They had been built before the First World War, at a time when few had family cars, and so most of the houses had no garages. Two-car families and the splitting of family homes into flats meant that there was insufficient room for all the cars in the street, and they lined both pavements from end to end, frost glistening on their roofs. A careful observer would have noticed an exception; one car, a maroon Rover almost at the end of the road. Indeed, the condensation on its windows indicated that it was occupied, and had been for some time. On the other side of the road, almost directly opposite the Rover, was a new block of flats, the only break in the line of identical houses. To the left of the flats was a small service road which led to a row of garages behind the block. Behind the garages however, the service road continued and then turned right to run parallel to and along the back of the Victorian houses. It eventually emerged onto the main road next to the Express Dairies, London North depot; but just before it did so, it served the Dairies' rear entrance, which featured a tall concrete wall topped with wire, interrupted by ten-foot steel gates.

The depot did not deal in milk; it dealt in money. Every large supermarket in the area was supplied daily with cartons of milk. The bigger supermarkets demanded such quantities that a lorry was required to make their deliveries. And once a week security guards, divided into four teams each responsible for a different area, would make a tour of the supermarkets in their area and collect what the dairy was owed. These were hand-picked men. Not for Express Dairies the retired policemen, bouncers, and assorted thuggerie often employed as security guards. They selected and employed only the best. Their men were intelligent, well-trained, and hard. Many were ex-Army. They had never been robbed successfully in the seven years since the present system had been introduced.

Robbie Sands opened his eyes and looked at the clock on the dashboard. 5.52 am. He closed his eyes again. Plumber sat next to him, looking worried. Once again Plumber felt in his anorak pocket. The gun was heavy, bigger than he had imagined. He had examined both weapons carefully the night before and would have been unable to distinguish them from the real ones he'd used as Corporal Plumber during the war. Sands had told him that the barrels had been blocked originally but that they had been drilled out to make them look real from the point of view of someone staring down the barrel. Plumber looked, and felt, deeply uneasy.

He checked his other pocket, also not for the first time. He could feel the cold metal of the handcuffs, four pairs, and the wool of a balaclava mask. He too looked at the clock. He reached into his inside jacket pocket and took out a chocolate bar.

'What, another one?' said Sands. 'No wonder you're getting so fat.'

'I need it. I get all sweaty and shaky if I don't eat. 'Specially if I'm on a job and the old wossname's running. Adrenaline.'

'Suit yoursel'.'

Plumber demolished his bar in two bites and folded the wrapper carefully before putting it in his pocket.

'That's better,' he said.

'Okay. Time to move,' said Sands, opening the passenger door and stepping onto the pavement. He looked up and down the road. It was deserted.

'Shut the door,' pleaded Plumber. 'It's friggin' freezing.'

Sands closed the door quietly, and walked to the vehicle in front, an inconspicuous white Commer van. He opened the door and sat inside. His breath came in white clouds, and within seconds the inside of the windows were covered in condensation. He reached forward to wipe them clear, and then stopped. There were footsteps approaching from the far end of the road. Sands slipped down in his seat and held his breath. A young man wearing a duffle coat and a long green scarf appeared, walking towards the two occupied cars. He stepped off the pavement three cars up from where Sands sat and crossed to the far side of the road. He approached the service road. He was out of Sands's vision, but Sands heard the sound of his footsteps change from sharp clicks to the crunch of gravel as he left the pavement.

Behind Sands's vehicle Plumber turned the ignition key

and the Rover engine coughed into life. Plumber's hand delved into his left pocket and drew out the balaclava. He pulled it on, the wool scratching his face and neck, and saw Sands in the Rover doing the same. Plumber signalled his readiness and Sands half-turned and reached underneath his seat, pulling out a plastic bag. He fumbled inside with one hand, and drew out a short, heavy gun with a wooden stock. It had two barrels, sawn off about eight inches from the stock. He slipped it inside his jacket, took out the imitation revolver and put it beside him on the seat, turned to wave again at Plumber, and pulled away from the pavement. Plumber moved off behind the van. They turned into the service road. The van passed the flats and bounced across the bumpy forecourt of the garages. Plumber caught sight of the man in the duffle coat just as he disappeared around the bend in the service road. Sand's van accelerated hard, slid sideways as he took the corner slightly too fast, but corrected well enough and barrelled towards the man, who spun round. Sands drove straight at him, and he scrambled backwards until his back was flat against the wall of the depot. Sands braked hard and leapt out. He grabbed the man's hair with one hand, and shoved the revolver under his chin.

'No' a peep outta you, sonny, or you're dead meat!' he snarled.

The man turned as green as his scarf and twisted his head away from the gun as far back as it would go. Plumber drew up behind the van in the Rover.

'Keys!' demanded Sands.

'In… in my coat… left pocket,' stammered Duffle Coat. Sands reached in and took them out. He handed them to the man.

'Open up!' Sands ordered, whirling him round, and shoving him towards the gates, a few feet away down the road. He did as he was told. Sands pushed him through the gates, and propelled him across a tarmacked yard towards the door to the building. A featureless brick wall faced them, broken only by a short open flight of metal steps leading to a flush steel door.

'You're gonna unlock that door for us, and then you're gonna turn off the alarm, right?' There was no response. 'Right?' shouted Sands, giving him a further hefty shove in his back that sent him sprawling onto the bottom steps. Sands reached down, grabbed the hood of the duffle coat, and dragged the man to his feet. He had grazes on his face and chin and there were tears in his eyes. He looked terrified.

'Yes, okay, okay, okay! I'll do whatever you say, but please don't shoot me!'

'I'll no' shoot you if you do as you're told. But if you mess with me, laddie, I'll blow your fuckin' head off, and that's a promise.'

Sands pushed him up the remaining steps to the door. Duffle Coat's hands shook violently as he tried to get the key into the lock.

'How many locks?' demanded Sands.

'Two – plus the combination.'

'Do them!'

Plumber's Rover had followed them into the yard and Plumber parked it by the wall in one of the parking bays. He slammed the door shut and raced back into the service road. He dived into the van and drove it past the yard entrance and further down the road. He parked it in a bay next to some dustbins and ran back just in time to follow Sands into the building. Duffle Coat was crouched just inside the door, turning a key in the alarm. Sands yanked him to his feet.

'Is it off?'

'Yes.'

'If you've left tha' on, and the police arrive, do you understand what'll happen?' The other nodded, and then shook his head.

'Imagine this,' explained Sands. 'The police are outside, and they've got their cars, and their guns, and their blue lights. I'm inside, and all I've got is you. How am I to get out? Answer: I use your wee body as a shield, right? If they shoot at me, they hit you first. If they dinnae shoot me, I take you with me, and then *I* shoot you. So, we dinnae want the police, do we? And that means…?'

'Turning off the alarm, yes, I get it. It's off, I promise.'

'Good.' Sands indicated to the door, and Plumber slammed it shut. 'Now, today's your turn on the door, right?'

'Yes.'

'And you sit in this wee cabin –' Sands pointed to a cubicle by the door ' – and look at your fancy new camera, and you open the door when the staff arrive.'

'Yes.'

'Get tae work then.'

Duffle Coat opened the cabin door, and sat on the stool inside. He stared at the gun still pointed at him.

'Do you always sit in your coat?' asked Plumber. The man shook his head.

'Take it off then,' ordered Sands. He did as he was told.

Sands indicated to Plumber and pointed away from the cubicle and into the building. Plumber nodded and turned round. He was in a corridor that ran straight back from the door. He hesitated a second and then set off. A few feet down, to his left, the corridor opened out into a bay into which was set a door, and a glass-fronted cashier's desk. Plumber peered through the glass. He could make out desks, filing cabinets and a safe. He continued down the corridor. Another door opened off to the right. He opened it – a broom cupboard; a final door marked W.C. on the right, and the corridor ended in swing doors. He pushed the doors open and looked out. Stairs ran upwards to his right. To his left was a lift, and before him, the front door of the building. He turned and made his way back to Sands.

'Okay?' asked Sands.

'Sweet.'

•

STATEMENT OF LORNA WESTON

Age: 18
Occupation: Cashier's Clerk
Address: 20 Denham Close, Wood Farm Road, Hendon
NW4

This statement consisting of 3 pages each signed by me is true to the best of my knowledge and belief and I make it knowing that, if it is tendered in evidence, I shall be liable to prosecution if I have wilfully stated in it anything which I know to be false or do not believe to be true. I have read this statement.

At about 7.30 am on Friday 5th. February 1960 I arrived at my place of work, Express Dairies, North London depot, where I work as a cashier's clerk. I was a bit late because my father's car would not start and I had to take a bus. I went up to the security door and through the intercom I identified myself, and asked Tim, who was on duty that morning, to be let in. He opened the door for me. As I went through the door, a man wearing a blue donkey jacket and a mask grabbed me from behind and shouted at me to keep quiet. He held me round my chest with one arm and with the other hand (I think it was his right hand) he pointed a gun at the side of my head. It looked a heavy gun, with one barrel, but I was too frightened to notice anything else about it. He pushed me into the cash office. The door to the cash office is usually kept locked, but it was open on this occasion. As I entered the room, I could see all my colleagues lying on the floor. They were in pairs, and were handcuffed, with the handcuffs going round the central heating pipe that ran along the skirting. I was told to lie down, and I was handcuffed alone to the leg of Mrs Webster's desk. We were all told to keep quiet, or else they would kill us.

We lay there for about twenty minutes, and then the crew of Round 4 called in on the radio. Tim was operating the radio, and, at the direction of one of the men, he told them that it was all clear. Five minutes later the crew knocked on the door, and Tim let them in. The man who had grabbed me was waiting for them in the same way, and he brought them into the cash office and handcuffed them too. One of the men, I think his name is Trevor, would not lie down at first, and the man who had grabbed me hit him on the side of the face with his gun. Two other crews came in, and they were caught in the same way. I cannot remember the order they came in. I only remember the first crew because Trevor was hurt.

The last Crew to come in was from Round 3. Round 3 had an extra call on it that day, as a new supermarket had opened, and Bill Wright, the team leader asked Tim to arrange for someone to help them in with the boxes. The robbers would not allow him to go out or to send anybody, and he made up an excuse about there being an inspection from Head Office and that no one could be spared. I was able to see the screen from where I was lying, and I could see that Mr Wright came up to the security door alone. He asked to be let in, but once the door was open, he stayed just outside. The robber who had been standing by the door prodded Tim with his gun, and Tim asked Mr Wright what he was playing at, just standing there. Mr Wright must have suspected something, because he called out to his van 'Code Red' which means that the police must be alerted. He ran away from the door. I cannot say in what direction because he went off camera. The two robbers ran out of the door. I do not know if they were running after him, but the next thing I heard was this loud bang. From outside I heard the robber who had done all the talking shouting 'Go! Go! Go!' A second later they both came running in, picked up the cash bags they had already accumulated and ran out.

I was released by the fire brigade about an hour later.

My description of the two men is as follows:
(1) The man who did all the talking was about five feet eight inches tall, with a pale complexion. He was quite slim, and had thin, reddish brownish hair. He was wearing a donkey jacket, jeans and sneakers. He wore a balaclava mask and I saw none of his face. He had a Scottish accent.
(2) The other man was about the same height, but he had a heavier build. I didn't see his hair because it was completely covered by his balaclava mask. He wore a green anorak, brown trousers and brown leather shoes. He also wore a balaclava mask. I did not hear him speak. He also carried a gun, but I did not see it well enough to describe it.

I have checked the accounts from the various stores whose money the men stole, and the total taken is £138,530, 16s and 6d.

Signed Lorna Weston.
Signature witnessed by P.C. Clarke 517

•

'Is that you Plumber?'

'Yeh, it's me. You've got a fucking nerve phoning me, Sands.'

'We gotta talk.'

'I've got nothing to say to you. This time I mean it. You seen the papers? That geezer's probably going to die, you fucking lunatic! And I swear, I *swear* Robbie, I won't swing for you!'

'It won't come to that, Del. Calm down and listen tae me – '

'No I fuckin' won't! How could you do it, you Scots maniac? You swore they would be imitation! And you go and take a real shooter, without telling me, AND USE IT!'

'Listen Derek, I know you're upset now, but you've gottae mind what I'm saying. We were both there; we're both in it.'

'No we bloody ain't! I never took no gun, and I never shot no one. That's down to you. So it ain't *me* who's going to hang. I'm getting outta London now, and you can do what you bloody like.'

'Don't be a fool Plumber. We've both got form, and I only got out a few weeks ago. The Bill will be round, asking questions. This is no time tae go off on holiday. Stay put, act like normal.'

'And what if they start asking me about shooters? I'm not going down for murder on account of you.'

'You mean you'll grass me?'

For the first time, Plumber's furious flow was halted. He suddenly realised what danger he might be in, not only from the police.

'I didn't say that,' he prevaricated.

'Now just listen for a sec Derek,' said Sands, in a soft, almost friendly tone. 'You know and I know that even if you do grass me, regardless of what that might do to our friendship, the Old Bill will never wear it. They'll have you for an accessory at least, and that's assuming they believe you when you say you didnae know I had a real shooter. Whatever you say, you've had it. Think about it.'

Plumber had already thought about it, and he knew Sands was right. 'I know,' he whispered, his bluster totally evaporated.

'But I have a solution,' said Sands with confidence. 'Are you listening Derek?'

'Yeh,' he replied wearily.

'They'll never work out who we were, right? But just in case they do, remember this. I've been speaking to a brief I know, and this is what he reckons. The police know there must have been three guns, the two imitations seen inside and the shotgun too, right? If we both swear that we

had the imitations, and never knew that the third gun was
real – '

'How could we not know?' interrupted Plumber. 'One
of us had to carry it to shoot the fuckin' thing!'

'We didn't know it was real, 'cos the third man carried
it.'

'What third man?'

'The third man who was the lookout.'

'Don't be ridiculous, they'll know – '

'How will they know? That first geezer was shitting
hisel' so much, he wouldna ha' known how many there
was of us. As for the rest, they never saw anything anyway.
Who's to say we didnae have a lookout outside?'

'They'll never believe it,' said Plumber, shaking his
head.

'So what if they don't? They've got three guns, and two
men, both denying they carried the shotgun. How can
they prove which of us it was? How can a jury be sure one
way or the other? This solicitor reckons that if we were tae
stick to our stories, no jury could convict us of murder.'

'What about the men outside? They saw you running
out and shooting their mate!'

'I doubt it. The guard himsel' was running away, and
the two in the van were diving for cover. But, anyway, we
both had masks on. We're near enough the same height
and build. Even if they don't believe the third man story,
they'll never prove which one of us was. It'll work.'

'Yeh?' asked Plumber, sceptically.

'Aye. It's cast iron,' assured Sands.

'As cast iron as the job was, eh?'

'You get any better ideas, pal?'

'Do a runner, like I said.'

'That's as good as puttin' up a neon sign saying "Come and get me". Use your loaf, Derek, act like nothing's happened. Okay?'

The line went quiet while Plumber thought about it. Sands listened to his breathing slow.

'Yeh, okay,' sighed Plumber, resigned.

'Right. Now don't contact me for a bit, okay? And for God's sake Derek, don't go splashing your money about. Put it somewhere safe.'

'I know. Bye.'

'Bye.'

•

STATEMENT OF PETER RODERICK MITCHELL

Age: Over 21
Occupation: S.O.C.O.
Address: West Hendon Police Station

This statement consisting of 2 pages each signed by me is true to the best of my knowledge and belief and I make it knowing that, if it is tendered in evidence, I shall be liable to prosecution if I have wilfully stated in it anything which I know to be false or do not believe to be true. I have read this statement.

the brief

*I am a Scenes of Crime Officer presently attached to West
Hendon Police Station. On 8 February 1960 I had occasion
to examine a White Commer FC Van bearing registration
plates number AHX 458. The van was stationary in a
service road at the rear of Corringham Road, Wembley.
Its side doors were open and embedded in the brick walls on
each side of the road, so that access to and egress from the
road was impossible. I examined the tyre patterns left by the
vehicle in the road, and concluded that it had been reversed
at speed up the road with its doors open, apparently with
the aim of blocking the road, the driver making his escape
through the rear doors.*

*I requested assistance from the Fire Brigade, and the vehicle
was moved.*

*On 9 February 1960 at West Hendon Police Station together
with S.O.C.O Paul Smith I examined the van. Behind
the driver's seat I found a plastic bag, which I produce as
Exhibit PRM 1. I sealed the bag in a plastic container and
sent it to New Scotland Yard for further examination.*

*Signed Peter Roderick Mitchell.
Signature witnessed by PC Clarke 517.*

STATEMENT OF WILLIAM JAMES BELLIS.

Age: Over 21.
Occupation: Fingerprint Officer.
Address: New Scotland Yard, London SW1.

*This statement consisting of 1 page signed by me is true
to the best of my knowledge and belief and I make it
knowing that, if it is tendered in evidence, I shall be liable to
prosecution if I have wilfully stated in it anything which I
know to be false or do not believe to be true. I have read this
statement.*

*I have been engaged in the identification of persons by
means of fingerprints for the last eight years. In that time
I have never known impressions taken from different fingers
or thumbs to agree in their sequence of characteristics. On
23rd. February 1960 I received a sealed container which
held a large plastic bag marked PRM 1 from S.O.C.O.
P.R. Mitchell. This bag was examined and chemically
treated. Marks were found on the outside of the bag. These
were developed. The bag was passed to the Photographic
Department and on 17th. March 1960 it was sent to the
Fingerprint Department of the Criminal Records Office
in Bridgend together with photographs and negatives of
the developed impressions. On 11th April 1960 I received
from the Criminal Records Office a card containing a full
set of fingerprints marked "Robert Reginald Sands" which
I produce as exhibit WJB 1. I have examined the ridge*

57

characteristics of the marks taken from PRM 1, and I can state that they are similar in sufficient respects for me to be in no doubt that they were made by the same person whose fingerprints appear on WJB 1.

Signed William James Bellis.
Signature witnessed by D.I. Wade 334.

CHAPTER FOUR

The cold morning air of Deptford was shattered by the simultaneous sounds of breaking glass and the splintering of wood, as the rear kitchen window and the front door of the terraced house were breached. Footsteps thundered up the stairs, and three men charged into a bedroom. The first leapt towards the bare mattress that served as a bed, and, arms held in front of him, pointed a handgun at the head of the dazed occupant of the bed.

'Get the blanket!' he shouted.

Another man grabbed the end of the blanket and yanked it off the mattress. Sands lay there in his underpants, shivering.

'Mr Robert Sands?' asked the gunman, rather less excitedly.

'Yeh?'

'My name is Detective Sergeant Franklin of the robbery squad, and this is Detective Constable Pearce and Police Constable Khan.' The detective flashed his warrant card at Sands.

'So?' asked Sands, calmly pulling the blanket back round him.

'You are under arrest on suspicion of robbery at the Express Dairies depot, Wembley. You are not obliged to say anything unless you wish to do so, but anything you say will be taken down and given in evidence. Do you understand?'

Sands did not reply. He lay back, careful to leave his hands where they could be seen.

'Note "No Reply",' said the sergeant to the two young officers with him, 'at...' he looked at his watch, '...6.28 am.'

'How long you been in?' asked Sands of Franklin. Franklin ignored him. 'You did that very nicely; very correct, very polite. One of the prettiest arrests I've seen.'

'Do you want to put some clothes on, sir, or are you coming to the station in your Y fronts? Stay with him while he gets dressed, would you Bruce?'

•

Sands sat at one side of a table in the small room, his back to the wall. Opposite him were two officers in plain clothes. One, Detective Sergeant Franklin, had some sheets of paper in front of him and a pencil. Sands could see that some at least of the papers were witness statements, but he had tried, and failed, to read them from where he sat. The other officer was older, greyer, and sour-looking. He had small black eyes and a sharp pointed nose, and he wore a short bristly moustache that seemed only tenuously attached to his top lip. He reminded Sands of a shrew. His name was Detective Inspector Wheatley, and he and Sands knew one another of old.

Wheatley was bent. Not bent in the sense that you could bribe him – no, that had been tried. Bent in the sense that there wasn't a rule he wouldn't bend or break into small pieces to get a conviction. He had form for planting evidence, fabricating confessions and threatening witnesses. More than one of his suspects had suffered accidental falls down the cells steps before reaching the safety of a Magistrates' Court. One had actually died "assisting the police with their enquiries." But judges and juries loved him, this decorated war hero, with his spine of steel and clipped no-nonsense style of giving evidence. Sands knew he'd have to be on his guard.

'Well, Robbie, I think you know everyone present,' started DS Franklin. 'I'm going to be questioning you about a robbery that occurred at the Express Dairies depot in Wembley on Friday 5 February this year. I will make a note of my questions and your answers. Before I start, I remind you that you are not obliged to say anything unless you wish to do so but what you say may be put in writing and used as evidence. Do you understand?'

Sands flicked a glance at the older detective who was yet to speak. This formality was unusual, and it worried him.

'I can tell you now,' he answered, 'that I refuse to answer any questions until I have seen ma solicitor, and only then in his presence. That's my answer now, and that will be my answer from now on.'

'It has been explained to you that it is felt that the presence of a solicitor might well hinder the recovery of the property stolen in the robbery. I therefore propose to interview you now. Where were you on the morning of 5th February 1960 at about 6.30 am?'

'No comment.'

'You are being given your chance to explain your side of

the story. If you're innocent, I am sure you'll want to tell us where you were at that time.'

'No comment.'

'Have you read about this robbery, or heard about it on the news?'

'No comment.'

'You must know that firearms were used.'

'No comment.'

Sands watched as the sergeant's pen laboured its way across the ruled notepaper, recording every word spoken. The recording caught up with the interview and Franklin spoke again.

'You realise also that a man has been very seriously wounded, and that he's still in intensive care.'

'No comment.'

'At present you have only been arrested on suspicion of robbery, but there may well come a time when I shall arrest you for attempted murder. Are you sure that you wouldn't like to take the opportunity of explaining what happened?'

'No comment.'

'Do you know Derek Plumber?'

'No comment.'

'He's done a number of jobs with you in the past, hasn't he?'

'No comment.'

'And he's the only one of your erstwhile colleagues at liberty – or alive in fact – at present, isn't he?'

'No comment.'

Franklin looked at his superior officer. Wheatley looked up from the documents he had been reading and stared at Sands with a blank expression. He spoke slowly, as if measuring each word.

'Before Sergeant Franklin terminates the interview, Mr Sands, you might like to think about this: we know you were there. We know you took part in this robbery. The Rover was stolen just around the corner from your digs. You left a plastic bag in the back of the van with a print on it. I shall allow you at a later stage to read the statement of the Fingerprint Officer if you wish. Derek Plumber has also been arrested, and I've interviewed him. He admits being on the robbery, but he says another person, a third person, took the shotgun without telling him, and used it without warning. I suspect that that person was you. Do you still wish to make no comment? This is your last chance to put your side of the story. As far as I am concerned, the robbery is open and shut and you're just wasting everyone's time. It is the gun aspect that concerns me.'

'Still no comment.'

'Very well.'

Wheatley stood, hitched his trousers up, and collected the papers on the desk. 'Take him back to the cells,' he directed Franklin.

'Yes, guv,' replied the younger man. 'Up you get.'

Sands remained where he sat, staring at the table. Franklin looked across at Wheatley, who raised his hand commanding the DS to wait. After a while Sands looked up at Wheatley, and smiled. 'Hang on a sec,' he said.

'Yes?' asked Wheatley.

'I've decided to talk,' said Sands. Wheatley sat down again, and indicated that Franklin should do the same. 'Well?'

'There were three of us. I'm not gonna name the other man. All I'm gonna say is that neither I nor Derek Plumber knew that the third man was going tae carry a real gun.'

'What part in the robbery did you play?'

'I went in with Derek. He drove the Rover, I drove the van.'

'You went into the depot?'

'Yes.'

'You were one of the two men who used handguns to force the employees to lie down?'

'Imitation guns, yes.'

'What part did the third man play?'

'He was the lookout.'

'Did he enter the building?'

'No.'

Franklin put his hand on his superior's arm and raised his eyebrows. He wanted to ask a question. Wheatley indicated to go ahead.

'What vehicle did he arrive in, this third man?'

Sands paused. He had not thought to agree that with Plumber. It would have to be the van or the Rover, but which? If he said one, and Plumber said the other...

'I can't... I refuse to answer questions about what either

of the two other men did. I will answer questions only about what I did.'

'Why then,' asked Franklin, 'did you volunteer that you and Derek went in?' Sands did not reply. 'Wasn't it because you and he have made up this third man, and that one of you two shot the security guard?'

'I've said everything I'm going tae say. I was part of the robbery but I had nothing tae do wi' the shootin'.'

'I shall therefore end this interview here,' said Wheatley. 'I must however inform you that you're now under arrest for the attempted murder of Mr William Wright. Do you wish to say anything? You are not obliged to say anything unless you wish to do so, but anything you say will be taken down in writing and given in evidence. Do you understand?'

'I understand.'

'Put him back in his cell.'

Sands was taken back to his cell, puzzled. He'd prepared and planned for every line of questioning he could imagine, every trick, sleight of hand and beating he might receive at the hands of the police. But DI Wheatley playing it by the book? That was unfathomable.

•

Sands lay on his bunk, his hands behind his head, and stared at the single bulb in its caged recess in the ceiling. He had no way of telling how long he had been there – his watch and other personal belongings had been taken from him when he had arrived at the police station – but he calculated that it must have been around tea time; his stomach was growling. He had refused the greasy egg and chips offered to him for lunch. He knew Plumber was probably in a cell along the same corridor, but he dared not risk calling out. It wouldn't have been the first time that police had waited in such situations for a careless word between cells. He just hoped that Plumber had had the sense not to attempt to make up unrehearsed details of the third man's involvement.

The iron gate that barred the end of the corridor clanged, and Sands heard footsteps approaching his cell. Tea? The door opened, and Wheatley stood on the threshold.

'Stand up Mr Sands,' he said. 'This is a big moment for you. You've just graduated to the big time. Robert Reginald Sands, I must charge you that on the fifth day of February 1960, together with Derek Plumber, you did murder William Wright.'

'What?'

'Yes, Robbie. The guard just died. You are not obliged to say anything, but anything you do say will be written down and given in evidence.'

CHAPTER FIVE

Bow Street Magistrates Court was still a beautiful Victorian building, almost directly opposite the Royal Opera House and a stone's throw from Covent Garden, but it was shabby and it smelt. The corners of the entrance hall were littered with rubbish and cigarette ends, and it stank of stale cigarette smoke and unwashed bodies. It had been raining hard since dawn, and the lobby was packed with defendants, witnesses, lawyers, policemen and reporters sheltering from the rain, and as Charles entered the lobby he was suddenly struck by a smell reminiscent of a damp sheep pen – wet wool.

The lobby was heaving with people, far more than was usual for even a busy Friday. Charles recognised a colleague from chambers in Kings Bench Walk and pushed his way through to him.

'Morning Brian. What's this circus all about?'

'Oh, hello Charles. It's the committal of the Kray twins' arson case. I'm trying to get my plea on before they're brought up. What're you here for?'

'First remand of the Express Dairies murder.'

'Lucky you. Oh – I can see my instructing solicitor! See you later.'

Charles pushed his way through the crowd to the door leading down to the cells, pressed the bell, only once as the grubby notice pinned to the door required, and waited. There was a long pause, and then in the distance, from the other side of the door, he heard the jangling of heavy keys. The wicket in the door opened and a face peered at him.

'Yes?'

'Counsel, to see…' Charles paused, and looked down at his notebook where he had written his clients' names, '… Plumber and Sands.'

The gaoler closed the wicket, and Charles heard him fumbling with the keys. The door swung inward.

'Come in, sir', said the gaoler. 'They've just arrived.' He closed the door behind Charles, and led him to another constructed of heavy steel vertical bars. 'I'm afraid both interview rooms are occupied sir, so you'll have to speak to them in the cell.'

'That's alright, I shan't be long.'

'Down on the left,' pointed the gaoler, 'last door.'

Charles led the way down the narrow corridor. The gaoler opened the cell door. 'Counsel to see you,' he said to the occupants. Plumber and Sands were seated on the bench opposite the door. Plumber stood.

'I'm afraid I'll have to lock you in sir,' said the gaoler.

'That's alright,' replied Charles. The door closed behind him.

'You know where the bell is, don't you?' called the gaoler.

'Yes, thank you.'

Charles held out his hand to Plumber, who stood and shook it, and then to Sands, who shook it also but remained seated.

'My name's Charles Holborne. Mr Cohen has asked me

to come down and represent you on the remand.' Charles drew a deep breath, and then wished he hadn't. As his practice had grown, he did Magistrates' Court cases less than he used to, and he had forgotten the smell of the cells. There was no other like it on earth, an extraordinary blend of fried food, sweat, urine, faeces and fear. The last was the most pungent ingredient – bitter, sharp and completely unmistakeable. Charles had noted that for some reason the cells in The Assizes did not have quite the same smell; perhaps because by the time he had reached The Assizes an accused man had worked out his defence, had met his barrister, and was at least prepared for his trial. The prisoners at Magistrates' Courts on the other hand had often come straight from their interrogations, in some cases had been taken straight off the streets; they still smelt of the chase, animals at bay.

This cell smelled particularly bad, and Charles peered into the lavatory bowl set into the floor in the far corner. It was full.

'We've asked them twice tae flush it,' said Sands, seeing Charles's expression. 'They're too busy.'

'I'll give it a try,' said Charles. He pressed the button on the wall, and shouted through the door. 'Gaoler!'

There was a pause, and then a voice called: 'Are you finished sir?'

'No, but would you please flush this toilet?'

There was no reply. A few seconds later the toilet flushed, operated by the gaoler from outside.

'Okay,' continued Charles. 'Mr Cohen rang me and

gave me very brief details. This is the first time up, right?'

'Yes,' answered Plumber.

'No application for bail?' asked Charles for confirmation.

'Hah!' snorted Sands with a smile.

'I didn't think so,' said Charles. 'It'd be a waste of time, at least until we've seen the prosecution statements. When we know the strength of the case, then we can reconsider.'

'So what're you doin' here, then?' asked Sands. 'PR?'

Charles smiled. 'Frankly, yes. Just holding your hands –'

'And making sure we dinnae sign up with another solicitor,' interrupted Sands.

Charles grinned, not upset. 'It just so happens that I do have Legal Aid forms here for you to fill in. Of course, you're free to nominate any solicitor you like. I understood that Mr Plumber has been with Cohen in the past…'

'Yeh, I was, and very happy I was too,' said Plumber turning to Sands.

'Ach, it's no skin off my nose,' said Sands, stretching out on the bench and putting his hands behind his back.

'Mr Sands, I shall be quite happy to represent Mr Plumber alone, and get the duty solicitor for you, if you like.'

'No. Sign me up – at least for the present. We'll get a silk in, in any event, won't we?'

'You're entitled to a Q.C. on a murder charge, yes, but I'm afraid you may not find one at the Magistrates' Court today.'

'Fair enough,' said Sands. 'Gi' us the form, and show me where tae sign.'

'Just a few questions first,' said Charles, opening the document. 'Is there room for me to sit down for a moment?' Sands swung his legs down, and Charles sat. 'Okay. You first, Mr Sands. From the top: full name of applicant.'

•

Charles pulled open the door of the public telephone booth on the corner of Bow Street. The wall in front of him was plastered with pictures of scantily-clad women offering massage and escort services. Most were in Soho, less than a two-minute walk from where he stood. He smiled, fished in his pocket for some pennies, and dialled Cohen and Partners. He waited for the receptionist to say "Hello?" and pressed button A. He listened for the coins to drop and then spoke.

'Hello, this is Mr Holborne at the Magistrates' Court for Mr Cohen senior please.'

'Please hold, Mr Holborne, and I'll connect you.'

The solicitor came on the line almost immediately.

'Hello Charles. Have fun?'

'God, I'd forgotten how revolting Magistrates' Courts are.'

'I thought you'd enjoy it – can't have you getting too big for your boots. What do you think?'

'Well I'll fill you in when I get back to Chambers, but have you met them yet?'

'I've known Derek Plumber for years. I represented him

on his first driving offence twenty-five years ago. I've not met Sands. I just got a call from the nick asking if I'd like a murder case, and if so, get down to the Court.'

'Blimey. What does that arrangement cost the firm?'

Cohen laughed. 'We're on a rota, but I do know the desk sergeant at the police station quite well. I think he said the first couple of numbers he tried were engaged. So we were lucky I guess.'

'OK. Plumber is straightforward enough, and my sense is that this is well out of his league. Sands on the other hand – quite a character. Reckons he's a hard bastard.'

'Is he?'

'Probably. Can you get his CRB record and we'll check his previous? Anyway, I had a chat with the officer in the case and he gave me the general position. They've both admitted the robbery, both denied the shooting.'

'They've got a run then?'

'It gets more interesting. They both claim a third man was with them, and *he* carried the sawn-off shotgun.'

'What's the police view of that?'

'They think it's a con, but I'm not sure they can prove it.'

'Where does that leave our clients then?'

'If the jury are sure one of them did it, but can't make up their minds which one, they both have to be acquitted.'

'Both?'

'Of course. To convict, they must be satisfied so that they're sure – beyond reasonable doubt. If it could have been either, they can't be sure beyond reasonable doubt which one is guilty. You know, "It's better to let ten guilty men go free than to convict one innocent man", and all that stuff.'

'I see,' said Cohen. He digested the information. 'What if it's a joint charge?'

'Ah, that would be different. If they can be proven to have agreed to the carrying of real weapons and to their use if necessary, I suppose the Crown might prove a joint enterprise in relation to the shooting. But that doesn't look likely in these circumstances. There were, after all, two imitation guns, and from what I can remember of the statements I was shown, our clients were both seen inside the depot with one each. It does tend to support their story of a third man with the real gun.'

'Okay. It looks as if this could be quite an interesting case. Any ideas for a leader?'

'A leader? I thought I was doing this one solo,' laughed Charles.

'Sorry Charles; next time perhaps,' joked Cohen. 'We'll need a silk on this. What was the name of that lady you were talking about recently?'

'Barbara Whitlam. She's excellent. Unfortunately, she's now a judge.'

'Oh. Any other ideas?'

'I don't know. Maybe. I'll make a few calls and let you know. For the present, you'll no doubt be glad to know that Legal Aid was granted subject to their means being within the limits.'

'You mean their declarable means, excluding the £138,000,' joked Cohen.

'Correct. Remanded for seven days.'

'Get your clerks to put the return date in the diary. I don't expect you to do it – do you think there will be a pupil available?'

'I should think so. If there's a problem, I'll give you a call.'

Charles ended the conversation, and dialled Chambers. Stanley picked up almost immediately.

'Stanley? It's Charles Holborne.'

'Yes, sir?'

'I'm on my way back, but could you get me the number of Mr Michael Rhodes Thomas? He's somewhere on King's Bench Walk. Number 5 I think, or maybe 7.'

'Do you want to speak to the clerk or to Mr Rhodes Thomas himself, sir?' answered Stanley.

'Well, if he's in, I'll speak to Mr Rhodes Thomas. Back in 15.'

Charles hung up, pulled his collar up, and stepped out of the phone box. The heavy rain had given way to a thick drizzle. He splashed his way through the puddles and broken paving stones towards the Aldwych. Fifteen minutes later he was back in the Temple, hanging his saturated coat on the back of his door, when it opened slightly and Sally put her head in.

'Afternoon sir,' she said. 'The clerk to Mr Rhodes Thomas is on the line for you. And I thought you might like this.' She had a mug of steaming tea in her hand.

'You're an angel, Sally,' said Charles. 'Can you put it on my desk?'

Sally came in, and Charles saw that she was wearing a dress he'd not seen before, tight in the bodice and flared. It revealed much more of Sally's chest and calves than he had seen before.

'My God, Sally, you're going to give half of Chancery Court apoplexy dressed like that!'

Sally's face flushed. 'Don't you like it, sir?'

'You look great. I just wonder what some of the more… conservative members of Chambers will say.'

'Stanley's already had two complaints,' she admitted. 'He says it's too modern for the Temple.'

'There you are then. But you'll get no complaints from me.' Charles grinned at her, and she smiled back. He's got such lovely eyes, she thought to herself.

'Put Rhodes Thomas through, will you?'

'Right away sir,' said Sally, leaving the room.

The telephone rang again a minute later, and Sally announced the Q.C.

'Hello, Michael?'

'Yes Charles, how are you?'

'Not bad, thank you. How's the family?' asked Charles.

'Growing more expensive by the day, thank you for asking.'

Charles had worked with Michael Rhodes Thomas Q.C. on a case some eighteen months before. He practised from a different set of Chambers, where they dealt with a wide mixture of common law, including quite a lot of crime. The members of the set were by and large friendly, and Charles had co-defended with a number of them over the years. Rhodes Thomas himself was very able, with an affable personality and a common touch that juries appreciated. Charles felt that their approaches were similar, and on the last occasion Rhodes Thomas had led Charles they had not only been successful but they'd had a lot of fun too.

'I know you're extremely busy – ' began Charles.

'Overloaded, as always,' interrupted Rhodes Thomas.

' – But I wondered if I might interest you in a little murder.'

'Yes?' asked the other, interested.

'It won't be up for a while – it's not been committed from the Magistrates' Court yet – but it's a goodie. The Express Dairies robbery.'

'I didn't know they'd charged anyone with that.'

'This morning. I've just seen them – it's a two-hander – called Plumber and Sands.'

'That's not Robbie Sands is it?'

'It is,' replied Charles, surprised. 'Do you know him?'

'Yes. I represented him on the Shell Mex Payroll job, about six years ago. Got him off, too. Small world, eh?'

'Indeed it is. What do you think?'

'Subject to availability, I'd be delighted, assuming the solicitors are happy.'

'They're alright. They've asked me to suggest someone.'

'Fair enough. I assume you don't want me before committal.'

'I don't know yet, but I doubt it. I'll get the solicitors to have a word with your clerk if necessary. Otherwise, perhaps we can organise a conference at the prison after committal.'

'Fine. How are you keeping?'

'Me? I'm okay.'

There was a pause before Rhodes Thomas spoke again. 'How's Henrietta?' he asked.

Charles cast his mind back, and remembered that he had introduced Henrietta to Rhodes Thomas one day when they had met him in the Temple. 'She's fine, thank you.'

'Saw her a few weeks ago,' said Rhodes Thomas.

'At Peter Ripley's retirement dinner?' asked Charles.

'Well, yes, but after that too. At the Ellisons'.' There was another pause. 'I expect you were burning the midnight oil again.'

'Yes. I expect so,' said Charles, absently. 'You do mean Simon and Jenny Ellison?'

'Yes. He's in your Chambers, isn't he?' asked Rhodes Thomas.

'Yes, he is. I just didn't know Henrietta saw them socially.'

'Oh, I think it's something to do with Jenny's charity work. I got the impression that Henrietta was involved too.'

'That must be it then.' There was another pause.

'Let me know if you fancy a drink after court one day, Charles. For a chat, you know?' he said sympathetically.

'Will do, Michael. Thanks.'

•

Ralph Cohen led the way up the narrow stairs and knocked on the door at the top. The door was unlocked and opened by a prison officer. Charles and Rhodes Thomas followed Cohen inside, the door was locked behind them and the lawyers turned to face three prison officers.

'You've all been here before haven't you, sirs?' asked one of them, evidently in charge. The lawyers nodded their assent. Charles had visited clients in most of the prisons in London, especially this one, HM Pentonville, where one section housed prisoners on remand awaiting trial, but he never got over the thrill of being on the inside. It was like entering a secret country with its own language, customs, sounds and smells.

'If you'll just empty your pockets in the bowls, and your briefcases on the table? Then take off your jackets please and hand them to my colleague.'

Charles had already taken out his loose change and keys. He placed two packets of cigarettes on the desk. Charles didn't smoke, but prisoners on remand were allowed cigarettes and Charles had learned that to visit a remand client in prison without cigarettes was a cardinal offence. Even if the client didn't smoke, a pack of cigarettes provided him with ready currency on the cellblock to buy soap, shampoo, phone calls and favours.

Charles had also learned not to bother to take a briefcase. He carried the bundle of case papers tied with pink ribbon, and he undid the ribbon and fanned the papers out on the table. The year before there had been the infamous prosecution of the bent solicitor who'd smuggled in a hypodermic in a hollowed out part of prosecution depositions, and ever since he had expected the prison officers to leaf through the papers. He took his jacket off and handed it to one of the other prison officers, who checked it thoroughly while Charles was frisked expertly from head to toe.

It took ten minutes for the three lawyers to be searched, after which they were allowed to dress and gather their possessions. Cohen led them to the far end of the room where a fourth officer sat behind reinforced glass windows.

'Solicitor and counsel to see Mr Plumber,' said Cohen, speaking into a microphone mounted on the wall. The officer took their details, and they were eventually shown into a small room. A few moments later, Plumber entered.

'Hello Mr Cohen, Mr Holborne,' he said amiably.

'Hello Derek,' replied Cohen. 'May I introduce you to Mr Rhodes Thomas? He's the Q.C. who will lead for the Defence.'

Plumber put out his hand. 'Pleased to meet you sir,' he said to Rhodes Thomas.

'Take a seat, Mr Plumber. Am I mistaken, or do we get offered tea at Pentonville?'

'You're dead right, sir. He'll be along in a sec,' answered Plumber.

Tea having arrived, Rhodes Thomas took the ribbon off his brief, spread his papers on the table, and began.

'Now, I've got a great deal to ask you, but what I want to know first is what's happened to Mr Sands?'

'Beg pardon?'

'He's instructed new solicitors, hasn't he?'

'That's right, yeh.'

'You two haven't fallen out, have you?'

'No, not at all. He's used Oppenheims a couple of times before, that's all. Why?'

'Mr Holborne and I were just a bit concerned. If you're both going to get off the murder charge, you've both got to stick to your guns. Sorry about the pun. There's no apparent conflict between your stories, and so we wondered why he wanted to change solicitors.'

'I don't think there's nothing, wossname, suspicious, about it.'

'Good.'

'Do you mind if I ask a question?' asked Plumber.

'Not at all,' replied Rhodes Thomas.

'Do I have to plead guilty to the robbery?'

'Well, as I understand it Mr Plumber, you've said in your interview to the police, and to Mr Cohen here, that you did take part in the robbery. Is that the case?'

Plumber looked embarrassed. He turned round to Cohen, but received no assistance. Charles intervened.

'I'm sure you understand Mr Plumber, once you've told Mr Cohen that you did do the robbery, neither he nor myself, nor Mr Rhodes Thomas can represent you if you plead not guilty. We are not able to lie to the Court on your behalf. You'd have to find other solicitors – and if you tell them that you are guilty, you'll lose them too.'

'Oh,' said Plumber, clearly disappointed.

'There is however, one exception to that rule,' continued Charles. 'You are entitled to plead not guilty, despite what you've told us, and we are allowed to test the prosecution evidence. We're still prevented from actively suggesting to the Court that you're not guilty, and we certainly can't call any positive evidence on your behalf. But if the prosecution evidence doesn't come up to scratch, you'd be acquitted. On the other hand if at the end of the prosecution's evidence, there's enough evidence to go before the jury, you'd have to plead guilty at that stage. Probably sounds rather artificial to you, but we are bound by rules of conduct.'

'Do you understand all that?' asked Rhodes Thomas.

'I think so. The thing is, see, I was wondering: if I plead not guilty to the robbery, at least at the outset, the prosecution might drop the murder if I offered to change me mind, and put me hands up to the robbery.'

Rhodes Thomas smiled. 'They might indeed.'

'Do you reckon?'

'Put it this way Mr Plumber: if the evidence comes out exactly as it appears in the prosecution statements, I do not think a jury could properly find either you or Sands guilty of the murder. I think further that the prosecution will be well aware of that. That *may* make them amenable to an offer. On the other hand, you've made a full confession, and it will be hard to persuade the Crown that there's any risk of your getting off the robbery in any event. They may therefore decide to take their chances, and see if they can get you for both.'

'I'd like to have a bash anyway.'

'Very well. I'm sure Mr Cohen here will inform the Court that both charges are to be contested, and I will certainly have an informal word with the prosecution leader to sound him out. But just in case they do proceed with the murder charge, I suggest we have a look at some of the evidence.'

The conference continued for another two hours and three cups of tea. Unknown to the participants, in an adjoining block at Pentonville Prison, Robbie Sands was also receiving a visit. The conversation with his visitor only lasted forty-five minutes, but at the end of it Robbie Sands returned to his cell with a smile on his thin face. The visitor, Detective Inspector Ronald Henry Wheatley, departed with a full notebook. He did not break the habit of a lifetime and smile, but he was no less satisfied.

PART TWO

THE TRIAL

CHAPTER SIX

Although his practice had taken him there every now and then for the last ten years, Charles still experienced a particular thrill, a special lightness of step, as he entered the Old Bailey. This was the sharp end of criminal practice, the Court where the seasoned practitioners worked, met, and discussed cases, judges and trials. It was the heart of the web of British criminal justice.

Charles climbed the wide stairs and entered the Great Hall. The building work to repair the Blitz bomb damage had been completed a couple of years after he started work at the court, and for several months the barristers mingled with stonemasons and plasterers. Many at the Bar had been irritated but Charles wasn't among them. Instead of using the Bar Mess he had queued for lunch in the public canteen with the workmen, doffed his wig and sat with them, picking through the weekend's football or complaining about the price of a pint. He had told Henrietta that it was essential for a jury advocate to have a sense of what the man on the Clapham omnibus was thinking, but in truth he felt more at home with them than he did with his fellow barristers.

Charles climbed the stairs to the robing room. The place was buzzing with barristers in various states of undress as they changed into tunic shirts and wing collars, a couple of the younger men jostling to stand in front of the mirror while they struggled to tie their court bands.

Charles's wig tin joined the shoal of identical black oval tins on the robing room table and he lifted the lid. He took out his wig and, as usual, sniffed it cautiously. After a hot summer of sweat-inducing high-stress cases, horsehair wigs could smell dreadful. Cleaning them was a delicate, not to mention expensive, operation.

'Deceased?' asked a voice behind him.

Charles turned to see Philip Jewell, a barrister with fair, almost white, hair, pale blue eyes and a shy grin. Jewell was a couple of years older than Charles. His soft voice and diffident manner concealed a sharp mind and great courage. He had been a Hurricane pilot in the Battle of Britain, downing eleven enemy planes, despite twice being shot down himself.

'I'd say not in the best of health, but not quite moribund.'

'Mine's dreadful. I forgot to get it cleaned during the summer vacation. The first time I opened the tin this term, it tried to crawl out on its own.'

Charles laughed. He liked Jewell. They had gone up to Cambridge in the same year after the war, and when they came down to London for their Bar Finals they had often sat in the same tutorial groups. Their paths had crossed socially too.

'What brings you here?' asked Charles.

'Oh, murder and mayhem, as usual,' replied Jewell.

'The same,' said Charles. 'You're not in Plumber and Sands are you?'

'Certainly am. I'm your co-defendant. You're for Plumber, yes?'

'Yes. Are you being led?' asked Charles.

'Robin Lowe is leading me, but he won't be here today.'

'Why not?' asked Charles, puzzled.

The other did not answer, but grinned mysteriously. 'Court Two, isn't it?' he asked.

'Yes.'

Jewell picked up his case papers and winked. 'See you down there, then,' he said, and disappeared into the crowd of black-robed barristers heading down the stairs.

Charles walked right to the end of the line of lockers where there were a few for visiting barristers from other circuits. He was in fact a member of the South Eastern circuit, but as the only dedicated criminal practitioner in Chambers it was not considered necessary for a locker to be reserved for him. So, purely from habit, Charles used the locker his pupil master had let him use years before, when Charles was still a pupil.

He pondered Jewell's words. If the case were to start, it would be most unusual for the defence not to be represented by its silk. On the other hand, if Sands were simply applying for an adjournment, something Jewell would have done alone, why the mystery? Puzzled, Charles changed his everyday stiff collar for a wing collar, tied his bands, donned his wig and gown, and collected his papers. He glanced at his watch – 9:45 – time for quick cup of tea.

He pushed his way against the flow of barristers and hurried quickly to the Bar Mess. He found an empty table and sat down. A waitress approached him.

'Good morning Mr Holborne,' she said.

'Hello Sylvia. Enjoying the new job?'

Charles knew almost everyone in the building. He particularly liked the junior staff at the court. They were an invaluable source of gossip and they always knew what was going on. Charles was aware that Sylvia had recently moved from the cleaning department to work as a waitress in the Bar Mess.

'I am, thank you, very much. Although it's doing nothing for my waistline.' She leaned forward conspiratorially. 'The chips are too good.'

'I know,' replied Charles. 'But I'll tell you a secret: they're even better downstairs in the cells.'

'Is that right? Tea and toast?'

'Yes please.'

She disappeared to collect Charles's order.

'Hello there. It's Charles Holborne, isn't it?'

Charles looked up to see another barrister. It was Marcus Stafford, the junior for the Crown. He was enormously fat, with piggy eyes lost in great red cheeks, but he had the reputation of having one of the best minds at the Criminal Bar. He and Charles had spoken on the telephone a few days before about the evidence in the case.

'Yes. Stafford?'

'Yah. Haven't seen my illustrious leader by any chance?' asked Stafford.

'Sir Richard Hogg QC? No, not yet. And I don't suppose you've seen Mike Rhodes Thomas?'

'No, sorry. Do you mind?' Stafford indicated the seat next to Charles.

'Not at all.'

Stafford sat down. 'Is this still to be a fight?' he asked.

'That's up to you,' replied Charles. 'As we've already discussed, he'll plead to the robbery if you drop the murder. We both know you can't make it stick against either of them.'

Stafford smiled. 'We'll see.'

This sort of friendly sparring was not new to Charles – it happened frequently – but there was a confidence about Stafford which made Charles wonder what was going on. He didn't have long to wait before discovering what it was. A short middle-aged man bustled up to them.

'Morning Marcus,' he said, and sat opposite them.

'Hello Richard. This is Charles Holborne. Charles, Richard Hogg.'

'Ah,' said Hogg, rifling through his papers, 'got something for you.' He handed Charles a document. It was a statement headed "Robert Reginald Sands". 'I expect you'll want some time to consider that with Michael, and your client of course. I don't suppose the Crown could object to an application for an adjournment if you decide to make it. In any event, I've spoken to the clerk and told her we'll need some time before arraignment.'

Charles scanned the document. It was a statement dated that day. In it, Sands retracted his earlier statement and said that only two men had been on the robbery, himself and Plumber. He claimed that Plumber had taken and used the shotgun without his knowledge. His reason for his earlier statement was that Plumber had threatened the lives of his family.

'May I take it that Sands is prepared to give evidence to this effect for the prosecution?' asked Charles trying to appear unconcerned.

'You may,' answered Hogg.

'May I also take it that the Crown is proposing to call him as a witness of truth?'

'You may,' repeated Hogg. 'We shall offer no evidence against him on the murder, and I shall apply to the Judge to sentence him for the robbery before he gives evidence against your client.'

'I'd better get some instructions,' said Charles. 'If you'll excuse me…'

Charles went to the public canteen where he found Ralph Cohen and his son, Daniel, at a table.

'Good morning – ' started Cohen senior. Charles silently put the new statement in his hands. Daniel craned his neck to read over his father's shoulder.

'Fucking hell!' he breathed.

'Language,' chided Ralph quietly as he continued reading. 'So,' he continued, when he had finished.

'Yes. It's clever. As long as the two defendants stuck to their stories the Crown was always likely to fail on the murder charge. No jury could be sure which one of them did it and would have to acquit both. This way the prosecution at least has a shout at getting one of them.'

'But probably the wrong one,' said Daniel.

Charles nodded, but shrugged. 'But it's not for us to

say, is it? That's for the jury. Have you seen Mr Rhodes Thomas?'

'We agreed to meet him outside the cells – ' Daniel looked at his watch ' – right now.'

'Let's go then,' said Charles.

The three men descended to the basement. Michael Rhodes Thomas was waiting for them outside the main door.

'Well met,' he said as the others arrived.

'Wait till you've seen this,' said Charles heavily, indicating that Ralph should hand the QC the new statement. Rhodes Thomas read it while they waited for the gaoler to arrive. 'Well, we did suspect they might try this tactic, didn't we Charles?' He handed the document back to Ralph.

'Yes. Poor Derek Plumber is now facing the gallows on his own.'

'Indeed. He's going to need very gentle handling. And we may have to reconsider our tactics.'

The door opened. 'Good morning gentlemen,' said the prison officer. The door was locked behind them, and they followed the officer up a short corridor to another locked door. The air was redolent of frying bacon.

'I swear, the food down here smells better than that in the Bar Mess upstairs,' said Rhodes Thomas, echoing Charles's comment of only a few minutes before.

'Oh yes, sir. We're the first Michelin starred restaurant in HM Prison Service,' said the gaoler with a grin.

Five minutes later Plumber was shown into the tiny cell

already cramped with the four lawyers. Without speaking, Rhodes Thomas gave him Sands's statement. Plumber read it, his face growing ashen, his slack jaw dropping.

'Jesus Christ,' he whispered, 'I'm done for.'

'Sit down Derek,' said Rhodes Thomas. 'Take a few deep breaths, and start telling us the truth.'

Plumber sat, but his hands holding Sands's statement shook violently and he was gasping for air. 'I'm getting dizzy,' he said, and indeed he was swaying like a plant blowing in a breeze. 'I think I'm having a heart attack!'

Charles scanned the cell quickly and saw Daniel's open briefcase. He reached in and took out a large crumpled manila envelope. He tipped out the contents, colour photographs of the Express Dairy building, and handed them to Daniel.

'May I?' he asked, holding up the envelope.

'Sure.'

Charles compressed the opening of the envelope and blew into it, forming a bag. He held it out to Plumber.

'Put that in front of your mouth and breathe in and out of the envelope. Go on!' Plumber put up a trembling hand, took the envelope, and applied it to his mouth. 'Either cover your nose or just breathe through your mouth,' ordered Charles.

Plumber did as instructed, and within a few seconds his breathing began to return to normal.

'Better?' asked Charles.

Plumber nodded.

'He was hyperventilating, that's all,' explained Charles.

The other lawyers looked at Charles in surprise. 'I didn't know you had any medical experience,' commented Rhodes Thomas.

'I don't. I grew up with a hysterical mother.'

It took Plumber a couple of minutes to calm down sufficiently to talk.

'There was only the two of us on the job. God, I never wanted to go, I swear it. I'd gone straight for four years. I had a job and everything. But he called me, I guess within a day or so of getting out, and threatened to grass me on the last job. It was cast iron he said, this would be the last job ever, and it would set us up for life. He persuaded me to take a wossname, an imitation shooter. You can look up my record: I've never touched a gun – real or fake – in thirty years of being a villain till this job. I never even knew he had a sawn-off, on my baby's life, I swear it.'

'Very well,' said Rhodes Thomas. 'Why make up a third man?'

'That was his idea. He reckoned if we both stuck to our stories, we'd neither of us be convicted.'

'He was right. But he hasn't stuck to the story. And for some reason the prosecution believes him rather than you. They're proposing to drop the murder charge against him. Why should they believe him Derek?'

'I don't know. What're we gonna do?'

'That's up to you. They're obviously not going to take an offer on the robbery alone, and on your instructions, you can't plead guilty to the murder. The case will depend on which of the two of you the jury believes.'

'A cut-throat,' said Charles.

'Yes,' agreed Rhodes Thomas. 'A cut-throat defence: each defendant blaming the other.'

'What does that mean?' asked Plumber.

'In practical terms,' answered Charles, 'a dirty trial. No holds barred. Your credit with the jury is all-important. Subject to what Mr Rhodes Thomas thinks, you'd be advised to plead guilty to the robbery and tell the jury the whole story. It'll look dreadful if he admits it, and you don't.'

'I agree,' said Rhodes Thomas. 'The question I need to have answered now is this: do we require an adjournment? The Crown won't oppose us asking for one, if there's any point. But I have your instructions on this new statement, and I personally cannot see what purpose would be served by delaying the trial.'

'What do you think, Mr Cohen?' asked Plumber, turning to the man he'd known the longest.

'I think counsel are right. I see no reason to delay. It'll only give Sands the chance to make up more convincing detail.'

'Okay then,' said Plumber, sounding a lot more brave than he looked. 'Let's go for it.'

The lawyers left the cells and went directly to Court Two. The prosecution team and Sands's barrister awaited them.

'Well?' asked Hogg.

'Very, thank you,' answered Rhodes Thomas with a smile.

'Still fighting?' asked Hogg.

'Oh my dear fellow,' replied Rhodes Thomas, 'I should hate to deprive us all of a few days' work. We're still fighting.'

'Fair enough. I've asked the clerk if she can arrange for us to see the Judge in Chambers just to explain the position.'

'Why?' asked Charles.

'There are other matters which you'll understand I can't mention now, that have to be aired in Chambers.'

A grim-faced, grey-haired woman of about fifty wearing court robes approached the barristers.

'His Lordship will see you now gentlemen, if you're ready.'

'Are we ready?' asked Hogg, turning to Rhodes Thomas.

'We are.'

The five barristers followed the clerk to a door behind the Judge's bench and out onto a carpeted corridor, the walls of which were hung with paintings. They filed down the corridor for some distance until they came to a panelled door. The clerk motioned for them to wait, and knocked.

'Come,' said a voice from behind the door.

The clerk entered, half closing the door behind her, and then opened it wide to usher the barristers in.

'Good morning Judge,' said Hogg.

'Good morning gentlemen. Do sit down if you can,' said the Judge. His Honour Judge Galbraith Q.C. had been a recent, and popular, appointment to the bench.

He was of the new generation of judges, those who were not so prosecution-minded as the old school. He was non-interventionist too; he let the barristers get on with the cases in their own way with a minimum of judicial interference. On his appointment as a full-time judge he had commissioned a small polished triangle of wood to sit on the desk in front of him with the words "*Be Quiet*" embossed in large gold letters. Every morning he carried the little sign into court with his case papers, and placed it carefully on his bench facing himself.

Sir Richard Hogg introduced the other barristers, and explained who they each represented.

'There are a number of matters I'd like to explain with your permission, Judge,' he continued. 'The indictment contains two counts, robbery and murder. As I expect you will have read, the prosecution case on the first is strong, whereas I concede we would have had difficulty on the murder. The position has now changed, in that Sands has offered to give evidence for the Crown.' He handed to the Judge a copy of the statement. 'That is a Notice of Additional Evidence served on the Defence this morning.'

He paused to allow the Judge to read it. The Judge turned to Rhodes Thomas. 'Are you asking for an adjournment?'

'No, Judge.'

'That presumably means that you will no longer proceed against Sands,' said the Judge to Hogg. Charles now understood why Sands did not need a Q.C.; he wasn't to be tried at all for the murder.

'If you accept this evidence as the truth,' continued the

Judge, 'it means that you accept that he didn't know of the shotgun.'

'It certainly means that we cannot prove otherwise,' replied Hogg.

'What gives this statement credence in your view?' asked the Judge. 'It might as easily have been Plumber who approached you. It's still a cut-throat.'

Charles smiled. This Judge was no fool.

'That brings me on to the other matter that I wanted to raise, Judge, and it's a matter that would be best not aired in open court. Sands has been of great assistance to the police in relation to other matters. He has provided information that has led to a number of arrests, and I am instructed that charges will follow. He appears to have been entirely frank in relation to those matters, some of which may result in charges against him personally.'

'And of course, you, Mr Jewell, want me to take these "other matters" into account when sentencing him,' asked the Judge.

'Yes, Judge, I do.'

'And I expect you both want him sentenced for the robbery before we start the trial of Mr Plumber, so there can be no suggestion that he is buying a light sentence with false evidence?'

'Yes,' said Jewell and Hogg in unison.

The Judge leaned back in his chair and considered what he had been told. 'If the only evidence against Plumber is that of a potential co-defendant, the jury will have to be warned in any event against convicting him on Sands's word alone. There will have to be corroboration, won't there, Mr Hogg?'

'That's right, Judge. The prosecution says that there is evidence capable of being corroboration, subject, of course, to your ruling.'

'I see. What do you have to say about this Mr Rhodes Thomas?' asked the Judge.

'There's nothing I can say, Judge. The prosecution have taken a view of the evidence. I cannot change that. We're entitled to know exactly what information Mr Sands has given to the police, so we can consider if we want to cross-examine on it, and what other charges may follow.'

'Yes,' said the Judge. 'I think that must be right. I shall need a note signed from a responsible police officer setting out what Sands has told the police, so that it may be put in the file. I shall make no express reference to it in Court. I must say that I am not entirely happy with the turn of events, Mr Hogg, but I cannot prevent you from taking this course. If you decide to offer no evidence against one of two defendants, I can't stop you.' Hogg did not answer. The Judge turned to Rhodes Thomas. 'Is Plumber proposing to plead guilty to the robbery?'

'Yes, Judge, he is.'

'Well, thank you gentlemen. How long will you need before we can swear in a jury?'

'I would have thought we'd need ten minutes before we can start,' answered Hogg. 'We should then be in a position to deal with the guilty pleas and the sentence of Sands. I suppose the jury in waiting could be asked to stand by for midday.'

'Very well,' said the Judge.

Once outside the Judge's Chambers, Rhodes Thomas winked at Charles. 'I am beginning to think we might have some fun with this, Charles,' he whispered. 'I wonder if Hogg's bitten off a bit more than he can chew.'

They returned to the cells to see Plumber.

'He's turned grass,' said Rhodes Thomas.

'What?' exclaimed Plumber, incredulous.

'He's given the police information regarding other crimes. That's why they believe him.'

'Where does that leave me?' asked Plumber.

'Mr Holborne and I have been chatting about it on the way down. We're not optimistic, but we don't think all is lost. It gives us a lever over Sands. What I'd like to do, Mr Plumber, is keep a very low profile for almost the whole of the case. You admit that you took part in the robbery, and you do not deny the witnesses' accounts of the shooting. You simply say that it wasn't you with the gun. The dead man can't say which of you it was, and the other two members of Team 3, Gilsenan and…'

'Barrett, or Barnett,' offered Charles.

'Yes, well, they were both unsighted by their van and by Wright himself. In my view it's simply a question of which of the two of you the jury believe.'

'Do you agree, Charles?'

'Yes, I do.'

'Very well,' continued Rhodes Thomas. 'I propose to ask no questions at all of the other prosecution witnesses. We shall save the whole attack for Sands himself.'

CHAPTER SEVEN

Sands got nine years. It would have been less but for his bad record, and it would have been more but for the assistance he had given, and had promised still to give, to the police. With remission and discounting parole he would probably serve between four and five years. By the time he had been sentenced it was almost 1 o'clock and the Judge adjourned for lunch.

At 2 o'clock the jury was sworn in, Plumber pleaded guilty to robbery and not guilty to murder. The trial began. By the end of the afternoon, almost half of the Crown's case had been completed, and the Defence had not asked a single question. The jury were looking decidedly puzzled. Charles looked across at them every now and then, and could see them looking at the bench where the Defence team sat, wondering what was going on. There was no doubt: by the time Mike Rhodes Thomas stood to cross-examine Sands, the full attention of the jury would be on him.

The Judge adjourned at 4.15 pm, and Charles headed back to Chambers. He hesitated outside Mick's, tempted to stop for a cup of tea, and saw a group of barristers at one of the tables. He was about to move on, when one of their number saw him, and waved for him to enter. Charles looked at his watch and went in.

Charles arrived back at 2 Chancery Court at 6.30 pm. suitably warmed with several cups of tea and rounds of toast. He walked into the clerks' room. Unusually, Sally was still there. She had bowed to the pressure and replaced the miniskirt and leather boots with her more familiar dark blue suit and cream blouse, but Charles still found her very attractive. She was petite, little more than five feet tall, but with a perfect hourglass figure, a little turned up nose, and large brown eyes. Her hands – always instantly visible because of the ever-changing brightly coloured nail varnish she wore – were very small but extremely deft. Charles loved watching her tying the ribbon used for legal briefs – slick, efficient and effortless. More than once he had thought about those little white hands undoing the buttons of his shirt.

'Hello there,' said Charles, as he peered into the pigeon-hole reserved for his briefs (and more importantly, cheques) as they came in. 'What are you doing here so late? We're not paying for overtime are we?' he joked.

'You're kidding, right? No, I'm going out tonight and me boyfriend's picking me up. So, as I had to wait anyway, Stanley asked me to hang on for Mr Clarke's brief to arrive. It's being sent over by hand. Are you staying, sir?' she asked.

Charles didn't answer. A large brief had been awaiting him in the pigeon-hole, and he undid the ribbon on it and skim-read the instructions. 'Damn!' he said softly as he read. 'Sorry, Sally, did you ask something?'

'Yes. Are you going to be staying, as I've locked up on the other side.'

The set of chambers was split into two sets of rooms

divided by a central landing, and each "side" required its own keys.

'Well,' answered Charles, 'I *was* going to go straight home, but they want an indictment drafted by tomorrow *and* an Advice on Evidence,' he said, tapping the papers in his hand. 'Why they always leave it to the last minute I shall never understand. The sooner we get a central prosecution service, the happier I shall be.'

He gathered the papers together and left the clerks' room. He opened the door to the corridor, still reading as he walked, and bumped straight into someone coming in the other way. He knew by the smell who it was, without even looking up.

'Evening, Kellett-Brown,' he said, stepping back. Ivor Kellett-Brown was the oldest – and the oddest – member of Chambers. He had come to the Bar in the late 1930s having failed at a number of other careers, and had promptly failed in the Law too. However, incredible as the members of 2 Chancery Court found it, he appeared to have friends in high places. Mr Justice Bricklow, who had been head of Chambers until 1936, had brought Kellett-Brown in, and he had stayed ever since. He had no discernible practice but, unlike in most other professions, every now and then a complete duffer managed to survive at the Bar, living off the crumbs from other barristers' tables. As long as he paid his Chambers rent – and no one knew how he managed even that, as his earnings from the Law were certainly insufficient – and he caused no one any trouble, he was permitted to occupy the corner of the pupils' room.

He lived in a single room in Lincoln's Inn with a dozen budgerigars whom he permitted to fly free within the confines of the room. Droppings and feathers covered every available surface, and the floor crunched underfoot with decades of dried filth. Kellett-Brown himself invariably wore threadbare striped trousers, the seat of which was so shiny that the pupils in his room on one occasion all wore dark glasses to protect their eyes from the glare. The joke had been utterly lost on the wearer of the trousers. He owned one jacket, the cuffs of which he trimmed regularly, and over that he wore, like an overcoat, the evidence, visual and odiferous, of his domestic companions.

To add to this prepossessing appearance, Kellett-Brown had an "unfortunate manner" as some of the more charitable members of Chambers termed it. As far as Stanley, the senior clerk, was concerned, he was an argumentative old fool who should have been kicked out years ago. He frequently appeared in Chambers in the late afternoon, plainly the worse for the subsidised sherry served in Hall at luncheon, when Stanley was sorting out the diary for the next day. He would peer over the clerk's shoulder, a tipsy, disgruntled vulture, and remind Stanley repeatedly that he was available for anything that might be going spare.

Charles wrinkled his nose with distaste. Kellett-Brown bore his usual pungent air of sherry and decrepitude.

'Sorry, Ivor,' said Charles, attempting to circumvent Kellett-Brown and get to his room.

'I beg your pardon?' said the other with very great

dignity, turning slowly to face Charles after he had spoken, and peering at Charles from under heavy lids.

'I said sorry, Ivor. For bumping into you,' explained Charles. He watched as Ivor swayed slightly. 'Forget it,' said Charles with impatience, as he continued on his way across the landing.

Charles unlocked the far door and walked down to his room. He threw the papers onto his desk, reached across to the desk lamp, and settled himself down to read his new brief.

Charles was unaware of the passing of time, but he had read about a hundred pages when there was a faint tap on his door. It was so quiet that he ignored it at first, but then it was repeated, slightly harder.

'Come in,' he said, putting down his pen. The door opened very slowly, and Sally's head appeared timidly round the door. 'Yes, Sally? What are you doing still here?' He looked at his watch. It was almost 8 o'clock. 'You've not been stood up, have you?'

Sally looked down at the mass of papers spread about Charles's desk and the pile of law books on the floor.

'Oh…no… it really doesn't matter if you're busy, sir…' she said in a strange voice.

She stepped back and began to close the door behind her. Charles pushed his chair back and followed her. She looked back at him like a frightened rabbit. Charles led her gently by the arm back to the circle of light around his desk and turned her round. Her eyes were red and she had been crying. Her eyeliner, which, was usually applied

– albeit in large quantities – very carefully, was smeared, and her hair was awry.

'What on earth's the matter?' asked Charles gently.

Sally was usually so competent and brisk that he was quite startled to see her upset. She took a deep breath as if to start speaking but her voice broke and all that emerged was a deep sob. Charles led her to the one comfortable chair in his room, an old leather armchair in the corner, and sat her down. He returned to his desk, searched his drawer, and came up with some tissues and handed one to her.

'Now. Take a deep breath and tell me what's happened. Is it your boyfriend?'

'He didn't come…' she started.

'Oh, I'm so sorry. Well, more fool –'

She waved her hand to stop him. 'That ain't it.' Charles waited for her to take another deep breath and let her start again. 'I was waiting for him over there,' she said between gulps of air, pointing to the clerks' room, 'when Mr K…K…Kellett-Brown came in…'

'Yes?' asked Charles, crouching beside her.

'Oh, Mr Holborne sir, I don't know…what's best…I'd better not…' Her voice rose sharply with each phrase. She was on the verge of hysteria.

'Just take it slowly. One word at a time.'

'I…can't… I'll get into trouble, Mr Holborne.'

'No you won't, I promise you.' He lifted her chin with his hand and looked up into her smudged eyes. 'If something's happened, you must tell me.'

She looked straight at him, and nodded. 'Mr K–B came in. I was waiting for Johnny. He…Mr K–B…he asked me if I didn't think it would be better if I shut the outer door, so no one could come wandering in.' Her voice was calmer but she spoke very quickly, as if afraid that if she paused she would be unable to continue. 'Stanley told me about downstairs being burgled, so I thought perhaps I should. Johnny'd always knock anyway.'

Now she had started talking the words tumbled out in a cascade. 'So I did, I shut it, and went back to my desk. I was typing a letter, for Mr Smith, when Mr Kellett-Brown called on the 'phone. Wanted me to bring him in some paper. So I went in there, and he wasn't at his desk. I turns round, and there he is…behind the door…' She laughed, a peculiar high-pitched giggle that turned into a cry. 'He had his…thing…you know? Sticking out his trousers. He kept saying he wouldn't hurt me…wouldn't hurt me… just wanted me to…to…' She had to stop again.

Charles stood up, and moved towards the door. Sally grabbed at him. 'Please don't go! Don't go Mr Holborne!' she cried.

'I'm not going. I just want to see if he's still there.'

'He ain't. He left after…after…'

'After what?' asked Charles, turning back to her. 'Are you saying he… did something to you?' he asked gently.

She shook her head violently. 'No, he never, but he grabbed at me…' She opened her jacket, and showed Charles her blouse. Two of the buttons in the middle of her chest were torn off. Charles averted his eyes from her breasts.

'I pushed him away, and he fell over. I ran to the loo and locked meself in. I've been there nearly 'alf an hour. I heard the door go, but I was too scared to come out till now.'

'My God, you poor thing,' said Charles. 'Let me get you a drink. I keep a bottle in the desk for –'

'No,' she replied firmly. 'I don't want nothing. I just want to go home.'

'Stay here,' he ordered. 'I shall be a minute at most. Lock the door after me if you're worried.' He crossed swiftly to the other side of the building and pushed the door to the clerks' room open. The place was empty. Charles picked up Sally's coat from the back of the door and returned to her.

'He's gone,' he reported. Sally was sitting where he had left her, looking forlorn. Charles drew up another chair alongside her.

'Now, what do you want to do?'

'Like I said, I want to go home.'

'No, I mean so far as Kellett-Brown is concerned. You are quite entitled to call the police and have him charged with indecent assault. Or maybe even attempted –'

'No!' she replied very firmly. 'No,' she repeated, 'I couldn't do that.'

'I'd come with you,' Charles offered. 'Maybe we should give your mother a call?'

'It's not that,' she said. She took several deep breaths to calm herself. 'He's a horrible old man…a dirty old – no

– ' she said, seeing Charles's half-smile, 'I mean he don't wash. And he smells, too. But…I know what you're going to say, Mr Holborne… but I feel sorry for him. He's lonely – '

'Doesn't matter how lonely he is! That doesn't give him the right to go flashing, and grabbing at you like that!'

'I know. But I couldn't get him sent to prison – '

'It might not be prison, you know – '

'I don't care,' she said adamantly.

'I think you ought to think about it, Sally. Don't make any snap decisions. You could easily have been raped.'

'No I couldn't. I could punch his lights out any time, if it came to it,' she said vehemently. Charles looked at her with surprise and some admiration. He believed it too. 'I was just a bit frightened,' she went on. 'That's all.'

'So you're happy just to forget it? Smile and say "Good morning" to him tomorrow? Pretend it didn't happen?'

Sally looked at him with wide eyes. She hadn't thought about that.

'I…don't know. I'll have to talk to me Mum.' She paused, her brow contracting in thought. 'Ooh, I'm gonna have to give up the job, ain't I?' And this time the tears began to fall in earnest, thick and fast. 'I could never face him again,' she said between sobs. 'And they're never gonna throw him out are they?' She looked up at Charles, eyes streaming rivulets of black mascara down her cheeks.

'I don't know. My guess is that, if Sir Geoffrey finds out about this, even if you don't report it to the police, it'll be the final straw. But if you're absolutely sure you don't want me to call the police, I agree you should go home. I'll walk you up to Fleet Street, and you can get a cab.'

'I ain't got enough for a cab from here to Romford.'

'That's alright. It can come out of petty cash. It's the least Chambers can do.'

Charles helped her into her coat, handed her her bag, and leaving his papers where they lay, escorted her out of Chambers.

'It might be a good idea not to come in tomorrow, eh?' he said. She nodded in reply. 'I'll tell Stanley you weren't well tonight, and that I sent you home. Okay?'

She nodded again, and sniffed. 'Tell him it's me throat. I've been coughing all day anyway.'

'Fine.'

Charles locked the doors behind him and they set off. Sally felt for his hand as they walked down the stairs.

'Thanks Charlie,' she said, looking up at him with a smile, and squeezing his hand. It was the first time she had ever used his first name, and it was, according to the protocol of the Bar, quite wrong. She could never have done it with any other member of Chambers, and they both knew it. Charles was flattered. He smiled back at her. 'I don't know what I'd have done, if you wasn't in,' she continued. He squeezed her hand in reply.

CHAPTER EIGHT

Charles left home the next morning at 6.30 am. He had to complete the work he had left unfinished before he went to the Old Bailey. He also had business in Lincoln's Inn.

Relations with Henrietta over the past few days had been less tense, but she had spent the last three nights in her own bedroom. Charles didn't wake her before he left.

From Paddington he took the Tube to Chancery Lane rather than Temple and walked down towards the Thames. It was a bright, clear morning, and at 7:15 am the streets were deserted and seemed fresh and clean. The leaves on the plane trees were beginning to emerge, and Charles could smell spring round the corner.

The part of Lincoln's Inn where Kellett-Brown lived had been built in the 16th century, and had barely changed since. The building in which he had his room was occupied on the ground floor by barristers' chambers, and Charles paused as he passed the board that announced the names of the barristers practising inside, noting that he didn't recognise a single name. He had little to do with Chancery practitioners. Their working lives were so different from his that they might have been in different professions altogether.

He climbed the staircase to the upper floors. The staircase was oak, blackened with time and hundreds of years of footfalls, unchanged except for a lick of paint since the time of Dickens.

The second floor housed a book-binding business and

the third a firm of solicitors of whom Charles had never heard. The staircase leading to Kellett-Brown's room on the top floor was particularly ill-lit and Charles had to feel his way up step by step. He finally came to a door at the head of the staircase. There appeared to be no bell or knocker, so Charles rapped on the oak door with his knuckles. There was no sound from within. He repeated his knock, much harder this time and, after a few seconds, he heard movement.

'What do you want? Do you know what time it is?'

'It's Charles Holborne, from Chambers.'

There was a pause. 'What the bloody hell do you want?'

'Will you open the door, Ivor? This is very important.'

'For God's sake, Holborne, go away. I'll be in Chambers this afternoon if you want me.'

Charles could hear Kellett-Brown's footsteps retreating from the front door.

'I suggest you open up now Ivor. I doubt you'll want me to shout through the door, but if you give me no alternative, I shall. It's about Sally.'

The footfalls ceased. Charles could imagine the old man, motionless, only a few feet away from him on the other side of the door, debating whether to open up or not. Eventually, curiosity – or fear – got the better of him, and the footsteps approached again. Charles heard a chain being withdrawn, and a bolt sliding out of its place. The door opened. Kellett-Brown faced him, wearing an old blue dressing gown, skinny pyjamaed legs sticking out of the bottom.

'You'd better come in,' he said.

Charles walked past him into a smelly darkened room, overcrowded with heavy furniture. There were a number of small birds on perches dotted about the room, apparently asleep. Kellett-Brown closed the door and turned to Charles.

'Well?' he whispered, apparently so as not to disturb his pets.

'I'll come straight to the point,' replied Charles. 'I was in Chambers last night when you assaulted Sally.'

'Assaulted Sally? What on earth are you talking about?'

'You can pretend not to know if you like Ivor, but if you take that line, you'll have to continue it with the police. I'm not here to mess about. I know what sort of state Sally was in last night after you finished with her, and if necessary I'll give evidence of exactly what I saw.'

'The girl's raving!'

Charles shook his head. 'Very well,' he said quietly. 'You may expect a call from the police.' He took a step towards the door but Kellett-Brown didn't move. 'Do you want to reconsider?' asked Charles. 'I have told no one about it as yet, and if you choose, that's the way it can remain.'

'How do you mean?'

'I mean that I'm sure Sally won't press charges, and last night's events will be forgotten.'

'And what am I supposed to do to prevent these false charges being brought against me? You do realise that this is blackmail? You could be prosecuted yourself for this!'

'I am trying, Ivor, to save your reputation, such as it is,

and prevent this whole thing being dragged through the courts. I am also trying to save a young girl's job.'

'I repeat, what's the price?'

'Your resignation from Chambers, effective as from today.'

'Preposterous!' replied Kellett-Brown.

Charles pushed past him and opened the door. 'It's entirely up to you. If, by the time I return to Chambers this afternoon, I've heard nothing, I shall report the matter to the head of Chambers. What he does then is up to him. Likewise, it will be up to Sally to decide whether or not she wishes to prosecute. In my view, there's absolutely no doubt but that she should. Good morning.'

Charles left the stinking apartment, slammed the front door behind him turned and descended the staircase. There was a considerable fluttering and squawking behind him.

Once at Chancery Court, Charles continued reading his new brief until 9.00 am, hastily jotted some notes for the typists to decipher, and walked down to the Old Bailey. Before leaving he left a note on Stanley's desk saying that Sally had become ill the night before while still at Chambers and that she'd not be in for the day.

In the Old Bailey's Bar Mess he ordered an enormous fried breakfast and settled down with a cup of coffee to read the newspaper.

At 10.20 it was announced that Mr Justice Galbraith was dealing with a bail application and that all parties in the case of *The Queen versus Plumber* were released until

11.00 am. That was in due course extended to 11.30 am, and then midday. The case finally resumed at 12.15 pm. By 4.20 pm the evidence for the Crown was completed apart from the evidence of Sands. The judge adjourned until the morning. It had been a frustrating day for the Defence, and the team was on edge.

Charles walked directly back to the Temple. As he entered the clerks' room, Stanley beamed at him in a most unusual way.

'Have you been drinking, Stanley?' asked Charles with a smile.

'Not a drop, thank you sir. Mr Kellett-Brown has resigned from Chambers. Came in at lunchtime, paid a quarter's rent, took his desk, and departed. Ill-health, he said.'

'Well I never,' said Charles. 'He always looked perfectly well to me.'

Charles went into his room, and closed the door. He picked up the telephone and called Sally.

'You can come back tomorrow,' he told her. 'Mr Kellett-Brown has resigned, and he has already gone.'

'Have you said anything, sir?' she answered, reverting to formality. Charles was surprised to find that he was disappointed. His short moment of intimacy with the bright nineteen year-old was over, and would never be referred to again.

'I had a word with Kellett-Brown, that's all. Otherwise it's between us and no-one else,' he assured her.

'I'll see you tomorrow then, Mr Holborne. I'll phone Stanley now and tell him I'm feeling better.'

'Fine. Goodbye.'
"Bye sir.'

•

Henrietta was in the garden when Charles arrived home, wearing trousers and a sun hat, a pair of pruning shears in her gloved hands. She didn't often wear trousers, considering them too American and too modern, but Charles approved when she did. He found it difficult to take his eyes off her swaying hips as she moved, and on this occasion he watched from the kitchen door for some minutes before she sensed his presence. She turned and took her hat off, brushing the hair out of her eyes with her upper arm.

'What are you doing here?' she called with surprise.

'I live here,' he said cheerfully, crossing the lawn and approaching her. 'Might I be addressing the lady of the house?' Charles kissed her on the cheek. She absently kissed the air beside his face.

'Yes, but it's only six-thirty. You've not been home this early for years. Are you ill?' she asked, almost serious.

'No. I'm perfectly well. I thought we might spend some time together, that's all.'

'Good God, Charles, this is all rather unexpected. After all this time, you want to play at being husband for a night?'

Charles looked at her with his large brown eyes, the exaggerated pout on his lips not entirely hiding the fact that the remark had stung.

Henrietta was almost his height, slim, with an oval face framed with silky chestnut hair. She looked, if anything, more beautiful than she had the day he met her at Cambridge, eleven years before. On that day he'd been dressed as a penguin – part of some student rag accosting passers-by – and she'd been late for a lecture. He'd held her by her skinny arms until she either made a donation of at least half a crown or had promised to meet him for a drink. Having almost no money with her she had been forced to accept the alternative.

That meeting had been only two weeks after Charles's decision to change his name, one week after the awful scene with his father. The full implications of his decision had yet to sink in, and he was still exploring his new identity, Charles Holborne, English gentleman. Perhaps that was why he had the courage to grab her wrists in his flippers and demand a date with her, because it wasn't Charlie Horowitz asking, but this new, dangerous, dashing Charles Holborne.

Everyone knew Henrietta of course. The Hon. Henrietta Lloyd-Williams, eldest daughter of Viscount Brandreth, one of the fastest of the "fast set" as Charles's father used to call them, and yet with an unpretentious, easy manner and, so it was said, a good brain too. What persuaded her to go out with this dark-eyed persistent penguin she didn't know. His arrogance was quite unlike the self-assurance of the well-bred languid young men with whom she had grown up. It was dangerous, almost bellicose. It invited challenge, so much so that for the first few months of their relationship part of the attraction was her anticipation that something, *anything*, might happen when she was with him. There had been a couple of fights in Cambridge pubs in which Charles had demonstrated a thrilling ability to look after himself. There was also a bitterness about him, but softened by a gentle self-deprecating humour that made him appear vulnerable. It was certainly his ability to make her laugh that persuaded her to see him again, but it was the "little boy lost" that so endeared him to her. That so big a man, both in intellect and in size – although Charles wasn't tall, he was as broad as a bull – could at times look so perplexed by the universe was indeed endearing.

For Charles's part, he sensed something in Henrietta with which he identified. Her relationship with her father the Viscount, an exacting impatient man, was fraught and punctuated with long periods during which the two of them would not speak. Charles was unaware of it at the time, but Henrietta's third year at Cambridge when they first met was one such period. That year had been the most intense of their lives – romantic weekends away, shared books, music and ideas, and sex at all times of the day and night, and in increasingly dangerous places. They couldn't keep their hands off one another. They inhabited their own private, intoxicated, world. And barely ten months after they first met, post-coital on a desolate Northumbrian beach, Henrietta proposed to Charles, and he accepted. A week later, still during term, they were married in Cambridge without a word to either family.

Two days before the ceremony Charles told Henrietta that he was Jewish by birth, but not practising. Charles didn't think to mention that to be Jewish doesn't require practice. She couldn't actually say she'd met a Jew before, practising or otherwise, but it didn't matter to her, she said, as long as they could continue to eat bacon and oysters.

Her parents loathed him of course, albeit politely. Her mother had been heard to say that there was nothing wrong with Jewish furriers from the East End of London, of course, nor indeed with their clever sons. They were just so... *unsuitable*, as in-laws. The Viscount took it as a personal insult by his daughter, the most successful means she had yet found to demonstrate her contempt for him, which in many ways it was.

So far as Charles's parents were concerned it was much simpler. When they learned of the marriage they said *Kaddish*, the prayer for the dead, mourned Charles for a week and never mentioned his name again. As far as they were concerned, their eldest son, the apple of their eye, had died. Henrietta's family were, of course, quite grateful for this attitude. One Jew connected to the family was quite enough; an entire brood would have been intolerable.

At the end of term Charles took Henrietta to his parents' home to introduce her. His parents refused to come to the door and David, Charles's younger brother, apologetically barred his way at the threshold. Charles, hurt beyond description, shouted some unforgivable words from the doorway before Henrietta managed to drag him away. He still remembered some of those words with shame, but he had no further contact with the family in the intervening years.

Once, a couple of years after that event, Harry Horowitz discovered David eating breakfast while reading a court report in The Telegraph about a case where Charles's name was mentioned. David was by then in his early 20s, but his father still beat him as efficiently as his sixty-six year-old arms and heart condition would allow. Five years after that, when viewing a development plot in one of his rare property cases, Charles discovered by chance that the family had moved. The entire street in the East End where his childhood home had stood had been demolished. Where his parents were and whether they were both still alive he neither knew nor, he told himself, cared.

'I thought perhaps we could go out for a meal,' said Charles.

'I'm sorry, Charles,' Henrietta replied, with sincerity, 'but I can't. I've been invited to the Robertsons' for dinner; they have some friends over from the States, and they're holding a small party for them.'

'I'm sure Helen wouldn't mind if I came too.'

'She didn't invite you because you've never once kept a mid-week dinner arrangement since we've been married,' she replied, continuing with her pruning.

'I've told you a million times, don't exaggerate.'

'Alright, maybe not "never". But you have let them down on more than one occasion. It's a bit unfair to ask at this stage, don't you think? It's a small party, and it's starting in two hours. You'll throw her into a tizzy if you ask to come now. But if you really want me to 'phone, I will.'

Charles pondered, and decided against it. 'Okay; forget it.'

Henrietta rested her forehead on his chest and Charles drank in the smell of her hair – cut grass and sunshine. She looked up. 'It was a nice idea. If you do it more often, I'll get used to it.'

She took his face in her muddy, gloved, hands, pulled his head towards hers and kissed him on the mouth.

'You smell nice,' he said.

'You smell nice too.'

'What of?' he asked.

'Just Charlie,' she answered, hugging him.

'I don't suppose…' he suggested.

'What don't you suppose?' she replied, snuggling closer to him.

'That you might develop a dreadful headache at about ten o'clock tonight which might mysteriously clear up on your arrival home?'

'Charlie! Whatever has come over you?'

'Nothing's come over me. I was hoping to come over you.'

'You're disgusting,' she said with a grin. 'Still, I'll see what can be arranged.'

Henrietta took his arm and they walked slowly down the garden.

'Charlie?'

'Present.'

'Can we both make a special effort? I know I've been a real bitch the last few weeks. And you – '

'I've been working too hard – ' he interrupted.

'You've been distant, cold and thoughtless,' she corrected.

'Hmm.'

'I was adding it up this morning. I haven't seen you for more than six hours this whole week. That's three breakfasts, one trip to the shops, and an hour on Monday night – and that was only because the power cut prevented you from working.'

He sighed. 'It's this murder. And there's the fraud next month. They're both important – '

'I know they are, and I'm proud of you, even though I think you're wasted doing this stuff. What does Daddy call it?'

'"The Verbals".'

'Yes, that. But I sometimes wonder how high our marriage is on your list of priorities.'

'We've been through this before, Etta. If you got yourself a proper job which actually stretched you, you wouldn't be waiting at home with nothing – '

'"Proper job"?' she exclaimed. She was about to launch into an impassioned response, but she bit her lip, took a deep breath and looked up at him. 'Don't you see how such comments demean me?' she asked. 'Do you never wonder how someone might feel, on the receiving end? Anyway that's not the point. I don't want a different job. I want – '

'I know what you want. You want a child. I know, Etta, really I do. But we've been through this, and we agreed to wait a year or two – '

He was interrupted by Fiona calling from the French windows.

'Is Charles in yet? Oh, you *are*. There's a chap called Stanley on the 'phone. He says it's very urgent.'

Charles looked at Henrietta. 'I'd better take it. I'll be right back.'

He ran up the lawn and into the house where Fiona handed him the telephone. Henrietta returned to her gardening, shaking her head to herself.

'Stanley?' Charles asked.

'Hello, sir. Sorry to trouble you at home, but I've just had a call from Tony, the clerk to Mr Rhodes Thomas. Mr Rhodes Thomas has had an accident. It's not life-threatening, but apparently he's broken his leg, and he'll be out of commission, in traction, for at least six weeks.'

CHAPTER NINE

'For fuck's sake! What was he doing? Now what? Will we be adjourned? How long am I going to have to stay on remand?' wailed Plumber.

Charles, Ralph Cohen and their client sat in a conference room at HM Prison Brixton, to which Plumber had been moved at the start of the trial.

Cohen replied. 'He slipped down the stairs at the Old Bailey. It must have been just after I left him last night. He's in Bart's, just opposite the court. He says he'll be in hospital for as much as six weeks. But we're pretty confident that we can get the case adjourned.'

'What, for six weeks?'

'I don't know about that. It will probably be more than six weeks before he's back at work, maybe three or four months. It's a very bad break. I'm not sure the Court will allow as long as that. It may be better to get a new silk in before then.'

'You mean start the trial again?' protested Plumber.

'Del, we're going to have to do that, whatever happens,' replied Cohen, sympathetically. 'I understand how you feel. But a jury can only be sent away for a couple of days, certainly not for weeks. They'll have to be discharged.'

'And how long will it take to find another silk?'

Cohen looked at Charles to answer. 'I don't know,' he said. 'The case isn't difficult in terms of what's got to be assimilated; it's just a question of finding someone who's free at very short notice. Good silks get booked up early.'

'So it means I've to put up with someone who's second rate? With me life on the line? You gotta be fucking joking!'

'Please calm down Mr Plumber,' answered Charles. 'There is no question of you being represented by anyone second rate. Mr Rhodes Thomas was my first choice, but there are plenty of excellent leaders.'

'Yeh, but I'm under pressure to find one quickly. I've been on remand for months. I can't go through this again, Mr Holborne. I can't sleep, I can't eat, and I'm at me wits' end. I don't want to put the case off at all. Why can't you do it? Don't you feel up to it?'

'It's not that. You're charged with a capital offence, and you're entitled to leading counsel.'

'I'm entitled to counsel of my choice, right? Well, one of 'em's crocked but I've still got one left, and I've got confidence in him. I don't want the case put off or started again.'

Charles looked at Cohen, who shrugged. 'You are aware,' said Charles to Plumber, 'that I have less experience than a Q.C. would have?'

'Yeh. But, like I said, I have faith in you. I know you'll do as well as anyone.'

Charles paused. 'Thank you for that vote of confidence, Mr Plumber. I appreciate what you've said. But I need a little time to think about this. I have a professional duty to do the best I can for you, and if that involves getting in another silk, that's what I have to do. Would it be okay if I give you my answer tomorrow?'

Plumber nodded.

•

'Well?' asked Charles of Cohen as they stepped out of the prison gates onto the forecourt.

'You've had express instructions from the client, Charles. He wants you to carry on. It's a murder, yes, but this is about as straightforward a case of murder as you can get. All you have to do is discredit one witness, and you've done that hundreds of times. I think you can cope.'

'But if I mess it up, our client's going to hang.'

'True. But that doesn't make me any less confident that you can do it. To be honest Charles, you're better than half the silks I see every day. And I think the jury'll warm to you. You talk like them, you come from the same part of London, and there's no front on you. It's your decision of course, and if you decide it's a bit too early, I'll take your advice and we'll find someone else.'

'Okay. I'll think about it overnight.'

•

R. v. Plumber – Transcript of Evidence
Friday, 18 November 1960

Sands: Examination in chief

MR HOGG:	Would you please give the court your full name?
WITNESS:	Robbie – er, that's Robert – Reginald Sands.

MR HOGG: Your present address.

WITNESS: Brixton Prison.

MR HOGG: Yesterday, you pleaded guilty to robbing
             the Express Dairies, London North
             Depot of approximately £138,000 on 5th
             February this year.

WITNESS: Aye, I did.

MR HOGG: Did you commit that robbery alone or
             with others.

WITNESS: I did it w' him.

JUDGE: Let the record show that the witness
             pointed to the Defendant, Plumber.

MR HOGG: Were any others involved?

WITNESS: No.

MR HOGG: Were any firearms used in the robbery?

WITNESS: Aye. We each took an imitation, at least
             that's what I thought.

MR HOGG: Would you please show the witness
             Exhibits 4 and 5?

WITNESS: They're the ones. I cannae say which
             was mine or Plumbers, 'cos they were
             identical.

MR HOGG: Who obtained these replicas?

WITNESS: I did.

MR HOGG: When you obtained them, were you
             anxious to obtain real or imitation
             firearms?

WITNESS: I wouldnae have gone on the job at all had I
             known that real shooters were to be used.

MR HOGG:	What was your part in the robbery?
WITNESS:	We both went in. I stood by the door and collared the employees as they came through; Plumber handcuffed them to the pipes. We took two cars, well, a van and a car. Plumber was the getaway driver. The van was used to block the alley after us.
MR HOGG:	There came a time when a member of one of the crews returning to the Depot was reluctant to enter, did there not?
WITNESS:	There did.
MR HOGG:	Will you tell the jury what happened then?
WITNESS:	The wee laddie on the door opened up, but the fella wouldnae come in. He must have been suspicious, 'cos he ran off, shouting something.
MR HOGG:	What happened then?
WITNESS:	I rushed out to grab him. He was about ten yards ahead of me, running to his van.
MR HOGG:	Where was Plumber at this stage?
WITNESS:	I thought he was still inside, 'cos that was his job, right? Guarding the employees. But then I heard something behind me, and the next second there was this bang. The guard caught it right in the middle of the back. Blew him off the ground and down by the van.
MR HOGG:	Did you see what had caused the noise?

WITNESS: Not till I turned. There was Plumber wi' that in his hand and smoke coming from it.

JUDGE: Let the record show that the witness indicated Exhibit 2. Have a look at it Mr Sands please.

WITNESS: That's the one.

MR HOGG: Show us how Plumber was holding it, please. (Witness takes exhibit) You are holding it at waist level with your right hand on the butt and the left supporting the barrels. Where was it pointing?

WITNESS: Straight at the dead man, or at least, where he had been when he was upright.

MR HOGG: What happened then?

WITNESS: I ran up tae Plumber. He was, eh, stunned, like.

MR HOGG: How do you mean?

WITNESS: Well, he was, like, frozen in position. I shouted at him.

MR HOGG: What did you shout?

WITNESS: I cannae recall that now, "Let's go!" or something like that.

MR HOGG: Did he react?

WITNESS: Not immediately. I had tae grab him, turn him round. We ran back inside, grabbed the money, and left. I'm sure he didnae mean tae do it. It was just the panic.

JUDGE: It's for the jury to decide if he meant to

	do it or not, Mr Sands, not for you. Please don't make comments like that. You are here to answer questions.
WITNESS:	Certainly, my Lord. I just wanted, eh, tae help him out if I could.
MR HOGG:	Wait there Mr Sands; there will be more questions for you.

[End of examination in chief]

Sands: Cross-examination

JUDGE:	Mr Holborne?
MR HOLBORNE:	Thank you my Lord. Mr Sands, who planned this robbery? (Pause). Mr Sands?
WITNESS:	We did it together, Plumber and me.
MR HOLBORNE:	Mr Plumber was the driver of the getaway car, wasn't he?
WITNESS:	Aye.
MR HOLBORNE:	And he planned the getaway, isn't that right?
WITNESS:	Aye.
MR HOLBORNE:	But he didn't plan anything else did he?
WITNESS:	Eh...not as such, no.
MR HOLBORNE:	It was you who had the idea, and you took the proposal to Mr Plumber. You recruited him, rather than he recruited you.
WITNESS:	Aye, that's right.
MR HOLBORNE:	And as far as you were concerned, two

imitation guns were to be taken on this robbery?

WITNESS: That's right.

MR HOLBORNE: You've told us that you were responsible for obtaining them?

WITNESS: Aye.

MR HOLBORNE: So you know where one can obtain such things?

WITNESS: Aye, I do. Lots of shops sell them.

MR HOLBORNE: What shop did you buy them from?

WITNESS: Er, I didnae buy them from a shop.

MR HOLBORNE: You got them through less orthodox channels.

WITNESS: You could say that.

MR HOLBORNE: Illegally?

WITNESS: I don't know.

MR HOLBORNE: You got them from a man in a laundrette. That's not likely to be a lawful source is it Mr Sands?

WITNESS: No.

MR HOLBORNE: That "unorthodox channel" is the sort of channel that could have provided you with a real gun, had you wanted one.

WITNESS: I don't know. I didnae ask him.

MR HOLBORNE: If you were only after imitation guns, which you have noted can be bought legitimately from "lots of shops", why did you get them from a man you met in a laundrette?

WITNESS: (pause) I don't know.

MR HOLBORNE: It was not because you wanted a real gun too, and that had to be obtained illegally?

WITNESS: No.

MR HOLBORNE: Why then?

WITNESS: I don't know. I suppose I didnae want the police asking at shops an' that.

MR HOLBORNE: Let's move on. How did you feel about Mr Plumber's having taken a real gun with him?

WITNESS: I've already said. I wouldnae have gone had I known.

MR HOLBORNE: By that, I take it that you disapprove of real firearms.

WITNESS: Aye, I do. They're liable to go off.

MR HOLBORNE: You must have been furious with Plumber then, for taking the shotgun and for using it?

JUDGE: That's two questions Mr Holborne. First, Mr Sands, were you furious that he had taken the shotgun?

WITNESS: If I'd known before we went, I wouldnae have been exactly furious, but not happy. I woulda told him to leave it behind.

JUDGE: Were you furious that he had used it?

WITNESS: I couldnae believe what he'd done. He had no need to. Once the guy had seen the imitation, he woulda stopped. They're no' armed, those men. Aye, I was furious.

MR HOLBORNE: Why?

WITNESS: You ask me why? Jesus, the guy had been shot in the back. Robbery's one thing – murder, that's something else altogether.

MR HOLBORNE: Your concern then was that you might be implicated in a murder that you had no part in?

WITNESS: Exactly.

MR HOLBORNE: Did you express that concern to Mr Plumber?

WITNESS: I don't follow.

MR HOLBORNE: You've told us that you were unhappy that he took a real gun along with him, and furious that he used it. Did you tell Plumber that?

WITNESS: Well, I gave him a right bollocking in the car, but what could I do? He'd already shot the guy by the time I knew what was going on.

MR HOLBORNE: So by the time you are in the car, your principal concern is to get away.

WITNESS: Obviously.

MR HOLBORNE: You don't want to hang around where someone has been shot?

WITNESS: Correct.

MR HOLBORNE: You don't want to be tied in any way to a murder of which you say you are innocent.

WITNESS: Correct.

MR HOLBORNE: Where did you go immediately after the robbery?

WITNESS: To my flat.

MR HOLBORNE: What did you go there for?

WITNESS: To divi up.

MR HOLBORNE: Did you go there directly?

WITNESS: We did. Well, we changed cars once on the way, and dumped the guns and balaclavas and that.

MR HOLBORNE: Where did you do that?

WITNESS: We left them locked in the car, and scrapped the car.

MR HOLBORNE: When you say "locked in the car", it is true is it not, that they were left hidden under the rear seat.

WITNESS: Aye.

MR HOLBORNE: And when you say "scrapped", what do you mean?

WITNESS: A compacter. We sold the car tae a scrap metal dealer I know, and he agreed to squash it. He didnae do it though. He got greedy.

MR HOLBORNE: I'm sorry?

WITNESS: Well, we paid him over the odds to squash it, but he obviously took a fancy to it, 'cos it was still in the yard when the police went there.

MR HOLBORNE: I see. And how did you get back to your flat from the scrap dealer?

WITNESS: In ma own car.

MR HOLBORNE: You scrapped the Rover before you went back to your flat?

WITNESS: Yes. I've already said.

MR HOLBORNE: Within minutes of the robbery?

WITNESS: Not minutes, no.

MR HOLBORNE: How long then?

WITNESS: Within half an hour.

MR HOLBORNE: That's thirty minutes.

WITNESS: Okay, within thirty minutes.

MR HOLBORNE: And the reason you did that, I assume, was because you didn't want to risk being found in possession of incriminating evidence one moment longer than necessary.

WITNESS: You could say.

MR HOLBORNE: I do say, Mr Sands. What do you say?

WITNESS: Well, if you like. It's just common sense. I didnae want tae be connected to any of it.

MR HOLBORNE: Indeed. The one item of evidence that you would have been most concerned to get away from, would have been the shotgun.

WITNESS: Not necessarily.

MR HOLBORNE: But everything else ties you to a robbery. The shotgun ties you to a murder.

WITNESS: Well?

MR HOLBORNE: So the item you would most want to get rid of is the shotgun. (Pause) Isn't that right, Mr Sands?

WITNESS: I suppose so.

MR HOLBORNE: We know from the police evidence that Mr Plumber gave them the name of the scrap yard, and that they recovered the car, as you say, before it was compacted.

WITNESS: So?

MR HOLBORNE: They found the two imitation handguns, two masks, and some pairs of handcuffs, but no shotgun. What did you do with it?

WITNESS: I didnae do anything wi' it. Plumber had it. I never touched the thing.

MR HOLBORNE: So you placed the other items under the seat?

WITNESS: Aye.

MR HOLBORNE: And locked up?

WITNESS: Aye.

MR HOLBORNE: But you did not put the shotgun there too?

WITNESS: No.

MR HOLBORNE: Why not Mr Sands?

WITNESS: It wasnae mine.

MR HOLBORNE: But you have just told the jury that the thing you most wanted to distance yourself from was that shotgun. There you are getting rid of all the other evidence, but you keep the shotgun. Why?

WITNESS: I told you, I didnae keep the shotgun. Plumber had it.

MR HOLBORNE: And you let him bring it into your car,

	driving with it to your flat, when you wanted it nowhere near you? You couldn't have wanted to distance yourself that much from it: you let him hang onto it and travel around with it in your car!
JUDGE:	I think counsel's asking you a question Mr Sands, although he's not phrased it as such. Why did you permit Plumber to bring the shotgun with him in your car?
WITNESS:	I don't know. I just did.
MR HOLBORNE:	What happened when you arrived at your flat?
WITNESS:	We divi'ed up the money.
MR HOLBORNE:	That must have taken some time, counting out and dividing £138,000.
WITNESS:	Maybe.
MR HOLBORNE:	How long?
WITNESS:	I don't know; a coupla hours maybe.
MR HOLBORNE:	And you let Plumber leave the shotgun in your car all that time.
WITNESS:	No.
MR HOLBORNE:	In your flat then?
WITNESS:	(pause) I cannae remember what happened to it.
MR HOLBORNE:	From when do you not remember?
WITNESS:	I don't know. I'm not even sure I saw it in the car at all. Maybe he did leave it at the scrapyard, but someone found it.
JUDGE:	Mr Sands, in answer to a question from

	me, not two minutes ago, you said you didn't know why you let Plumber bring the shotgun in your own car, you just did. So you must remember it at that stage.
WITNESS:	I must remember it then, yes.
MR HOLBORNE:	So you remember it in your car. I suppose from what you've already told us, you would not have been happy about it being there?
WITNESS:	Not really, no.
MR HOLBORNE:	Even less happy about it being brought into your flat?
WITNESS:	Aye, correct.
MR HOLBORNE:	Why did you not tell Mr Plumber to get rid of it at the scrapyard?
WITNESS:	I didnae think to. I must have been in too much of a panic.
MR HOLBORNE:	Yes, but your panic was because of the shotgun. Are you really telling this jury that although you wanted nothing to do with the shotgun, and having had the opportunity to get rid of it, you allowed Mr Plumber to bring it into your car and maybe your flat?
WITNESS:	I don't know. I suppose so.
JUDGE:	Mr Holborne, would that be a convenient point at which to break for luncheon?
MR HOLBORNE:	It would, my Lord.
JUDGE:	Two o'clock, members of the jury. Please

keep in mind the warning I have been giving you: do not discuss this case with anyone outside your number.

•

R. v. Plumber – Transcript of Evidence
Friday, 18 November 1960 (continued)

Sands: Cross-examination (continued)

JUDGE: Are you ready, Mr Holborne?

MR HOLBORNE: Yes, thank you, my lord. Mr Sands: when you were first arrested for the offence of robbery, you were interviewed under caution, were you not?

WITNESS: Aye, I was.

MR HOLBORNE: And the police officers took notes of that interview, didn't they?

WITNESS: Aye.

MR HOLBORNE: Have you read those notes?

WITNESS: I have.

MR HOLBORNE: Your barrister has not suggested that the police officers made any mistakes when recording your interview. May I take it that you do not dispute their summary of what was said?

WITNESS: No, I don't dispute it. It's a fair summary.

MR HOLBORNE: During the course of that interview, you are recorded as having said there was a third man on the robbery, and that it was

	he who took and used the shotgun.
WITNESS:	I said that, aye.
MR HOLBORNE:	That was a lie, wasn't it?
WITNESS:	It was, but I only said it because he threatened me if I didnae.
JUDGE:	You pointed at the defendant. Are you saying that Plumber threatened you?
WITNESS:	I am. Well, ma family.
MR HOLBORNE:	When did he make this threat?
WITNESS:	On the telephone, the day after the robbery.
MR HOLBORNE:	And what, exactly, did he say?
WITNESS:	He said that he reckoned we might be caught, and that if we were, we should both give the same story, about the third man.
MR HOLBORNE:	Did you agree to this plan?
WITNESS:	No' at first. Only after he made the threats. He said that if I didnae agree, he would see to ma family.
MR HOLBORNE:	He wasn't going to see to you personally?
WITNESS:	You gotta be joking. Him?
MR HOLBORNE:	I take it that you are not personally afraid of Mr Plumber?
WITNESS:	Correct.
MR HOLBORNE:	Exactly what members of your family did he refer to?
WITNESS:	He didnae say.
MR HOLBORNE:	Does he know your family?

WITNESS:	I don't know.
MR HOLBORNE:	Well, what family do you have?
WITNESS:	I've got a mother.
MR HOLBORNE:	Is that all?
WITNESS:	Eh…I got an uncle too.
MR HOLBORNE:	Where does your mother live?
WITNESS:	I don't know. I havenae kept in touch. She remarried a while back.
MR HOLBORNE:	To whom?
WITNESS:	Some chap. I cannae remember his name.
MR HOLBORNE:	Where does your uncle live?
WITNESS:	He used to live in a place called Helmsdale.
MR HOLBORNE:	Where's that?
WITNESS:	It's on the north-east coast of Scotland, about 100 miles north of Inverness.
MR HOLBORNE:	Have you ever introduced Mr Plumber to your mother?
WITNESS:	No.
MR HOLBORNE:	To your uncle?
WITNESS:	No.
MR HOLBORNE:	So, to summarise: you neither know your mother's name nor her address, and your uncle used to live in the wilds of north eastern Scotland, but you don't know where he lives now. Correct so far?
WITNESS:	Aye.
MR HOLBORNE:	Mr Plumber has met neither of them, and probably didn't know that they existed.

WITNESS: Maybe.

MR HOLBORNE: And the threats were being made by a man of whom who you are not in the least frightened?

WITNESS: So?

MR HOLBORNE: You must've been quaking in your boots, Mr Sands. (Laughter). I suggest that your evidence that Mr Plumber threatened your family is completely untrue. You have made it up.

WITNESS: No. It's true.

MR HOLBORNE: I suggest that your evidence that *he* bullied *you* into saying there was a third man is also untrue. I suggest the bullying was the other way round. You threatened him.

WITNESS: No.

MR HOLBORNE: Mr Sands you have, I think, six convictions for robbery do you not?

WITNESS: Meybe. I have nae counted.

MR HOLBORNE: Well, I have. In 1948 you robbed a Post Office in Croydon of six pounds five shillings and four pence.

WITNESS: So?

MR HOLBORNE: The way you got the postmistress to hand the money over was to threaten her with a knife.

WITNESS: I don't remember.

MR HOLBORNE: I have all the details here, Mr Sands. I can ask one of the police officers to be recalled

	to read details to the jury if you need me to jog your memory.
WITNESS:	Whatever you say.
MR HOLBORNE:	Are you agreeing with me that you threatened the postmistress with a knife?
WITNESS:	Yes, I suppose so.
MR HOLBORNE:	After you came out of prison you were convicted in 1951 of three offences in which you robbed rent collectors in Sheffield. Is that right?
WITNESS:	Yes. But I served my time. It's got nothing to do with this.
MR HOLBORNE:	I say it has everything to do with this. How did you get the rent collectors to hand over their money?
WITNESS:	I dinnae know what you mean.
MR HOLBORNE:	Oh yes you do, Mr Sands. You understand me full well. You made the rent collectors hand over their money by threatening them with physical violence. One with a knife and two with an unloaded ex-army revolver. Isn't that right?
WITNESS:	If you say so.
MR HOLBORNE:	And during the last of those three offences, the rent collector, a Mr… forgive me, My Lord I have the document here somewhere… yes, Mr Thompson, gave evidence that you threatened to hurt his wife and baby if he didn't comply.

WITNESS: I never said that! That's a lie.

MR HOLBORNE: I have the sentencing remarks of the judge
               in front of me. He referred specifically
               to that as an aggravating feature when he
               sentenced you to prison. Lastly, in 1956
               you were convicted of another robbery
               were you not?

WITNESS: Aye.

MR HOLBORNE: On that occasion you didn't threaten
               violence. Instead you coshed a security
               guard over the head and put him in
               hospital for three weeks. So, I suggest
               Mr Sands that you have no compunction
               whatsoever in threatening or using serious
               physical violence to get what you want.

WITNESS: And what about him?

MR HOLBORNE: Yes, I was about to come to Mr Plumber.
               It is quite true that Mr Plumber also
               has a long criminal record. A full list
               of his convictions has been agreed with
               the Crown, my Lord. It is agreed by the
               Crown that Mr Plumber has never been
               charged with any offence in which he
               personally used or threatened violence.
               His involvement in robberies has always
               been as a getaway driver.

JUDGE: Is that agreed, Mr Hogg?

MR HOGG: It is, my Lord.

MR HOLBORNE: Now, Mr Sands, let's change subject. In

	August this year, you had a visit in Brixton from Detective Inspector Wheatley.
WITNESS:	Yes.
MR HOLBORNE:	You asked your solicitors to get in touch with him, and as a result, he paid you a visit?
WITNESS:	I don't remember.
MR HOLBORNE:	That's his evidence. Do you disagree?
WITNESS:	I suppose not.
MR HOLBORNE:	And at that visit, you told Inspector Wheatley that you had lied before about the third man, and that Plumber had carried the shotgun?
WITNESS:	Aye.
MR HOLBORNE:	You obviously felt by then that your dear lost mother was no longer in danger from Mr Plumber. (Laughter)
JUDGE:	That's a comment, Mr Holborne, not a question.
MR HOLBORNE:	I apologise my Lord. Let me put it this way Mr Sands, you tell us that you were forced into agreeing to making up the existence of a third man by Mr Plumber's threats to your mother. But at some point you decided, despite that threat, to request a visit from DI Wheatley so you could tell him your present story. Correct so far?
WITNESS:	Maybe.

MR HOLBORNE: Well, what part of what I have just said is wrong?

WITNESS: Nothing.

MR HOLBORNE: So the answer isn't "Maybe"; the answer is "Yes". So, what changed?

WITNESS: I thought about it some more, and realised that that pansy would never actually do it.

MR HOLBORNE: I see. So, on reflection, you decided that Mr Plumber was not really the sort of man to threaten violence to your family. Right?

WITNESS: Aye. I changed my mind.

MR HOLBORNE: Now, I want to ask you this: when you changed your story, did the Inspector believe you at first?

MR HOGG: My Lord, I object to that question. It is of no relevance to the jury whether the inspector believed this witness or not; the question is, do the jury believe him?

JUDGE: That's right, isn't it Mr Holborne?

MR HOLBORNE: Put thus, my Lord, yes. But the purpose of the question is not to usurp the function of the jury. I wish to ask about the witness's motives for discussing other matters at the same time.

JUDGE: You may certainly ask about other things spoken about, and Mr Sands's motives, but not about how they affected the officer's mind.

MR HOLBORNE: Very well. Mr Sands: in addition to telling

Inspector Wheatley about what you say
was Plumber's role, you gave the officer
other information, did you not?

WITNESS: (pause) Do I have to answer that question,
my Lord?

JUDGE: You do.

WITNESS: I…er…I really don't remember now. It
was a couple of months ago.

MR HOLBORNE: Do try and assist the jury, Mr Sands. I'm
sure you'll remember if you think hard
about it.

WITNESS: I cannae recall what we spoke about.

MR HOLBORNE: Let me refresh your memory, Mr Sands.
You gave the police information about
other crimes, didn't you?

WITNESS: I don't know.

MR HOLBORNE: You informed on a number of your
friends.

(Disturbance in the gallery. Shouting at the witness)

JUDGE: If this noise does not cease immediately, I
shall clear the court!

MR HOLBORNE: You turned grass, didn't you, Mr Sands?

WITNESS: No, I never!

MR HOLBORNE: Do you wish me to call Inspector
Wheatley to prove that that's a lie?

WITNESS: No.

MR HOLBORNE: Then the truth please, Mr Sands. You

                          informed on a number of your criminal
                          friends, did you not?

WITNESS: I… I was helping the police with their
                          enquiries.

(Continued disturbance in gallery)

JUDGE: Master at arms, take those men out! Any
                          further person making any noise from the
                          gallery will be committed for contempt
                          forthwith! Carry on Mr Holborne.

MR HOLBORNE: The reason you informed on your
                          colleagues was so the Inspector would
                          believe you. You wanted him to believe
                          that Plumber, and not you, used the
                          shotgun, isn't that right? (Pause) Do you
                          intend answering that question? (Pause)
                          May I take it that you have no answer?
                          (Pause) Very well. As a result of the
                          information you gave to the police, you
                          hoped to receive lighter sentence for the
                          robbery, didn't you?

WITNESS: I don't know.

MR HOLBORNE: Of course you know! By giving
                          information to the police did you hope to
                          receive a lighter sentence or not?

WITNESS: Well, I thought if I scratched his back…

MR HOLBORNE: Exactly. And having been originally
                          charged with murder in the alternative

	to Mr Plumber, the charge was dropped against you.
WITNESS:	Aye, it was.
MR HOLBORNE:	I suggest to you, Mr Sands, that in giving evidence to this jury you are not in the slightest motivated to tell the truth.
WITNESS:	I am telling the truth.
MR HOLBORNE:	I suggest that your sole motive was to escape the hangman, and if that meant dropping Plumber and all your other mates in it, then so much the worse for them.
WITNESS:	No.
MR HOLBORNE:	You were the one with the gun, Mr Sands.
WITNESS:	No.
MR HOLBORNE:	You threatened Mr Plumber into saying there was a third man who carried the gun.
WITNESS:	No.
MR HOLBORNE:	You then turned Queen's Evidence to avoid a murder charge, and falsely accuse Mr Plumber of carrying the gun.
WITNESS:	No.
MR HOLBORNE:	You murdered William Wright.
WITNESS:	No. Plumber did it, I tell you.

[End of cross-examination]

MR HOGG:	I have no re-examination. Does my Lord have any questions for the witness?

JUDGE:	No, thank you.
MR HOGG:	That is the case for the Crown.
JUDGE:	Mr Holborne?
MR HOLBORNE:	There is a matter of law, upon which I should like to address your Lordship.
JUDGE:	I suspected there might be Mr Holborne. Members of the jury, counsel has a point of law for me to decide, and, as questions of law are for me alone, I shall ask you to leave the jury box. I do not anticipate that this will take long. I shall send for you in about ten minutes.

CHAPTER TEN

R. v. Plumber – Transcript of Evidence
Friday, 18 November 1960 (continued)

JUDGE: Mr Holborne submits to me that Mr
           Plumber has no case to answer in respect
           of the murder charge. He concedes that
           in most cases the weight and credibility
           to be given to a witness are matters for
           the jury to consider and that the judge
           should not intervene. He however submits
           further that this is one of the borderline
           cases where the evidence is so tenuous,
           weak or inherently unreliable that no jury
           properly directed could safely convict
           the defendant, and that therefore I ought
           to stop the case. Mr Hogg agrees to the
           principle, but says that this is not such a
           borderline case.

           The foundation stone of the Crown's
           case is the evidence of a Robert Sands,
           who is conceded to be in the category of
           an accomplice. If, as in this case, there
           is no corroboration of Sands's evidence,
           and if that evidence is tenuous, weak or
           unreliable, the Crown cannot succeed.
           In such cases I cannot let the case go to

the jury. In deciding if the evidence is so tenuous or weak or inherently unreliable as to render it unsafe, I must apply my own judgment.

I reach my decision upon three grounds. Firstly, in my view Mr Sands was a patently unreliable witness. His evidence in relation to a central issue, his wish to distance himself from the shotgun used to murder Mr Wright, is contradictory and, in my opinion, unreliable. Secondly, I do not believe that any reasonable jury, properly directed, could conclude without reasonable doubt that it was Sands who was threatened by Plumber, rather than the other way round. Thirdly, his motives for giving evidence are suspect in the extreme. He obviously had the most powerful motive of all for lying to throw guilt on the accused: to save himself from the gallows.

In these circumstances I am of the view that no jury properly directed could rely on his evidence with any safety, and I shall therefore direct the jury when they return to acquit Mr Plumber. Mr Hogg?

MR HOGG: My Lord?

JUDGE: Before I ask the jury to return, I feel constrained to express the view that in the

light of the evidence that has been given,
I am most concerned at the decision taken
by the Crown to offer no evidence against
Mr Sands. I am not a jury trying him,
but it is at least possible, if not probable,
that he has wrongly escaped conviction of
murder. In the circumstances, I propose
referring the matter to the D.P.P. to see if
any further action should be taken.

•

'If you don't let go of my hand Mr Plumber, it will fall off!'

'I still don't know what to say, Mr Holborne, it was terrific! I'll never be able to thank you enough,' said Plumber, still pumping Charles's hand.

'Take it easy now; you do have six years to serve for the robbery.'

'Yeh, but even that's a result. I'd, wossname, resigned meself to the same as Sands got, you know, nine. To get six, on top of getting off the murder, well…'

'You don't have anything like as bad a record as he does,' said Cohen.

'Not only that,' said Charles, grimly, 'but your six will be a doddle compared to his nine. He'll have to spend it all under rule 43 – solitary.'

'That's right,' said Cohen. 'Life inside as a grass is not pleasant.'

'I'd not thought about that,' replied Plumber. 'Still,

serves him right. By the way, what was all that about the D.P.P.?'

'In simple terms, if the Crown can find a way, by hook or crook, to try Sands again for the murder, they'll do it.'

'Is that possible?' asked Cohen.

'He's technically been acquitted once, and he can't be tried again for the same offence unless there was some technical defect, for example in the indictment. Of course, the other possibility open to the Crown would be to charge him with attempting to pervert the course of justice. That, I'm pleased to say, is not my problem.'

In fact Charles's problem awaited him in the form of an envelope addressed to him in his pigeon-hole when he reached Chambers.

Holborne
You may think you have won, but I assure you, no filthy little Jew and his whore shall defeat me. The disgrace you have made me suffer will be as nothing to what I shall cause you. I shall repay you with interest. Isn't that what your race expects?

The note was unsigned and there was no clue from the envelope, which had been delivered by hand, but Charles had a suspicion. He lifted the notepaper to his nose and sniffed. There was no doubt: it had the same musty bird smell as Kellett-Brown's clothing and budgerigar-infested flat. Charles read it again, laughed, and threw it in the bin.

•

"SERIOUS CRIME FILE E4/1379/82 [Murder/ robbery – EXPRESS DAIRIES, LONDON NORTH DEPOT 5/2/60]
Memorandum:
Central Criminal Court Indictment No: 61/0012 (see linked indictment 60/1375-6)
Robert Reginald SANDS (CRO E/6563/20) convicted on 23 March 1961 of attempting to pervert the course of public justice. Sentenced to 5 years imprisonment to run consecutive to present sentence of 9 years for armed robbery. No further action re: murder William Wright. File ends."

PART THREE

1962, PAYBACK

CHAPTER ELEVEN

The rain stopped almost as suddenly as it started, and as the black clouds scudded off towards the east, they seemed lit from underneath by the horizontal orange shafts of the setting sun.

'Look at that,' said Charles, nodding through the windscreen at the sky. 'Amazing. If you painted those colours, people would think you were making it up.'

They had not spoken since getting into the car almost an hour earlier, and Henrietta deliberately turned her head to look out of the passenger window without responding. Charles sighed, and leaned forward to turn on the radio. Without a word Henrietta turned it off.

'I thought you liked Cilla Black,' commented Charles. 'You were humming that yesterday.'

Henrietta turned slowly and stared at Charles's profile. 'The music's fine, Charles,' she said, after a pause. 'I just don't want to pretend anymore, okay? I don't want this to be normal – it's not. We're not listening to pop songs, having a nice little drive on the way to a party, as if nothing was wrong.'

'I thought perhaps we could make a special effort, you know, draw a line under the last few days and have a nice evening?'

'I'm too angry.'

'Couldn't you just put that to one side for a few hours?'

'No. I'm not like you, Charles.'

They remained silent for the rest of the journey. When they arrived at the Temple Henrietta got out of the car before Charles had turned off the ignition, and clip-clopped in her high-heeled boots across the wet cobblestones to the wooden staircase leading to the top of Chancery Court. Charles watched her blue nylon slacks disappear up the stairs and sighed. Yet again he wondered what had happened to them. There had been a time, until about a year before, when despite Henrietta's disdain for him and the cold bitterness of their rows and the nights spent apart, he was always able to locate in himself the deep tenderness he had felt for her from the first. It took much to make Charles really angry, and once roused the storm soon passed. Half an hour of pottering in the garden, working on some papers or watching television, and the substance of the row no longer seemed important, and all he wanted was to ambush her with a hug, and watch how the corners of her mouth would, despite her resistance, crease with a reluctant smile. And then they would have make up sex which brought them oblivion and then stillness, if only for a short while.

But now…well, now, he was just exhausted by it. It was such hard work, just keeping the peace. Once or twice Charles had let himself be goaded into responding in kind and, with a glorious and dangerous freedom, he had let the brakes off, reducing Henrietta to tears. Now however it was as if the brake lever was useless in his hands. Whatever he said or didn't say made no difference. Their marriage had become a runaway train, rattling downhill at an increasingly terrifying speed towards an inevitable wreck.

Charles got out of the car and locked the door. He followed Henrietta up the staircase towards the sound of animated talking and music. The door was just closing having admitted Henrietta, and for one moment Charles toyed with the idea of simply turning on his heel and leaving. Henrietta would barely notice his absence, and an hour or two of walking along the Thames embankment at dusk appealed to him. But as he hesitated, the door opened wide and Sebastian Campbell-Smyth looked out.

'I did wonder for a moment if Henrietta had come alone,' he said. 'Has she?'

Charles sighed, and stepped inside. 'No, although you did catch me wondering if I could bunk off.'

Sebastian smiled grimly. 'Still no better?' The state of the Holbornes' marriage was an open secret in Chambers. Charles shook his head. The other barrister leaned forward confidentially. 'I did wonder about the wisdom of buying that flat.'

Charles shook his head. 'That's nothing to do with it. It's convenient, and Henrietta agreed it made sense. It takes me exactly three minutes from here to Fetter Lane.'

'Sure. But what message did it send, eh?'

Charles thought about it, and nodded slowly. 'I know. If truth be told, I needed…an oasis,' he sighed. 'Somewhere to regroup.'

Sebastian put a friendly arm round Charles's shoulder. He was about to say something else when someone dropped the heavy brass knocker on the outside of the door, and he resumed his door keeping duties.

Charles followed party sounds through the panelled corridor into the reception area. Chambers was laid out for a party. To his right the double doors into Sir Geoffrey's room, the largest in Chambers, were wide open. The room had been cleared of office furniture and now contained two large tables laden with food and drink. In a corner were the unattended instruments of a jazz trio. Two waitresses circulated among the guests with champagne and *hors d'oeuvres*. Most of the members of Chambers were already there with their wives. The only female member, Gwyneth Price-Hopkins, clinked champagne glasses with her husband. The guest of honour, Sir Geoffrey Duchenne, soon to be Mr Justice Duchenne, had still to arrive.

Charles scanned the room for Henrietta but couldn't see her. He wandered over to the makeshift bar and waited to be served. He looked to his left and saw Sally.

'Hello Sally,' he said. 'You look lovely.'

'Thank you sir,' she replied, blushing slightly at the compliment. She wore a strapless, and almost backless, evening dress in crimson. Her hair had been cut in a very short bob. Charles found the contrast between her full figure and tomboy haircut enticing. He found himself wondering how the strapless dress held itself up, and that thought led shortly to wondering what she would look like with no dress on at all.

'Is Mrs Holborne here?' she asked Charles.

'Yes... somewhere.'

Then he caught sight of her in the far corner, deeply engrossed in conversation with Simon Ellison. Their heads were close together, as if sharing some confidence, and they both laughed. She hasn't laughed like that with me for months, thought Charles bitterly, and then grimaced ruefully at his own self-pity.

Henrietta patted Ellison on the cheek. The gesture was affectionate but at the same time patronising, as if she was teasing a child who'd said something daft but endearing, and Ellison flushed. Then, as if suddenly aware that he was observing her, Henrietta turned round and caught Charles's eye. Her mouth hardened, and the smile died on her face. Charles considered for a moment if the whole scene might have been staged for his benefit. At a dinner party two weeks previously Henrietta had flirted outrageously with another of the guests and had become progressively more drunk and furious when Charles had ignored it. That evening had prompted an entire week of silence.

Ellison moved away from Henrietta and spoke quietly to Peter Finch, one of the senior members of Chambers. They had a brief whispered conversation, Finch nodded, and the two men slipped outside into the corridor. Plotting, thought Charles. Charles returned his attention to Sally, but she was no longer beside him. He took a second drink from a passing tray and stared out at the evening shadows lengthening over the manicured gardens of the Temple.

•

Peter Finch entered the panelled room on the opposite side of Chambers, followed closely by Ellison. The room was in half-darkness and it took a moment for Finch's eyes to adjust from the bright lights of the party. He reached for the light switch.

'Leave it off, there's a good chap,' said a voice from the far corner of the room. Finch started as he realised that his desk was occupied by someone else. 'I was just enjoying the last sunlight.'

Laurence Corbett sat with his feet up on Finch's desk and gazed out over the Thames. He slouched at an angle, his hand resting on the back of Finch's chair. Smoke curled lazily from the cigarette held between his index and middle fingers. His face was lost in shadow, but his head turned slowly as he followed the progress of a tug towing a wide empty barge upriver. As they laboured their way against the ebbing tide, the vessels' wakes created two wings of pink reflected sky.

'Get your bloody feet off my papers!' protested Finch.

'Certainly Peter,' replied Corbett, but he didn't move. After a few seconds he languorously folded his long legs like a crane fly and spun round, vacating the desk.

'Well? What do you want, Corbett?' asked Finch.

Finch was in his early 60s, with a long grey comb-over partially concealing his bald patch. When it was windy the thin mat of hair would sometimes fall forward over his face like a silver curtain, much to the merriment of his pupil. He had watery grey eyes, and he blinked frequently.

Corbett perched on the edge of the older barrister's

desk, making it difficult for Finch to skirt round and reach his seat. Finch cast an eye over his shoulder. Ellison was leaning nonchalantly against the door lighting a cigarette, and while he was not quite blocking Finch's escape, Finch felt uncomfortable, and stood awkwardly in the middle of the room.

'A few of the chaps and I have been chatting about the succession,' explained Corbett, 'and I have been asked to canvass your views.'

'I wouldn't have thought my views were very important,' replied Finch irritably. 'We all know who's going to be head of Chambers.'

'That's not a safe assumption,' said Ellison from behind him.

Finch turned. 'What do you mean?'

Corbett answered. 'Well…we wondered if *you* would like to stand?'

'Me?' said Finch, genuinely astonished. 'I have no ambitions in that direction.'

'Liar,' said Corbett quietly, without malice.

'We're not all as ambitious as you, Corbett. And I couldn't afford the rent. The Inn wouldn't have me.'

'They might, if a number of us stood as joint guarantors.'

Finch thought about that for a moment. 'You're saying that if I were to stand against Bob for the tenancy from the Inn, you and some others would support my application? Which others?'

'Enough.'

'No. I need to know exactly who. A contest for the

position would be extremely divisive, and...well, I may have had my differences with Bob over the years, but I'm not going to be responsible for splitting Chambers.'

'I can't tell you at the moment. Just believe me.'

Finch took a couple of steps towards the window, and looked at the river below him. In the space of only a few moments the pink flecks on the water had gone, and twilight was almost at an end.

'And what would you want from me?' he asked shrewdly.

Corbett smiled in the gathering darkness. 'Move Holborne on.'

Finch turned round. 'Oh, not again, Laurence. You've raised this half a dozen times, in Chambers meetings and outside. What *have* you got against the poor man?'

'You must be joking, Peter. Do *you* like his child molesters sitting in the waiting room? How do your banker clients enjoy sitting next to unshaven derelicts, smoking roll-ups and stinking of cider?'

'Granted – '

'And have you noticed how long Stanley's out every afternoon checking the criminal courts lists? During the busiest time of the day? A hugely disproportionate time is given to one man's practice, at the expense of everyone else's. How many times do I have to say it? We are not set up to do crime here. He would be far better off somewhere else.'

Finch listened patiently, a small smile on his face. 'All very good reasons, no doubt, but we all know the truth: you just loathe him, right? You just can't bear him.'

'Well, can you? He's an arrogant, common, barrow boy – like most of his clients. And he's a Jew. But that's really not the point. There are plenty of perfectly valid grounds for sacking him, if one needs them. The tenant of the Inn can give notice to any barrister in Chambers. Like everyone else, he'd be one of your licensees.'

'He'll appeal to the Inn. I would. He's done nothing to merit sacking. He pays his rent on time – which is more than many do – and he's never been caught with his hand in the till, or his trousers down.'

Ellison replied from the other side of the room. 'Not yet maybe, but have you seen the way he looks at Sally?'

'This is all academic,' said Corbett. 'There's no need to make life more difficult than it has to be. This wouldn't be a sacking; it would simply be a case of Chambers wanting to specialise in civil work, so those doing crime have to find a more suitable home. It's the way the Bar's going. It's what they did at Kings Bench Walk, and no one so much as turned a hair. Give him six months to find somewhere else, and he can't possibly complain.'

The door suddenly opened and Ellison found himself propelled further into the room. A couple of the junior members of Chambers entered. 'Oh, sorry,' the first apologised, giggling, slightly the worse for the champagne.

'That's alright,' said Corbett. 'Why don't you both stay?'

'Have you…' asked the other, indicating Finch.

'Just doing it,' replied Corbett. 'Well?' he asked, returning to Finch. The door closed silently, and the two young men stood next to Ellison.

'I'm not sure. I don't think there'd be enough support. Bob's got it sewn up. He's very popular. You'd need at least twelve to vote against him, and I can't see...' His voice faltered as he saw Corbett's face. 'You've got twelve?' he asked.

'Fourteen.'

'I don't believe it.'

Finch looked towards the others, and received a nodded confirmation. Finch wavered. His little pale eyes watered at the prospect, but then he began to shake his head. Corbett took several steps towards him, and leaned over the shorter man menacingly.

'Why don't you face facts, Peter? Your practice is going nowhere – ' Finch spluttered a half-protest but Corbett held up a finger to silence him ' – I've looked in the diary: you've only had two decent court appearances in the last six weeks, and your desk's almost empty. Don't tell me you're doing paperwork, because I know you aren't. You're, what, 62, 63? Your practice is winding down and you know it. If you're going to be able to keep the twins at university for the next two years, you need to get on the Bench. And the cachet of being head of Chambers... well, that would certainly help the CV, wouldn't it? Principles are fine, but not enough to support kids at university.'

•

Charles sat on a chair near the clerks' room, nursing his drink. Henrietta had disappeared some time ago. He wasn't sure whether she had gone home or was just in one of the other rooms, but he didn't care enough to go looking for her. Sally looked at him every now and then, feeling sorry for him. He looked so miserable! There were times when she could quite fancy him, even though he was a bit old.

Charles stood up, drained his glass, and made for the door, slipping behind the substantial bulk of his head of chambers. Sir Geoffrey had arrived an hour late, having been celebrating his elevation with some of the Benchers. He had made an impromptu and largely unintelligible speech and had started the dancing. Thus far, Charles had managed to avoid him. Geoffrey Duchenne's bonhomie was all he needed to give the evening the *coup de grace*, but as that very thought entered Charles's head, a heavy hand landed on his shoulder.

'Ah, Charles!' boomed Duchenne, 'I shall miss you, you and your tacky little clients.'

Charles stood. 'Will you, Geoffrey?'

Duchenne's ruddy face was redder than usual and his eyes sparkled. He was now unequivocally the worse for drink. 'I certainly shall. You know, I don't mind telling you now, I was against your coming in. But you came, and I don't mind admitting it: I was wrong. Thoroughly nice chap… and I can tell, you know, you're going places. I admire someone who doesn't let his background hold him back.'

'Thank you, Geoffrey,' said Charles, trying in vain to extricate himself. 'That will always be a great comfort to me.'

'You know, there's this Indian chappie. Bought the corner shop near me a few years back.' He frowned, trying to concentrate. 'Worked every hour God sent. Dammit if he doesn't own the whole bloody block now! Huge supermarket!'

'It's amazing isn't it? Sorry Geoffrey, but I really ought to find Henrietta.' Charles wrenched himself out of the other's grip.

'Certainly old chap. You really must bring her round some time soon. Ages since we saw you socially.'

'Never.'

'What?'

'We've never seen you socially, Geoffrey.'

'Oh, of course, no one's been to the new house – only been there a few months – '

'Not to the new house, nor the old house, nor any bloody house! For all I know, you live above your mate's supermarket.'

'You know, I could have sworn…'

Charles walked off. He opened the door and went down to the courtyard. The clouds had cleared completely, and the sky was alight with stars. He paused. For a second he couldn't remember where he had parked the car. Then he remembered, and looked over to the space. It was empty.

'Oh, Henrietta!' moaned Charles softly to the night air. So she'd gone home.

Charles looked across the cobbled courtyard to a battered orange sports car and peered at his watch, weighing his options. If he was lucky with a cab he might just make the last train back to the Buckinghamshire, but it would be tight. But what would be the point? By the time he got there Henrietta would be asleep or – worse – still up and so drunk they'd be bound to have another row. Resigned to another night on his own, Charles pulled his collar up, and set off for Fleet Street.

CHAPTER TWELVE

'Charles?' What on earth are you doing with that old jalopy?'

Charles withdrew his pounding head from under the rusty bonnet with some effort and squinted into the bright morning sunshine. It was the morning after the party. Back at the flat on Fetter Lane he'd opened a bottle of Scotch. He'd intended only to have a single drink, but by 2.00 am he had finished half the bottle. It then seemed like a good idea to phone Henrietta at the house to make sure she had reached home safely. There was no answer. Charles assumed she was either unconscious or more probably lying in bed deliberately not answering his call. So he decided to continue ringing every 10 minutes, which he did until he fell asleep in the armchair. Having failed to close the curtains he woke at daybreak and managed to stumble to the bed for another hour's fitful sleep. Now he was awash with coffee and aspirin, and feeling awful.

The voice was that of Simon Ellison, walking down the steps from Chambers, a large bundle of papers tied with ribbon under his arm.

'Oh, hello Simon,' replied Charles. 'Frankly, I begin to wonder. I can't get the bloody thing to start.'

'I saw it here last week,' said Ellison, 'and wondered whose it was. I didn't know you tinkered with cars. They take a bit of looking after, these Austin Healeys. And it doesn't look as though this one's had much love and attention.'

'I know, I know. It was a bit of an impulse buy. You know, a runaround for when I'm in town? The Inn said I could leave it here for a while till I organised permanent parking. But it's been standing here for a fortnight now, and the bloody thing won't start.'

'Here, let me have a look.'

'Do you know anything about these things?' asked Charles hopefully.

'Well, not about Sprites in particular, but a bit about cars,' answered Ellison. He leaned into the car, dropped his papers onto the leather driving seat, and returned to look under the bonnet.

'Have fun last night?' he asked.

'Not much. Henrietta took the Jag and stranded me.'

'Oh, you poor sod,' said Ellison sympathetically. ''Fraid I've no advice to offer there, old chap.'

'But you and Jenny seem very happy. How do you manage it?'

'No idea, Charles. I've just been very lucky. Let's have a look at this…'

Charles watched as Ellison inspected the rusting metal to which the distributor was fixed. Ellison grunted with effort and finally shifted the distributor cap. He came out from under the bonnet and showed Charles.

'I'm not surprised she won't start. This thing hasn't been serviced in years. The points are worn so badly they're almost useless. Look,' he said, pointing them out to Charles.

Charles looked over his shoulder. 'Now I know why it

was such a bargain.'

'If you want my advice, get yourself a nice new Mini. I'm not sure you're the sort of chap to be driving a neglected sports car.'

'Here – use this,' said Charles, handing Ellison a screwdriver. 'You'll never turn it with your fingernail.'

Ellison fiddled with the points for a minute.

'There,' said Ellison, 'let's try again.' He leaned under the bonnet once again. 'It may not get you as far as Bucks, though.'

'I've only got to get it to the flat for the moment. 150 yards.'

'I heard about your little London pad. Very convenient,' said Ellison, nudging Charles in the ribs.

'Nothing like that,' said Charles with a laugh. 'It's just for those nights when I finish too late to get back. Or can't get home for any reason. If I work until ten or later there's no point waiting half an hour for a train, and then getting home by midnight – by which time Henrietta's in bed – just to get up again at six.'

'Why move out so far then?'

'*Force majeure*. Henrietta wanted to be nearer her pals, and her parents.'

'You're near Thame, aren't you? I ride near there quite often,' said Ellison.

'You must pop in some time, then. We'd like to see you and Jenny.'

'Just give us a date, tell us how to get there, and we'll come.'

Ellison put the points back in the distributor and, without replacing the cap, sat in the car, and turned the engine over. Charles watched the distributor as he did so.

'It's opening,' called Charles. 'Let's try starting her.'

Ellison got out again, and they both stood at the front of the car.

'Been busy?' asked Charles.

'No. Far too quiet in fact. Keep it under your hat, but I may be leaving Chambers soon. I've applied for an appointment.'

'What, you too?'

'Yup,' said Ellison.

'Well, best of luck, your Honour,' said Charles.

'I'm not counting my chickens, but it's looking promising. I got great support from McDowell J.'

'How long before you know?' asked Charles.

'Shortly. Right,' said Ellison, 'do you want to get in and try starting her?'

Charles climbed in and turned the key. The car started immediately. He revved a few times, and leaned out, the engine running.

'Well done!' he shouted. 'I owe you a pint! I'll be off, before she stalls again,' he said, and closed the door. He handed Ellison his papers through the open window and moved off. Ellison grinned as he watched the car's spluttering progress towards the Temple gates, and shook his head as it disappeared.

•

Charles dropped the car keys on the shelf in the hall of his tiny apartment, reached immediately for the telephone and dialled.

'Hello?'

'Henrietta? It's me.'

'Yes, Charles.'

Charles paused to see if she would mention the night before and her premature departure from the party. She did not.

'I'm just calling to see how you are.'

'That's very thoughtful of you, dear. I'm very well, thank you. Are you still in London? I half expected you to call from the station.'

'No. I...I had hoped we might spend the day together, here.'

'No, sorry, Charles, but I have plans. I'm not coming back to town.'

Charles peered through the floor-to-ceiling blinds down at the sparse traffic on Fetter Lane. The city was wonderfully quiet at weekends, and he was disappointed. He'd planned everything: a lazy morning in bed with the papers, Brick Lane for fresh bagels, then the National Portrait Gallery followed by a walk by the river and a romantic meal at a new restaurant in Soho. Now the Healey was running they could even have a run out, to the Heath perhaps.

'I did mention spending the day in London,' he said gently.

'You did mention it, yes. But I didn't agree.'

'But if you didn't want to do it, why didn't you say? We could've done something else.'

Charles heard her sigh. 'I just didn't want another fight.'

'Fine. So if I come back to Thame you won't be there anyway.'

'Well, on and off, but basically, no. I've a tennis match this morning, and I said I pop into see mummy afterwards. You go and do whatever it is you wanted to do, and I'll see you Monday night.'

'Fine.'

'And by the way, I've been meaning to tell you: I'll be away next weekend. I've been invited to Shropshire.'

'With whom?'

'With friends, Charles. I have some, you know? I'm not cross-examining you about your plans for this weekend, am I?'

'How is that the same?' demanded Charles, his voice rising in frustration. 'My plans for this weekend involved *you*. I want us to spend time together. You, on the other hand, are going away without me.' He heard, and hated, the whine in his own voice.

'Please don't shout, Charles. I'm having a nice tranquil morning, and I don't want any of that.'

Charles drew a deep breath, willing himself to remain calm. There was silence from the other end of the line. 'Are you still there Henrietta?'

'I'm here.'

'Do you have nothing else to say?'

'Not really, no. If there's nothing else – '

'Oh, Etta –'

''Bye Charles.'

The line went dead.

Charles replaced the receiver. He stared out of the window for a while and then looked round at the papers on the small dining table, a two-day fraud listed for the following week. He made a decision, picked up his jacket and keys, and left the flat.

CHAPTER THIRTEEN

The walk along Lower Thames Street and past the Tower of London lifted Charles's spirits. The day was fresh and sparkling and a warm breeze spoke of summer round the corner. Charles paused at the railings in front of the Tower and watched for a few moments as a squabbling unkindness of ravens hopped about the battlements. He was asked to take a photograph of an American tourist family, and obliged, and then walked on towards Whitechapel.

Blooms, the kosher restaurant at Aldgate, was doing a brisk trade. A group of black-hatted Hasidic men emerged onto the pavement as Charles passed, talking volubly in Yiddish and gesticulating, reminding Charles of the ravens, and he smiled to himself. Blooms, an East End institution, had been a special Sunday morning treat for Charles and his brother David when they were children. Millie and Harry Horowitz would take the boys, usually with another family or two from their bridge club, and they would push together three tables at the rear of the restaurant. The rudeness of the harassed waiters and the size of the enormous portions were legendary, and the group would dally for up to three hours over their chicken soup ("with everything"), cholent or Vienna sausages and chips for the children, lokshen pudding and tall glasses of sweet lemon tea. No one cared if the group of children at the far end of the table made a noise or got in the way of the waiters. It was often dusk by the time they emerged, their throats sore from cigar smoke and shouting over the din.

Charles passed Aldgate East station and turned north up Osborn Street and into Brick Lane. For a century this had been the hub of East End Jewish life as successive waves of immigrants had arrived from Russia and eastern Europe, but over the last couple of years Charles had noticed an increasing number of Pakistanis moving into the area, initially single men but now, three or four years later, entire families. The first curry house had opened a couple of months before and both the clothing of the people on the street and the produce in the shop windows were more multi-coloured and varied. Waves of different intriguing cooking smells assailed Charles as he walked north, and he was suddenly hungry. He quickened his pace.

Halfway up the Brick Lane he turned into a kosher bakery and joined the queue. The bakery served fresh-baked bread and bagels 24 hours a day, 7 days a week to an ever-changing population of builders, taxi drivers, nurses and policemen coming off duty, students and, late at night, opera-loving refugees from Covent Garden in top hats and tails.

Charles ordered two plain bagels, paid for them and was about to leave the shop when someone spoke to him.

'Excuse me?'

Charles turned to see a slender dark haired woman in her late 20s with pale skin and very large almond-shaped eyes. She carried a grey duffel coat over her left arm, a plastic cup of coffee in her left hand, and a large bag of fresh bread clutched in the crook of her right arm. She was smiling and looked slightly embarrassed.

'Yes?' answered Charles.

The woman's smile broadened, and she nodded. 'Charlie Horowitz. I'll be dammed. I thought it was you. And you don't recognise me, do you?'

Charles frowned, and looked at her face more closely. There was indeed something familiar about her wide mouth and her large eyes, but Charles could not place her.

'I forgive you,' she said. 'I expect I've changed in the last 16 years. I was 11 when we last met. You were 18, and just going off to University.'

'I'm really sorry, but I can't remember …'

'Rachel,' she said, managing to extricate her right hand and offer it to Charles. 'Rachel Golding,' she said.

Charles searched his memory. A very faint bell of recognition rang about the name – friends of his parents? – but not about its owner. She was very attractive, and he was sure he'd have remembered had he met her before.

'We were at school together, and *chaider*,' she said, referring to Jewish Sunday school. 'Well, not *together* in truth, because you were a few years older than me. Still are, I expect.'

'I'm sorry, Rachel, of course I do remember your name but…. how on earth did you recognise me after all this time?'

'Perhaps it's something to do with the dreadful crush I had on you,' she said with disarming candour. Charles found her direct gaze unusual, and he was intrigued. 'To you,' she continued, 'I was a plump little girl – if you noticed me at all. But *you* were the success of the school – Cambridge, wasn't it? – and then a barrister. And our parents still meet at *shul*, so your name comes up every now and then. It's "Holborne" now isn't it?'

Charles smiled apologetically. 'It is.'

They left the shop together. 'Which way are you…?' asked Charles.

Rachel looked at her watch. 'I've only got another 15 minutes. So, back towards Whitechapel. You?'

'I'm just wandering. Mind if I walk with you?'

'That'd be nice.'

They set off southwards, back the way Charles had come. 'Only 15 minutes?' asked Charles. 'Do you have an appointment?' Charles hoped not; Rachel interested him.

'I have to get back to work. This is my lunch hour.'

The bag of bread in Rachel's hand tipped over suddenly but Charles caught it as it fell.

'Thank you!' said Rachel. 'It'd be a lot easier if I put this on – ' she indicated the coat on her other arm – 'but I didn't expect it to be this warm.'

'That's fine. I'll carry them. So, what do you do?'

'Well, I'm working in the Whitechapel Gallery for the moment.'

'Oh, I read about that,' replied Charles. 'Haven't you got that bloke…'

'Hockney? Yes, the exhibition opened last week. You should come.'

'Only if you explain it to me. What do they say? I don't know anything about art, but I know what I like.'

'You're asking the wrong girl, Charlie. I know little more than you. It's not my day job. I'm just filling in for a friend.'

'Oh, OK. What is the day job?'

'I dance. Well, I danced. I went to the Royal Ballet School.'

Charles heard the deep disappointment in her voice. 'But?'

'I was in the corps at the London Festival Ballet.'

'And…' prompted Charles.

'Sorry – I assume everyone knows. Well, basically, they're going bust, so most of us are out of a job. A friend offered me some hours at the gallery, but it's only part-time, and only temporary. Unless something comes up soon, I'll be back at Mum and Dad's. I don't have next month's rent.'

They walked in silence for a while, Rachel taking careful sips of her coffee every few steps. 'Anyway,' she said, forcing a smile, 'now I have before me the famous Charles Holborne, Barrister at Law. So how are you? Rich? Famous? Happy? Rich? Did I mention rich?'

Charles laughed. 'You remind me of a joke dad used to tell, about a Jewish tailor knocked down crossing the road. A policeman runs over and puts a jacket under his head and asks him "Are you comfortable?" The tailor replies: "Well… I make a living."'

Rachel laughed.

'And, well,' he shrugged, 'I make a living.'

'I like your dad,' commended Rachel.

Charles nodded. 'Yes, most people do.'

They turned left onto the main road. 'But not you?'

'It's… complicated.'

Rachel stopped, and turned Charles to face her. 'I heard. I'm so sorry, Charlie. That must have been really hard.'

Charles looked down at her thin, almost waif-like face, and her enormous brown eyes full of concern. He was about to make a glib comment, but as he inhaled to speak he felt a sob catch in his throat. 'God, sorry, I really…' he said, confused and embarrassed, '…that took me by surprise. It's been a difficult few weeks. Few months actually.'

Rachel put a sympathetic hand on Charles's arm. 'I noted you didn't say anything about happy.'

'No. Maybe that's it. Things are… like I said, difficult. At home.'

'I'm so sorry. Look…I know that's a terrible way to leave things, but I've got to go.' She pointed, and Charles saw that they'd arrived outside the gallery.

'No, of course,' he said.

'I feel so rude. I haven't seen you in half a lifetime and I've managed to make you cry!'

'I'm not crying,' answered Charles, now flushing.

'Don't be embarrassed. Now I feel really terrible. Look… I know this is going to sound very forward but I'd really like to carry on talking – only if you want to, right? – so –'

She darted over to a rubbish bin, threw her coffee cup in it, and returned to Charles's side. She reached into her duffel coat pocket and pulled out a pen. 'I haven't got any paper…'

Charles put out a hand. 'I'd like to. Put your number there.'

Rachel stared hard at Charles's face, took his hand, and wrote a telephone number on his palm.

'I'll never wash again.'

'Then don't bother calling. On the other hand if you *do* wash again, you have my permission to call,' she said. 'If you'd like to.'

Charles returned her steady gaze. 'I would like to.'

'Good.'

Rachel grabbed the bag of bread out of Charles's arm, waved, skipped across the pavement and pushed open the door to the gallery. Charles turned to go, and felt a hand on his arm. Rachel turned him round, and planted a kiss on his cheek. This time she blushed.

'Waited to do that for 16 years,' she confessed. ''Bye.'

CHAPTER FOURTEEN

The Barristers' Clerks Association did not need to meet formally all that often. The "Mafia," as the criminal clerks were sometimes affectionately known, had a number of watering holes where most nights, and many lunchtimes, groups of clerks would congregate to share gossip, discuss lists and list officers, and report on the rising young stars, the grand old men, and the fading lights of the Bar – their "Guvnors". The operation of this bush telegraph was informal and extremely effective. Most clerks knew long before any official announcement who was about to "be made up" – become a Judge – or who was having an affair with whom.

The term "Mafia" was not altogether inappropriate either. Barristers' clerks were powerful enough to dictate the course of the careers of their guvnors. Everyone knew of at least one story in which the clerk had ruined the practice of a barrister on the grounds of offence taken at a Chambers party, a perceived slight to the clerk's wife or simply a personality clash.

One of the most popular watering holes was the "City Squash and Tennis Club". Stanley had never played squash in his life and had last held a tennis racket at the age of fifteen, but then, despite its name, strenuous sports did not figure large in the City Squash and Tennis Club's activities. Its principal attraction, at least as far as Stanley was concerned, was its selection of 25 whiskies.

On this particular evening, Stanley had only popped into the Club for a quick one before catching his train home. Rita, his beloved, wanted to do some late-night shopping, and woe betide him if he were to return late. He chatted for a few minutes to a number of clerks he knew quite well, and downed the rest of his drink. As he was about to leave, he saw a familiar face. Peter McPhee was the clerk at a set of common law chambers in Essex Court. He and Stanley were old mates, having come into the Temple as juniors together thirty years before. McPhee waved at Stanley as he bustled up to the bar.

'Have another, Stan,' he said, somewhat out of breath. 'I've some interesting gossip.'

Stanley looked at his watch. 'I can't stay, Peter. I've got to get the 6.50.'

McPhee leaned over and peered at Stanley's wrist. 'Plenty of time,' he said. 'This won't take long. It involves one of your ex-guvnors,' he said tantalisingly. Stanley was hooked.

'Okay,' he said. 'Just a single. Highland Park.'

Peter obtained the drinks and the two of them moved away from the bar to a side table.

McPhee lit a cigarette and leaned forward confidentially. 'I've just bumped into your old favourite,' he said. His words were almost lost in the chatter of the drinkers and the click of snooker balls from the tables behind him. Stanley looked puzzled.

'Ivor Kellett-Brown,' announced McPhee with a flourish.

'My God,' said Stanley, 'I thought he was dead. Wasn't he dossing in Temple Gardens?'

'He was. I saw him myself. He was evicted by the Inn when he couldn't pay his rent. Nutty as a fruitcake, always talking to himself, shouting at thin air. One of my juniors once saw him addressing one of the statues on the Embankment as "My Lord".'

Stanley grinned and took a sip of whisky. He looked at his watch.

'Anyway,' continued McPhee, 'the point is he's come into some money. Quite a lot of money from what I could tell. He's driving a brand new MG Princess – almost ran me over actually – and dressed up like Fred Astaire, tails and all. I've never seen him look so…what's the word… opulent?

'Good heavens,' said Stanley. 'You sure it was him?'

'Certain. I spoke to him. He was parking in the Temple, and I had to jump out the way. When he got out I recognised him and said hello. He remembered I was your mate, and asked how you were.'

'Is he back in practice?' asked Stanley. 'I thought he'd packed up originally because of poor health.'

'That's what I'd heard – I think it was you who told me – but he reckons he was never ill at all. I tell you, Stan,' and here McPhee leaned over even further and dropped his voice almost to a whisper, 'he's barmy. He said, straight out, that he was being blackmailed.' McPhee leaned back in satisfaction, his punchline delivered.

'Blackmailed? Who by? And for what?'

McPhee shrugged and threw back his drink. 'He said it was someone in your chambers, and that they had a nasty shock coming to them. He was ranting on and on – it was like lighting a firework. I'd just asked if he was recovered enough to go back into practice, and he was off like a greyhound,' said McPhee, mixing his metaphors. '"There's nothing wrong with me!" He stormed. "There never was! I was forced out by that blackguard!"'

'"Blackguard?" Who says "blackguard" these days?'

'Ivor Kellett-Brown does. And he was shouting, weird stuff, like "Retribution shall be mine!" I was reminded of me old vicar. He had the same wicked look in his eyes, too. Then, without another word, he storms off, still ranting to himself.'

'And you've no idea who was supposed to have been behind all this?'

'Well, there's the thing. How many "Jew-boys" have you got in Chambers?'

Stanley looked at his colleague, mouth open. 'Holborne?'

McPhee shrugged, hands outstretched and open in a passable imitation of Fagin.

'That's enough of that, Peter,' said Stanley, sternly. 'Even in jest.'

'No you're right. Sorry. I'm not, you know, anti-Semitic. And from what I hear, your Mr Holborne's a decent bloke.'

'He is, Peter. Which is what makes this so odd. I'd never have him down as a blackmailer. And what could he possibly be blackmailing old K-B about?'

'No idea,' replied McPhee. 'I spect it's all in his head.

189

Anyway, I thought you'd like to know. Gotta run.' McPhee replaced his glass on the counter, patted his friend on the back, said 'See you,' and disappeared into the crowd.

Stanley remained where he was for a moment, idly examining his empty glass. Then he remembered the time, picked up his briefcase, and ran for the door.

A tall angular man with a hat pulled low over his eyes watched Stanley's departing back from a nearby table. He also knocked back the last of his drink, picked up his robes bag, and slipped out of the door.

CHAPTER FIFTEEN

Henrietta wove her way unsteadily through the hubbub and the guests to the far side of the room, oblivious to the contents of her champagne glass slopping over the edge and down her forearm. Her face was flushed and her eyes sparkled. She wore her hair up, accentuating her lovely neck and shoulders; but a few strands had escaped and fell over her eyes. She reached her destination but then stopped suddenly, unable to see the person she had been seeking. She frowned and squinted around, sweeping her wayward hair back over her forehead with an impatient gesture of her free hand. She eyed a group of men standing in a tight circle to her left. Most of the men at the party were in dinner suits and hard to distinguish from the rear, particularly to someone who had drunk almost two bottles of champagne. Henrietta appeared to recognise a member of the group and turned rather unsteadily towards him. She giggled to herself. She crept up behind a tall man with a broad back and flowing blond hair, slipped her hand up the back of his jacket and pinched his bottom.

The man whirled round, jogging Henrietta's arm in the process, and causing her to lose the final drops of liquid in her glass.

'Henrietta!' he hissed severely, but with a smile on his handsome face. 'Behave yourself!'

She shrugged and laughed. 'I want to dance,' she

pouted, taking hold of his arm, and tugging at him. 'Oh, come on Laurence, you've been talking for ages.'

Henrietta beamed an unfocused smile round the group of men she had interrupted. One or two of them smiled back politely.

'For heaven's sake,' replied Laurence Corbett, turning away from the group slightly, 'can't you be even a little discreet?'

'No one minds,' she protested. 'Why do you think Polly invited us both?'

Corbett lowered his head to speak confidentially. 'That's no reason to make a spectacle of yourself! Some people here know Marjorie. We've still got to be careful.'

Henrietta wasn't listening. She watched his lips as he spoke, noting his even, white teeth, and the pinkness of his tongue, and thought of what they had been doing to her nipples a few hours before while they were changing for the party.

She leaned towards him. 'Take me upstairs and fuck me,' she whispered wetly in his ear, just loudly enough to be heard by the others in the group. One or two smirked; others pretended not to have heard.

'For God's sake, Henrietta, stop acting like a whore!' replied Corbett. This time he made no attempt to keep his voice low and a number of people outside of the immediate group turned and looked at them. 'Just go away, and please: stop drinking!'

Corbett turned his back on her and resumed talking. Henrietta looked peeved for a moment, and then shrugged.

She turned and walked towards the door. An aisle of silence opened before her.

'You're boring Corbett, just boring,' she said with that curious distinctness that often characterises the speech of habitual drunks. 'Would someone *please* tell me where I can get a drink?' she asked plaintively as she made her exit.

Simon Ellison moved from the far side of the room where he had been talking to his wife, and joined the group of men.

'Hello, Simon,' said Corbett amiably. 'Do you know everyone?'

'Yes, I think so. Sorry, gents, but could I borrow Laurence for a moment?'

Ellison moved off and Corbett followed. They reached a quiet corner by the French windows.

'Chambers business?' asked Corbett.

'In a manner of speaking,' replied Ellison. 'Look, Laurence, I know it's none of my business, but don't you think you should ditch Henrietta Holborne? She's pretty much out of control, and it's only a matter of time before she spills the beans to Charles.'

Corbett smiled. 'That's half the fun.'

'My God, you really do hate him. But then...you don't actually care for her either, do you?'

'Not much. She's a bit of a shrew to be honest, 'specially when she's had a few. But my God, Simon, she's hot stuff in the sack.' He paused. 'As I think you know,' he added meaningfully.

Ellison's eyes suddenly narrowed dangerously. 'Just

exactly what do you mean by that comment?'

Corbett raised his eyebrows insouciantly. 'I'm sorry, Simon. Perhaps you misunderstood me. I thought Henrietta's reputation was well known.'

Ellison continued to stare threateningly at Corbett. Then he nodded slowly, and relaxed. 'The point I'm making is,' he continued, 'she's a loose cannon. You may not care if she tells Charles, but it won't stop there will it? Your Marjorie's bound to hear of it. And would she be as forgiving as she was last time, with the nanny, what was her name?'

'Gretchen' answered Corbett, with a wide grin.

'Gretchen. She was a bit of fun; over for a few months, and now safe back in Sweden – '

'Switzerland.'

'Wherever. But Henrietta Holborne is a different kettle of fish altogether. Like I said, none of my business, but wouldn't life be simpler if you just found yourself another nanny?'

'You're quite right, Simon, it *is* none of your business,' Corbett hissed, with cold intensity. His tone softened. 'Look, I realise you're just trying to be a pal. But honestly, there's nothing to worry about. Now,' continued Corbett, looking about the room, 'where's that lovely hostess of ours? Ah, there she is. Excuse me, but I'm owed a dance or two.'

Simon Ellison watched his colleague's back as Corbett threaded his way through the guests. Ellison's handsome brow furrowed in thought.

•

Henrietta wrapped her fur more tightly round her, and paced slowly around her car again. The country road was pitch dark and little used. She had waited in the car for twenty-five minutes listening to music on the radio, but then her legs began to get stiff, and so she got out, and had since been standing outside. Shortly after her "thing" with Laurence Corbett had started – it wasn't an "affair", which implied romance, and while this was dangerous and sexy, it was anything but romantic – she had begun to realise that the greatest part of it was not, as she had thought, snatched moments of passion, but waiting. She was always waiting for him to call, waiting at a hotel or waiting in restaurants – where all too often he never showed. And now she was waiting in the layby where they had agreed to meet on the way back.

The entire weekend had been a disaster. It had been the first time she and Laurence had ever planned a whole weekend together and she had been looking forward to it for weeks. Two whole days together without having to look over their shoulders, give false names or pretend they were strangers. Days of planning and lying had provided her with credible cover in case Charles had started asking questions. He never did. She found it infuriating. She couldn't work out if his determination to look the other way was because he didn't care or because he was too squeamish. He'd once told her that there had never been a divorce in his family, so perhaps that was it; they all just looked the other way.

Then Laurence had arrived two hours late. By the time he turned up, other guests were beginning to arrive and they had managed only a snatched half-hour together before going downstairs. And then, on top of everything else, it turned out that Simon and Jenny Ellison had been invited. Of course, Simon would never say anything, but she'd never met Jenny before and she had no idea if Jenny might say something inconvenient to Laurence's wife, Marjorie. So after all the planning and sneaking, once she and Laurence went down they had to pretend they weren't a couple – at least until she'd drunk so much she didn't care any longer. And every now and then she was aware of Simon Ellison's eyes burning into her back, which at first made her uncomfortable, then angry and, finally, reckless.

And then there was Laurence's lateness. His excuse? He had been held up on a case! The very same excuse Charles had given her 100 times over the years. She vowed to herself that the next time she committed adultery she'd pick a bus conductor; at least his sex life wouldn't be governed by the vagaries of the civil court process.

So they'd rowed, and then made up, which had been lovely, but the atmosphere had remained. She had drunk too much, and he had been rude, although quite how rude she couldn't remember. She knew that she'd been upset, but the precise events from the end of the evening were a bit fuzzy in her head. However she did remember quite clearly that Laurence and some other chap, an ex-member of Chambers she thought, were planning to do something horrid to Charles, and Laurence took great delight in gloating over it with a number of the people there. So she'd had enough. Henrietta had packed and departed. As she left she'd told Laurence she'd wait an hour for him, and then go home.

Not for the first time, Henrietta wondered if it was all worth it. So much effort for so little return. If I put half as much effort into pleasing Charles as I do Laurence, she thought, I'd probably have a successful marriage. The thought amused her at first. Then she considered it seriously, and was no longer amused. She got back into the car, feeling miserable. 'I'll give you five more minutes, Laurence Corbett,' she said out loud.

She turned the heater on but by then the engine had cooled completely and it blew freezing air onto her bare legs. She'd taken off her stocking and panties in preparation and usually the anticipation – sitting in the car, naked beneath her skirt – was so intense that she'd come almost the second he entered her. This had been "their" layby since they had fucked there for the first time in the back of his car. They had subsequently returned time and again to this lonely country road. Henrietta hated going to hotel rooms – seedy and unspontaneous – and she experienced a particular excitement making love only feet from complete strangers as they swept past, the black interior of the car suddenly ablaze as headlights swept across her while she straddled Corbett's thighs on the back seat.

But now on top of the prolonged wait and an emerging

the brief

headache the blast of cold air was the final straw. 'Fuck
you, Corbett!' she cried, and turned on the ignition. She
revved the engine and was in the process of moving off
when she saw headlights in her mirror. She waited for
them to pass, and then realised that they were slowing
down. Corbett pulled alongside. He wound down his
window.

'I was just leaving,' said Henrietta.

'Sorry. I got held up. Your place or mine?' asked Corbett
with a grin, referring to their two cars.

'Neither. I'm cold and tired, and getting a hangover,'
she said. 'I'm going home.'

'Just hang on a sec – ' he said, putting his car into gear
to pull in in front of her.

'No, really, don't bother,' she insisted, 'I want to go
home.'

'Can't we even talk?' he asked.

'I don't want to talk to you, Laurence. I'll speak to you
later in the week. I want to have a think first.'

'What about?'

'Everything.'

'What are you talking about, Henrietta?'

'I don't know. I just want time to think. This is all
so...' she searched for the right word, '...unsatisfactory.
I mean...I don't know. Maybe I need a break for a while,
just to think things through...'

'What's there to think about?'

'Everything...you, me, us, Charlie, Marjorie.'

'What have Charles and Marjorie got to do with it?'

'For heaven's sake, Laurence, we're married to them! What's more, Marjorie's my friend – my best friend, for that matter.'

'Look, will you just let me pull in, and talk to you sensibly. This is ridiculous,' he said, indicating their two cars standing side by side with their engines running. 'I feel like we're about to start a race.' He smiled his most winning smile but she was not to be budged.

'No! Stay there!' She didn't want him in her car. She knew what would happen. He would start whispering in her ear and stroking her neck; his other hand would travel up her thigh under her skirt; he would nibble her earlobes, his index finger would start making little circular motions, and she would be lost. In separate cars, with the cold night air on her face from the open window, she could be resolute. He looked at her with suspicion. His face hardened.

'Are you telling me it's over?' he demanded.

'No,' she said, quite surprised, 'at least…I don't know. Maybe I am, but I haven't realised it yet.'

'Well you can get that out of your head immediately,' said Corbett. 'You're not dumping me!'

Henrietta stared at him, astounded. 'What the hell do you mean by that?' she demanded. 'If I don't want to see you again, I bloody well won't!'

'You're being completely unreasonable! Everything was fine this morning, and suddenly you spring this on me – '

'I have nothing more to say, Laurence,' she said, closing her window.

'Well I've got something to say to you,' he said, getting out of his car, 'you gin-soaked, spoilt little – '

But Henrietta didn't hear the rest. She let out the clutch and her car shot forward, narrowly missing him, and swerved into the road. She put her foot down and raced off, looking back in her mirror to see him still on the road, staring after her. She caught sight of herself in the mirror. Her face was white and she looked frightened.

CHAPTER SIXTEEN

Charles sat at the kitchen table, reading the Sunday papers. The first arrests had been made in what was now being called the Great Train Robbery. Charles wasn't surprised. He knew Detective Chief Superintendent Butler, the officer heading the London end of the investigation. Butler was a strange man, but Charles had enormous respect for his policing skills.

He drained his coffee cup, and looked at his watch. Rachel was due to arrive at the flat in 10 minutes. He again scanned the apartment to make sure everything was in place.

Charles had phoned Rachel and they had met for a drink after work to swap outlines of their lives over the last 16 years. It had been very comfortable, and the following evening they'd gone out for dinner. That had been better still, but there had been nothing overtly romantic – no kiss goodnight, no touching, not even "accidentally" during conversation. At the end of that evening, standing outside the restaurant, Charles had asked her if she would like to take him round her Gallery on her next day off. She had agreed, and there had been a pause. Charles had wanted to kiss her and sensed that the moment was right, but he'd hesitated and the chance was lost. Rachel had said goodnight, turned, and walked away. As Charles returned to Fetter Lane he wondered if she'd have bolted anyway, and thanked God he'd not tried. He'd spoken a little about his marriage and his suspicions about Henrietta's affairs, and Rachel could see how unhappy he was. But the fact was, he *was* married, and until he sorted out the situation with Henrietta, Charles felt deeply uncomfortable about starting another relationship, no matter how much he was attracted to Rachel. And he sensed ambivalence in her, too. He thought she was interested in him, but not in an affair.

So he wasn't sure how to characterise this meeting. This was the fourth "date" in less than three weeks, so *something* was happening. But what?

Charles had not been back to Thame during the week, and he had not spoken to Henrietta. That more than anything had crystallised his thoughts about the marriage. However bad things had been, he had never before spent a week away from her unless he was away on a case, and even then he used to ring every night from his hotel room. The fact that Henrietta had neither called nor made any comment about his staying at the flat spoke volumes. Charles realised that divorce was now probably inevitable and had started, almost unconsciously, imagining a life without her. He would have to go back to Thame and sort things out.

Charles stood and rinsed his cup it and left it on the draining board. There was a light tap on the door. Charles took the single stride necessary to get him to the front door, and opened it.

'Hi,' said Rachel. Charles frowned. 'One of your neighbours opened the main door for me,' she explained.

She leaned forward and kissed Charles on the cheek. She was wearing a summer dress printed with large pink roses on a white background, and sandals. The dress was tight over her body and flared from her hips. She wore make up, a change from the other occasions Charles had seen her, when she'd been working, and she carried a pink beret in her hand. She looked younger than her 26 years.

'You look lovely,' complimented Charles. 'Come in.'

Rachel entered the tiny lobby, and the two of them danced round each other while Charles shut the door and took her bag.

'Would you like a drink before we go?' asked Charles.

'No thanks.'

'Okay. Take a seat. I'll just get my jacket and some money.'

Charles went into the bedroom and Rachel sat down where Charles had been reading the paper. She scanned the article. 'Do you have any professional interest in this?' she called.

'What, the train robbery? Not yet, but I have my fingers crossed. Every criminal barrister in the Temple wants one of those briefs. That's the sort of case on which careers are made.' Charles returned to the room, pulling on his jacket. He smiled at her. 'Shall we?'

•

The Holbornes' house at Putt Green, Buckinghamshire had once been a large farmhouse on the edge of the village. The last farmers of the land, brothers, had both been killed in action and after the war their executors had sold off the herd of dairy cattle, the land and the house to different purchasers.

By the time the Holbornes acquired the house in 1955 it was badly run down, but a gift from Henrietta's parents had restored it and it was now a stylish well-appointed family home, ideal for a couple with three or four children. But it was too large and rather isolated for a young wife who spent much of her time there alone.

Its garden, carved originally from one of the fields, was huge. Someone had clearly spent a great deal of time working on it, as the lawns were well manicured and the flower beds colourful and orderly. Outside the French windows, on a patio that ran the width of the house, stood an oak garden table and six chairs. A long striped seat with its own awning swung back and forth in the gentle breeze. The far end of the garden was separated from the rest by a massive clipped beech hedge through which there was an archway. Beyond the archway the garden was semi-wild, the grass taller and dotted with wild flowers. There was the stump of a huge old oak, now long dead, and several apple trees, ideal for climbing. It would have been an exciting place had there been any children in the household. Through the fence at the wild end of the garden was a stile leading to open fields.

Vehicles passed the front of the house infrequently and the noise of their engines was only just audible at the back. In the distance could be heard the voices of some children, and occasionally the sound of horses' hooves floated over from the stables in the lane.

Beside the stile at the rear of the house, hidden from the house by the hedge, a man shuffled from one foot to the other. He wore an anorak, heavy comfortable boots and thick socks, for his work often required waiting patiently in uncomfortable situations. He was short, with a round, jovial face and ruddy cheeks. He looked as if in another life he should have been an innkeeper. He'd been standing there for over two hours and he was getting tired. He looked at his watch. He took a pad out of his jacket pocket and made a note with a small stub of pencil. He replaced the pad, and chewed the pencil thoughtfully. It had been a dull shift, and he still had another two hours until he was relieved at 2.00 pm, when he would return to his car where a hot flask of tea and a sandwich awaited him. The subject had sat reading in the garden until the wind had picked up and it got a bit too cold, and then made herself something to eat. Thereafter she spent most of the time in the kitchen.

The only event to punctuate the dull surveillance had been when the telephone rang. The subject had picked it up and spoken, calmly at first. Then her voice started rising until she was shrieking into the receiver. She stood and started pacing back and forth as far as the telephone cable would allow. The call ended with her slamming the receiver down. There was a pause, followed by a further scream – frustration or anger – from the subject, and the man saw a fast movement. A second later he heard the sound of an object smashing, a vase perhaps. The watcher grinned. Temper, temper, he thought, as he recorded the event in his notebook, in slow careful pencil strokes.

•

INTERIM REPORT No. 4 to BSI ON
OBSERVATIONS AT 'The Old Farmhouse', Putt Green,
BUCKS.
Surveillance continued. Subject apparently retired for the
night and surveillance about to end when at 22.23 hours
lights were seen in the master bedroom. At 22.41 hours
the subject left the house and jogged to the junction of
Church Road and the A428 bypass. Waited for ten minutes.
Red Mercedes Saloon, Regn. No. LUC 800 approached
travelling east on by-pass, stopped, and subject got in. Vehicle
drove into church car park without direction from subject,
suggesting the car park had been used for rendezvous in past.
Due to lack of cover, an approach to vehicle deemed not safe,
and observation continued from corner of church at distance
of 150 yards. Driver: male Caucasian, late-thirties/early
forties, light colouring, no facial hair. Driver attempted to
kiss subject, was resisted, although parties clearly familiar
with one another. Discussion in car for ten minutes. Driver
continued to press himself on subject. It appeared driver
attempting to persuade subject. 23.05 hours subject descended
from car, slammed car door, and began to run out of church
car park. A few feet from car, subject turned and shouted
to driver. Subject's back was turned to operative, but words

appeared to be: "And don't 'phone any more. I mean it. I'll tell –" and here subject used a name, possibly "Melanie" or "Marjorie". Subject ran back to house. Vehicle remained stationary until 23.10 hours, then rejoined the A428 and continued in an easterly direction.

•

INTERIM REPORT No. 5 TO BS1 ON OBSERVATIONS AT 'The Old Farmhouse', Putt Green, BUCKS.
Surveillance recommenced 08.45 hrs. Subject seen to be up and about house. Visit from female neighbour 10.45 hrs. to 11.13 hrs. Subject left address driving Jaguar Regn. No. CLH 7. 11.54 hrs. Followed to local shops. Returned to address 12.48 hrs. Jaguar broke down outside address. Subject enlisted two male workers from adjoining farm to push it into garage. Subject returned to house. Worked in rear garden until operative relieved. No further incident.

•

The phone rang in the clerk's room and Stanley picked it up. 'May I speak to Mr Holborne, please?'

'Is that Mrs Holborne?'

'Yes, Stanley? How are you?'

'Not bad, thank you. A bit rushed this week as Sally's on holiday. Just putting you through. Mr Holborne? Your wife for you, sir. And your conference has arrived.'

Charles heard a click on the line.

'Charles?' said Henrietta.

'I haven't time for another flaming row, Henrietta. I have a conference starting right now.'

'The bloody car's broken down.'

'Okay. Where?' asked Charles.

'Just outside the house, thank God. I'd just been out shopping, and it conked out as I was driving back into the garage. I got some of Jim's men to help push it back in, but I've tried it since and it won't start at all.'

'What do you want me to do about it?'

'It's your bloody car.'

'Then I'll bloody manage without it until the weekend, won't I?'

'What am I supposed to use in the meantime?'

'I thought you just said it was my bloody car. What you mean is, it's my bloody car, but you want to drive it.'

'Charles, you know very well how isolated it is here. There's no way I can get around without transport. Particularly if you're not proposing to come up again until Friday. I've got arrangements this week.'

Charles took a deep breath and adopted as reasonable a tone as he could command. 'I'm really sorry, Henrietta, but I can't get there before Friday. If you need it urgently, book it into Breck and Co on the village green.'

'They're Vauxhall dealers.'

'They repair other cars too. They're very good. You might even persuade them to lend you a car while the Jag's in for repair. But I'm afraid I really have to go; my conference is waiting to begin.'

'You're a real bastard sometimes, you know that Charles?'

'That's a bit unfair don't you think?' started Charles, but Henrietta had hung up.

•

'Is that you, Mr Holborne?'

'Yes.'

'I've got nothing further to report. She stayed in all evening. No visitors. Went to bed about an hour ago. Do you want us to continue the surveillance?'

'Stand down your men for the night. It's late and she's got no car. I can't see her going anywhere tonight. Start again tomorrow morning?'

'Very well, sir. I'll report again tomorrow evening.'

•

It was 3.30 am, a dark and damp night. No lights showed from any of the houses in the deserted lane. A thin blanket of mist rose gently from the brook that ran parallel to the lane on the other side of the road to the houses. The clear water usually gurgled over its rocky path under a line of willow trees, but this night the mist seemed to muffle the sound of water, and the lane was unusually quiet. A tall man with broad shoulders, wearing overalls and a woolly hat pulled low over his ears, stood underneath one of the willow trees and observed the Holborne residence. He was completely still and almost invisible. Heavy drops of water dripped from the leaves of the willow onto his head and face. The house was in darkness. Satisfied, the man stepped lightly across the lane and walked softly up the drive of the

Holbornes' house towards the garage. He tried the main door but found it locked. He skirted round the garage, keeping to the shadows, and entered by the rear door. A minute later the main doors swung silently open. Then, like the silver snout of a large animal, the nose of the Jaguar emerged silently from the shadows. The man pushed the motor car from the driver's door, steering it with one hand. It was slow going at first and took an enormous amount of effort, but the drive sloped gently down towards the brook and after a couple of car's lengths the vehicle picked up speed and the man had to jog to keep up with it. Where the drive joined the lane he expertly steered to the left and allowed the vehicle to roll to a stop. He walked on a few paces to the tow-truck in which he had arrived, got in, and let off the handbrake so that it rolled silently backwards to within a few feet of the front of the Jaguar. Then he walked silently and quickly back up the drive and closed the garage doors, returning to the tow truck.

Curled on the back of the truck was a steel hawser with a hook at its end. The man silently uncurled the hawser, crawled under the front of the Jaguar, and attached the hook to the front axle. He returned to the tow-truck and operated the electric winder for three or four seconds, tightening the hawser, and the front of the Jaguar rose smoothly off the ground. The man then climbed swiftly into the cab of the truck, started up, and drove off, towing the Jaguar behind him. The operation had taken less than four minutes, and within seconds of the tail lights of the tow truck disappearing, the lane was again utterly silent.

CHAPTER SEVENTEEN

It was mid-morning in the Temple, and the ancient courtyards resumed their sedate pace following the early rush of barristers dashing off to court. Chancery Court was silent with concentration as members of Chambers settled down to draft documents and research the law in the Chambers' library.

Charles threw down his pen, stood, and paced about his room. He had been trying to draft what should have been a very simple Advice on a personal injuries matter for the last hour, and had written and crossed through the first paragraph four times. He could not concentrate and when he looked at the uncharacteristic chaos of papers and instructions lying on his desk, he realised that he had achieved almost nothing in the last two days.

Yet again Charles reached for the telephone. 'Peter?' he said as he dialled.

Charles's pupil Peter Bateman looked up from the papers on which he had been working.

'Yes?'

'Make yourself scarce for a few minutes, eh?'

'Sure,' replied the young man, and scurried off for a quick cigarette. Charles didn't permit smoking in the room, and the chance for a cup of tea and a smoke with the other pupils in Chambers was always gratefully received.

The call was picked up at the other end.

'Henrietta?'

'Yes?' she said, recognising his voice, and truculent.

'Do you agree that it would be sensible for us to have a discussion about the future?'

There was a long pause at the end of the line but Henrietta's voice when it came was sadder and gentler than Charles had expected. 'What do you propose?'

'I was thinking of coming up tonight, if you've got no plans.'

There was another pause at the other end. At first he could hear her breathing but then the line was silent. Just as he was about to check that she was still there, Charles heard a sob and realised she was crying.

'Etta, honey, don't cry. I'm sure we can sort it out – whatever the outcome. But we both know this can't go on. We're just making one another completely miserable.'

'Yes,' she agreed. 'I'll make something for dinner. You'll need to get a cab from the station.'

'Oh, yes, the car, I'd forgotten. Did you book it in?'

'Yes, but as it needs towing, they're too busy to come for a few days.'

'Okay. I'll be there around seven.'

Henrietta put the receiver down, and cried. She thought of calling her mother, but didn't think she could stand an hour's worth of "I told you so's". So she dried her eyes and went out to the garden. Gardening normally calmed her down, but she couldn't concentrate on what she was doing. After fifteen minutes she decided to cycle into the village. She put her gardening gloves on the garden table and went to the garage for her bike.

At first she didn't appreciate the significance of the emptiness of the garage. Then, with a shock, she remembered that Charles didn't have the car in London, that it was not in the drive, and that it should have been where she and the men from the farm pushed it the day before. She did all the foolish and illogical things one does when refusing to believe the obvious: she checked the drive and the road and even looked over the road to the stable yard. It wasn't there. Eventually she acknowledged with surprise that someone really had stolen it.

'What idiot would steal a car that doesn't run?' she said out loud in astonishment. She caught part of herself enjoying in anticipation Charles's frustration when he found out, but the nicer part of herself telephoned the local police. There wasn't a police station in the village but there was a police house with a blue lamp outside it where the local bobby lived. She rang the number but received no reply. She scribbled a note informing him that her husband's broken down car had been stolen from a locked garage. She read the note again, wondering if it would read like a practical joke, but shrugged. It fulfilled her duties as the owner's wife. She locked the house and cycled into the village to drop the note through the police house letterbox.

In fact, Henrietta need not have bothered. Late that night, while she was asleep, the same man that had stolen the car quietly drove up to the house in it, now repaired, carefully opened the garage doors as he had before, and backed the car into the garage. Had Henrietta looked in the garage the next day and seen the Jaguar there, she would no doubt have thought that she was going mad, or perhaps that she had been drinking too much gin. In fact she had no cause to go to the garage again on the following day, and she never realised that the car had been returned.

CHAPTER EIGHTEEN

Henrietta watched out of the window as Jo, the stable girl, closed the stable gates opposite the house. Jo waved goodbye to someone still in the stables and walked off down the lane, her riding boots crunching on the gravel at the edge of the road. There was no pavement on that side of the road. The tarmac disintegrated into gravel, and then there was a strip of tall grass, and the brook.

It was 6.40 pm. and Charles might arrive at any minute. The thought caused Henrietta to pick up her gin and tonic and gulp down what remained of it. She knew what was on the agenda for the evening's discussion. She had been hoping for a frank but kind conversation between the two of them for months – years in fact. But now it was imminent, she hadn't decided what she was going to say or what conclusion she wanted. About the only two fixed points in her emotional reference frame were that, firstly, she had been right to finish the thing with Laurence, and secondly she knew she still loved Charles. Maybe some counselling? She had heard someone at the tennis club talking about the Marriage Guidance Counsel. The idea of discussing their marriage with a total stranger filled her with embarrassment, but maybe they just had to. On the other hand, maybe it was best to call it a day?

Despite her earlier promise to herself, she took her empty glass back to the cocktail cabinet and poured another two inches of neat gin. She looked at herself in the mirror above the mantelpiece. She had made an effort with her makeup and she wore a long, quite formal dress which showed off her slim figure. The smell of Basque lamb stew, one of Charles's favourites, drifted from the kitchen. If it was going to end, she wanted Charles to see what he'd be missing.

She peered closer at her reflection, and saw that her eyelids were puffy and her eyes slightly bloodshot. Too much gin and too many tears, she thought, and for a second her nerve deserted her, and she thought of calling a taxi and disappearing.

She took a deep breath, smiled experimentally at herself in the mirror, and went into the kitchen to poke at the stew and check that the pommes dauphinoise were browning nicely. She had thought to calm her mood earlier by playing some music but she was so distracted that, an hour later, Albinoni still revolved soundlessly under the raised stylus. She threw herself into an armchair looking out of the window into the garden.

All of Henrietta's movements around the house had been observed by a man hiding at the rear of the garden. He was not the same man as the one who had stood in the identical position, observing the house over the previous days. He was smaller in build, and his clothes were clearly unsuitable for sneaking around others' gardens. He wore pressed pinstriped trousers hidden under a long mackintosh, well-polished black brogues, a hat, and he carried an umbrella. By his feet, and now becoming slightly damp from the grass, were a briefcase and a large blue bag made out of what looked like heavy curtain material, tied by a white rope drawstring. The last was a typical barrister's bag, used for carrying court robes.

The man had been watching Henrietta pace from room to room for the last hour. He looked nervous, or perhaps cold, as he kept shifting his weight from foot to foot and looking about himself. Every now and then he pulled a crumpled piece of paper from his pocket and consulted it, stuffing it back into his raincoat when he was satisfied, only to take it out a few minutes later. When he appreciated that Henrietta had at last settled in one room, he picked up his bag and briefcase, pulled the hat lower down over his face, and picked his way carefully across the lawn towards the back door of the house. He kept to the bushes and the lengthening shadows, and had just reached the corner of the garage and the house when he was alerted to a noise from behind him, at the rear of the garden. He scurried around the side of the garage, and watched.

Charles puffed, panted and cursed his way over the stile at the back of the garden. He was hot and sweaty, and extremely irritated. He had arrived at the station to find himself in a losing battle for the one taxi waiting there. He was thus forced to carry his briefcase and coat for a mile and a half across rutted and extremely muddy fields made all the more treacherous by the recent rain. He'd taken off his jacket and started to carry it just in time to slip and get it and his knees covered in mud and grass stains. His shoes heavy with adherent mud, he trudged across the garden, aware that he was leaving footprints on Henrietta's beautiful lawn, and clattered through the back door, throwing everything he had been carrying onto the floor. Henrietta, startled by the noise, ran into the kitchen to find him swearing as he tried to hook his shoes off without touching either of them with his hands.

She looked at him, aware of the risks of laughing, but unable to suppress giggling at him.

'You look quite a sight,' she said, holding her hand to her face to hide her laughter.

'Can you get some newspaper?'

'Okay, hold on. Just stay there.'

Henrietta opened a cupboard and took out an old newspaper which she spread on the floor in front of Charles. He attempted to hook a shoe off the heel of one foot with the toe of the other, managing only to spray gobbets of mud onto the clean floor.

'Mind out Charles!' shouted Henrietta. 'This is a decent dress. Be patient, and I'll do it!'

He obeyed, and looked down at her head as she crouched in front of him. He saw the stains all over his clothes, the mud on the kitchen floor and felt the sweat running off his brow.

'I had planned such a civilized, dignified entrance,' he said wryly.

'Right,' said Henrietta, standing up, having taken the second shoe off. 'I think the shoes have had it – they're saturated inside and out. You actually look as if you've been wading. And your socks and trousers are a complete mess. Why don't you go up and have a bath, get changed, and I'll put dinner on hold.'

'Won't it spoil?' he asked. 'I'm already late.'

'No, luckily, it's quite forgiving. 20 minutes won't do any harm.'

Charles did as he was told. To his surprise, while he was in the bath there was a knock on the door and Henrietta came in with a glass of sherry for him.

'Thank you,' he said, smiling 'that's kind.'

'Mind if I stay?'

'Of course not.' Charles patted the side of the bath. Henrietta got a hand towel and dried enough space for herself, and sat down. She leaned forward on impulse and kissed Charles on the lips. She meant it to be a light gesture of affection, but Charles's lips softened, and he bit her lower lip gently. She responded with her tongue, and leaned into him, bracing herself with her hands on the tiles above Charles's head. Charles would have touched her – earlier in their marriage he'd have pulled her into the bath on top of him, clothed or not – but he kept his hands to himself and after a moment Henrietta disengaged and sat up.

'Hmm,' she said. 'I'd forgotten how nice that was.' She looked down at his hairy muscular body, and the dark triangle of hair between his legs. 'I see you approve.'

Charles looked down at his growing erection and lay back in the warm water.

'You're not in the least shy, are you?' commented Henrietta.

'Not with you, no. God knows what I'd be like with someone else.' The comment, meant to be innocuous, touched a nerve in Henrietta, and she flushed as she remembered her brazen behaviour with several "someone elses."

'I'll see you downstairs, then,' she said, and left without making eye contact with him.

Twenty minutes later, cleaned and refreshed, Charles sat down at the kitchen table opposite Henrietta.

'Well,' said Henrietta brightly, as she took a spoonful of soup, 'you called this meeting.'

Charles took a deep breath and put his spoon down. 'Okay. Before anything else I want you to believe that despite everything, despite the fact that I may be the worst husband on the planet, and despite the fact that I know we have torn huge chunks out of each other, I love you. That has never changed.'

'Thank you for saying that.'

'But – '

'There's a "but"?'

'Yes. I've come to the conclusion that we can't live together. I don't know how to make you happy, Etta. And I don't think you really want me to try anymore.'

'But upstairs – '

'That's never been the problem, has it? The passion's always been there. But it's the rest. I can't live with this constant fighting. The ups are wonderful but the downs are too depressing, and too frequent. I would trade half the passion for some peace and quiet with someone who wants to share my life.'

'So what are you saying?'

'I'm saying I think we should divorce.'

Charles looked up as he said that, the first time he had looked at Henrietta since he'd started speaking, and realised that she had stopped eating too. She stared silently into her soup, her arms resting on the table either side of her bowl. He stood up and stared out into the darkening garden.

'I've known you been having an affair for some time.' Henrietta didn't reply. 'And it's so out of character for the girl I met at Cambridge. You were so repelled by your father's affairs over the years, so scathing of him, and yet here you are doing exactly the same. But I don't think that alone would make me give up on us. It's more that.. well... I think it just tells us how unhappy you are. And...' he paused, '... I think it makes you hate yourself, and me.'

He turned to look at her again, and saw a fat tear roll down her cheek and splash into her home-made tomato soup. She seemed unaware of the spots of red accumulating on the tablecloth and her dress.

'Oh, Etta – ' he said, from the heart, and rushed over to her.

'No, Charles! Don't touch me!' She shoved her chair back from the table, scraping noisily on the tiles, and retreated from him to the kitchen door, her shoulders heaving. After a moment she controlled her breathing enough to speak quietly, with deathly calm. 'I want you to go. Right now. Don't say another word, just leave.'

'But – '

'I mean it! Not another word. It's over. You said so. So, just leave.'

Charles hesitated, and then brushed past her into the hallway. He walked swiftly upstairs, packed a bag and collected a spare suit. He forced his feet into his ruined saturated shoes and within ten minutes he was walking back up the muddy lane.

The man in the garden, still hiding behind the garage, had watched through the lighted kitchen windows as the events unfolded. He smiled grimly and approached the back door. Henrietta was still in the kitchen, crying as she emptied the soup into the sink. She heard the back door and assumed that Charles had forgotten something. She didn't turn round when she heard footsteps behind her. She was unaware of the cosh as it descended onto the back of her head. She did however move at the last moment, and it ended its downward arc by striking her cheek and then her shoulder. She cried out in pain and surprise and turned for the first time. The man raised the cosh again, but before he could bring it down she lashed out with the heavy ironware saucepan in her hand. It struck her attacker in the eye, and he grunted with pain. He nonetheless got in his second blow, and this one landed directly on Henrietta's temple. She collapsed the instant it landed.

The man bent over the sink and washed cold water into his eye. It was extremely painful and already closing, but it wasn't bleeding very much. He bent and retrieved the saucepan which had rolled onto the floor. Holding it by his gloved hand, he rinsed it thoroughly under the hot tap and placed it neatly with the other utensils in the drying rack. Pressing a dishcloth to his face to prevent blood dripping onto the floor, with his free hand he dragged Henrietta's unconscious form by an ankle into the lounge. He placed her in the middle of the Persian rug, and took a cut-throat razor out of his coat pocket. Bending over her from behind, and careful to stand away from the direction of his swing, he brought the blade down swiftly and efficiently across her throat. Blood spurted out in a great leap, arcing over the coffee table and splashing in bright red washes over the wall. It continued pumping for a few seconds, and then gradually stopped, as Henrietta's life ebbed away.

The man stood, picked up a chair and threw it at the display case of vases given to Henrietta and Charles for their first wedding anniversary by her godparents. It smashed, sending shards of glass and porcelain over the room. He then turned over the occasional table and flung the decanters at the wall. At the same time he shouted; oaths, curses, meaningless words, a one-sided argument, concluding in a long, high-pitched shriek.

He raced back to the kitchen where he had left the briefcase and blue cloth bag, picked them up, and left by the kitchen door. He entered the garage. He unlocked the main doors from the inside but didn't push them open. He ran back to the house, sprinting through it to the front door, the cloth bag and briefcase sending an umbrella stand flying, and re-emerged onto the front drive. He pulled wide the garage doors, allowing them to crash back with force against the walls. He unlocked the Jaguar, threw the case and bag inside, got in, and started the engine. He revved it loudly, and then, just to make sure, drove the car at an angle out of the garage, so that the coachwork was dragged along the concrete doorpost. The screech of tearing metal could have been heard a street away.

The Jaguar shot out of the drive, sending dust and gravel into the air, and disappeared down the lane.

CHAPTER NINETEEN

It was nearly midnight when Charles reached the flat in Fetter Lane. He threw his things on the couch and sat down, staring out of the window. The streets were almost deserted. An occasional vehicle passed beneath his window, its true colours leached by the yellow sodium lights on the pavement. He was exhausted, having trudged both ways from the station to the house and back again, and then having to endure the last all-stations slow train back into London, but he knew that sleep would be impossible. After a while he got up, fixed himself a Scotch, and returned to the fraud papers he had left open on the kitchen table.

Half an hour later he realised that he had forgotten to bring Archbold, the criminal practitioner's Bible, from his desk in the Temple. With a heavy sigh he put his muddy shoes back on, threw on a jacket and walked down the staircase to the street.

The streets of the City were empty. Not a single vehicle was in sight as Charles crossed Fleet Street. There was an unnatural stillness, as if the night was holding its breath. Charles walked through the arch into the Temple. The trees were utterly immobile, their branches, now in full leaf, fixed against the night sky. His footsteps echoed around Chancery Court. He was about to climb the staircase to number 2 when he noted that one of the lights on the first floor had been left on. It took him a moment in the dark to find the right key for the great studded outer door. It stood open during office hours and the barristers, although supplied with keys, rarely had to use them. Eventually he got both doors open, and walked through the silent waiting room and up the stairs to the first floor. The light had been shining from a room opposite his but, having reached it, all the rooms on that side of the landing were now in darkness.

'Hello?' he called.

There was no answer. He reached forward to push open the door to his own room when the hairs on the back of his neck suddenly rose and he knew he wasn't alone. He whirled round, and remembered nothing more.

•

'Sir! Mr Holborne sir!'

Charles opened his eyes. There was a woman's black court shoe in front of him, and an ankle in stockings. Charles couldn't fathom why a shoe or an ankle should be on his pillow. He then realised that he was extremely uncomfortable and not after all in his bed. He tried to sit up and a wave of nausea overwhelmed him. He closed his eyes again to prevent the room spinning.

'Sir? Are you all right?'

Charles tried again, opening one eye just a fraction. 'Sally?'

'Yes, sir. Have you fainted, sir?'

'Do you want to try to sit up, sir?' said another voice, a young man's this time.

'Yes,' responded Charles, and he felt hands from each

side under his armpits pulling him into a seated position. Charles realised that he was on the floor just outside his room in Chambers. He was still disorientated.

'Sir, should we get an ambulance?' Sally asked.

'No…At least I don't think so. I don't understand… What's the time?'

'Just gone 8 in the morning, sir,' said the man. 'Have you been here all night?'

Charles moaned. His head was full of little men with big hammers. 'I'm not…yes, I must've been. The last thing I remember is coming up here late last night to get my Archbold. I remember… there was a light on… but then there wasn't…'

Charles opened his eyes further and saw Sally and Robert, the office junior, both crouched in front of him, looking concerned. 'Christ, my head hurts.'

Charles reached behind him and found a large lump on the back of his head. He took his fingers away and examined them, but there was no blood.

'Looks like you hit your head as you fell,' said Robert.

'Yeh…maybe…' replied Charles. 'Robert, can you help me into my room?'

'Don't you want to go to the flat, sir? You're pretty muddy, if you don't mind me saying so and maybe you need to change.'

Charles looked down at his clothes, shook his head, and wished he hadn't. 'Jesus, remind me not to do that again. No, I'd just like to sit down for a few minutes. I'll make my own way over in a bit.'

'Would you like a cup of tea?' asked Sally. 'I'm about to put the kettle on.'

'Sally, I could propose,' replied Charles with gratitude.

'Yes, but what, sir? Marriage, or something more interesting?' she said cheekily.

'I'm afraid it may be some days before I'm up to anything more interesting,' he replied.

Robert helped Charles back to his room and he collapsed in his leather chair. He had barely sat down when there was a knock at his door. Tea, he thought.

'Come in,' he called.

Sally entered, looking worried. 'Erm… sorry Mr Holborne… but there's a couple of men here to see you. They say they're policemen.'

Charles frowned. 'Better show them in,' he said, standing.

Sally stood back, and permitted two large men to enter the room. The first of them spoke.

'Mr Charles Holborne?'

'Yes?'

'I am Detective Constable Sloane, and this is Detective Constable Redaway.' The officer showed Charles his warrant card. 'We're from the Buckinghamshire Constabulary.'

'Yes, officer. Do you want to take a seat?'

'Er, yes, alright. You'd better sit down too, sir.'

'Yes, I know,' replied Charles, sitting back down cautiously. Standing suddenly had made his head swim, and he thought he might be sick. He felt the back of his head again.

'Something wrong, sir?' asked one of the policemen.

'Not sure,' replied Charles groggily. 'The clerks found me on the floor outside, with this on the back of my head. I must've been there since late last night.'

Charles turned his head gingerly and showed the lump to the two officers. He didn't see the look which passed between them.

'Mr Holborne?' said the officer who had introduced them, DC Sloane. 'Mr Holborne, I need you to focus on what I'm saying.'

Even in his befuddled state Charles recognised the stress in the officer's voice. He looked at the two men's grave faces and knew that he was about to receive very bad news. His heart was suddenly pounding. 'What is it?' he asked, aware of a slight tremor in his voice.

'Your wife, sir, Henrietta Holborne. I'm afraid there's been an incident at your home in Putt Green. I am very sorry to tell you that your wife is dead.'

'Dead? She can't be. I saw her yesterday evening.' Charles did not register that his answer was being quietly recorded by the second officer. 'What sort of incident? You mean a car crash?'

'No sir, I don't think it's that sort of incident. I've been asked to collect you sir, if that's convenient, and take you to Putt Green now to identify the…your wife. I'm sure the situation will be made clearer when we get there.'

'Yes, but…what happened? Please, tell me.'

'I'm sorry sir, I would if I could. But we're just chauffeurs, so to speak. We've been asked to come here and drive you to your house. I don't know any more detail than I've just told you,' he lied. 'Do you have a coat?' he asked, as he stood up.

'Jacket – yes – there,' replied Charles, pointing.

The second officer picked it up, noting the mud stains. 'I'll carry it for you, shall I sir? You won't need it in the car.'

'Yes... sure. I just need to speak to the clerks, tell them what's happening.'

'We've already had a word with them, sir. Best that we get a move on.'

•

During the journey that followed Charles tried several times to get the officers to divulge more detail about what had happened, but he soon realised that they either did not know or had orders to say nothing. By the time they came off the A40 the occupants of the police Ford Zephyr had been silent for forty minutes. Every now and then Charles was aware of being observed via the driver's mirror.

The car swung into the drive of The Old Farmhouse. There were already several cars there, two obvious police cars with their lights still flashing, two or three unmarked cars and, on the grass verge, an ambulance. A small crowd of onlookers had been confined to the opposite side of the road under the willows and Charles recognised a couple of the stable boys and Mrs O'Connell from the post office in the next village.

Standing on the doorstep was a man in a light grey

raincoat and a shiny grey suit speaking to several other men, all of whom wore plastic shawls and wellington boots. One had a dog on a lead. They departed, and went round to the back of the house. The man in the raincoat approached the car as it stopped, and opened the door.

'Mr Holborne?' he asked. He was tall, with thinning grey hair cut in a military short back and sides, in his late 50s. He sported a thin pencil moustache perched on an unusually long top lip. The moustache, which was so dark in colour that Charles wondered if it was dyed, moved precariously when the man spoke, as if it might fall off. Charles recognised the policeman from somewhere, but at that moment he couldn't place him.

'Yes.'

'I'm Detective Superintendent Wheatley, in charge of this investigation.'

'Would you please tell me what's going on?' Charles pleaded. 'All I know is that Henrietta's supposed to be dead.'

'That's right, sir. In a moment I shall show you inside –'

Charles tried to walk straight towards the house but found his arm grabbed from the side by DC Sloane and the Superintendent's hand firmly on his chest.

'In a moment, sir,' insisted the Superintendent. 'I must warn you that it is not a pretty sight. It appears as if your wife has been murdered.' Wheatley watched Charles's face intently as he gave this information.

'Murdered?' asked Charles, shaking his head in disbelief. 'Who by?' he asked stupidly.

'Now we don't know yet sir, do we?' replied the other. He led the way to the front door, and then paused. He turned back to Charles. 'All I'd like you to do at the moment sir is identify her. Please can I ask you to take off your shoes before we go in?'

Charles complied and found that DC Sloane was holding out his hand for them. With an instant's hesitation, Charles handed them to him.

Wheatley continued: 'And can you tell me where the keys for the garden doors are kept?'

'The French doors?'

'Yes.'

'They're usually on the bookcase to the left of the door, under the little window.'

'Thank you.' He nodded to DC Sloane, who hurried off down the hallway towards the back of the house. 'Follow me.'

Wheatley led the way through the front door. Charles quickly looked at the door frame and door: no signs of forced entry there, and judging by Wheatley's comments, none at the back either.

Two men were crouched by the overturned umbrella stand dusting it with silver powder. Wheatley guided Charles around it and into the lounge. Charles's heart was pounding so hard in his chest he was sure the police officers must be able to hear it. He rounded the door, and stopped suddenly. The walls were splattered with blood; there was overturned furniture everywhere; broken glass crunched under his feet. A blanket – the blanket he and

Henrietta used to take on their country walks – was spread over a bundle in the centre of the room, as if it had been laid on a grass hillock for some obscene picnic. From under the blanket emerged a viscous pool of almost black glistening liquid which saturated the thick pile of the rug.

'Just stay there please sir. I'm sure you appreciate it's important not to touch her or to disturb the crime scene,' said Wheatley. He took a step towards the centre of the room and lifted a corner of the blanket. Henrietta's white face was revealed, her eyes closed tightly, like a child's, waiting for a surprise. A wide black grin disfigured her neck.

'That's her,' said Charles, choking back tears.

'Thank you, sir.'

Wheatley replaced the blanket, and took Charles firmly by the arm, guiding him back through the carnage to the hallway.

'I shall ask an officer to take you to Aylesbury police station where we have an incident room. We shall need to take some details from you, and it would be better to do it there. He'll be able to arrange for some tea. Sergeant Bricker?' he called.

A stocky broad man who had been doing something on the stairs bent down so he could see them. 'Sir?'

'This is Mr Holborne.'

'Right, sir,' he said, coming down. He reached the foot of the stairs and turned to Charles. 'These yours, sir?'

He showed Charles a pair of black brogues which Charles hadn't worn in years.

'Yes. Where did you…'

'From your wardrobe, sir. The ones you arrived in are a bit wet, so we thought …'

'Thank you,' said Charles. He took the shoes and slipped them on.

'If you're ready, sir?' said Bricker.

'Bricker,' said Wheatley quietly. The other turned, and Wheatley leaned in and whispered to him. 'By the book, Sergeant. *Everything* by the book.'

'Understood sir.' The sergeant smiled to himself as he took Charles's elbow to escort him out of the house. That's rich, he thought, coming from you.

He walked Charles out through the open front door in a daze. Charles knew it was a cliché even as he thought it to himself, but he wondered if it was all a drunken dream, and that in a moment he would wake to find himself on the floor of Chambers' library. He had the detachment to wonder also if everyone in this sort of situation took refuge in hoping it was a fantasy, and decided they probably did.

•

Charles sat in the interview room, nursing his second cup of tea, now cold. Brief details had indeed been taken from him but that had taken ten minutes, and then he had been asked to await the return of the Superintendent. At that stage he had felt no compulsion about his remaining, but he had been left alone with his thoughts now for almost two hours, and he began to wonder. The officers who had spoken to him had been scrupulously polite but certainly not as friendly or sympathetic as Charles would have expected when dealing with a recently bereaved widower. The last time he had checked the door was still unlocked, so in theory he could just leave, but somehow he doubted that he would be permitted to do so.

The scene that greeted him as he'd walked into the lounge kept replaying in his head, over and over, the jagged glass, the horrible mound under the blanket and the metallic smell of the blood. And Henrietta's face. Most of all her beautiful face, so white, so frightened. It was a struggle to accept that it was real. In some alternate reality I'm at my desk drafting an indictment, Charles thought to himself, and everyone at Chambers is getting on with their day as normal. But somehow I'm in a police room at Aylesbury Police Station and Henrietta has been murdered.

He was about to get up and complain when the door opened and Superintendent Wheatley entered, flanked by another officer.

'I am sorry to have kept you waiting so long, Mr Holborne, but there were a number of matters that I had to deal with before speaking to you. I must now officially arrest you on suspicion of the murder of your wife, Henrietta Holborne. You are not obliged to say anything unless you wish to do so, but anything you say will be taken down and given in evidence.'

CHAPTER TWENTY

The dream-like impression that Charles had changed roles with one of his clients grew ever stronger. He knew the script all too well, it was one he read every day of his life, but he was acting the wrong part. He had been taken out again to the custody room, his possessions had been taken from him, and his personal details recorded. A custody record sheet bearing his name at the top had been opened, and he had been placed in a cell. His request for a solicitor had been refused on the grounds that the presence of a solicitor would lead to harm to the evidence connected with the offence. Charles knew that the grounds for the refusal were questionable at best, spurious at worst, but he was powerless to do anything about it. It was all very well scoring points in court; he was a long way from the armour of his wig and gown and the protection of a benevolent judge.

The temptation to do as he normally could – knock on the door, make some quip with the gaoler, and be let out – was almost overwhelming. The question kept returning: why would somebody want to murder Henrietta? Was it a burglary gone wrong? But if there was no damage to the doors and they were both locked, Henrietta must have let the burglar in. No, Charles corrected himself; that would depend on the time of the attack. The garden doors had been open when he'd left, so it may have happened later that afternoon.

He paced the cell, unwilling to sit on the filthy bunk and

the even more disgusting blanket which bore questionable brown stains. Now that his watch had been taken from him he found it difficult to judge the time, but he guessed from the growling of his stomach that it was past lunchtime. He remembered how so many of his clients used to tell him that the best way of keeping track of time was the state of one's digestion.

Finally he heard footsteps from the far end of the corridor and his door was unlocked. 'This way, sir,' said the gaoler, and he was led back to the interview room in which he had first sat.

Superintendent Wheatley and DC Sloane awaited him. Wheatley carefully cautioned Charles again, and the interview began. Charles found himself in such a familiar situation that he almost laughed. Time and time again throughout his career he had told clients: Say nothing! Even when you're innocent, say nothing! Words get twisted, displaced, muddled, only to be dissected in minute detail by experts, surgeons of syntax, in the harsh glare of a courtroom, until you don't remember what you said or what you were trying to say. And yet… and yet, the impulse to speak, to explain everything, to persuade them you're innocent so the nightmare can end! For the first time ever, Charles appreciated how experienced clever criminals, those who ought to have known better, spoke out, only to give themselves away. And yet, knowing all this, he still spoke.

Wheatley asked all the questions and DC Sloane made notes. The Superintendent went slowly, carefully, watching Sloane's pen to make sure that nothing said remained unrecorded.

'How was your married life Mr Holborne?'

'In what sense?'

'Were you and your wife happy?'

'Not very, no.'

'Did you live at home?'

'Er…yes. I have a flat in London which I use some week nights. But we live together.'

'Did you have arguments?'

'Yes, we argue. What couple doesn't?'

'Violent arguments?'

'I wouldn't say so, no.'

'So you would say it would be impossible for your neighbours to have overheard arguments on occasion?'

'No. It wouldn't have been impossible. But it would have been rare. I don't like to argue.'

The policeman looked at some papers in front of him, and then changed tack.

'You come from London, do you not?'

'Yes.'

'East London?'

'Yes.'

'Your parents are…what?'

'My father used to be a furrier.'

'And now?'

'I don't know. I'm not in touch with them.'

'But you'd agree that there's not much money in your family?'

'I can see you from a mile away, Superintendent.'

'I've no doubt, Mr Holborne. We're both experts at questioning. But let's not play games. Your wife is dead, and you are under suspicion of killing her. I'm trying to arrive at the truth, so just answer the questions if you will. She was the daughter of a Marquis?'

'A Viscount, but if you're asking if she was rich, the answer is, obviously, yes. If you're asking if I killed her for her money, the answer is, definitely, no.'

'You stand to gain a fortune from her death.' It was a statement, not a question.

'I have no idea.'

'Really?' sneered Wheatley.

'You'll have to ask her family. They didn't approve of the marriage. She gets her money through a family trust. I doubt any of it'll fall into her estate; they'll have made sure I don't receive a penny.'

'Did she have a will?'

'Er… yes. We did our wills together some years ago – unless she changed hers I suppose.'

'Might she have changed her will?' asked the super-intendent.

'It's possible.'

'Why?'

'Because, as I said before, we weren't very happy.'

'So divorce was a possibility?'

'Yes.'

'At whose instance?'

'I wanted to divorce her. I went there last night to talk

about just that.'

'And what do *you* say was her attitude?'

'I resent the implication that what I am about to say is a lie. That's hardly open-minded questioning.'

'I've already told you I suspect you murdered your wife. I am not open-minded. What was her attitude?'

'She was very upset. She cried, and shouted, and told me to get out of the house.'

'So you say that she was not happy at the prospect of a divorce?'

'It appeared that way.'

'Did you not write to her only last week, threatening her that if she divorced you, I quote,' and here he picked up a letter, '"It'll be something that you will regret, I assure you"?'

'May I see that?' asked Charles.

'No. I may show you a copy later. For the present I shall read it to you.'

He did. In it Charles told Henrietta that his career depended on being perceived as a happily married man, and that he would never countenance divorce, threatening her in veiled terms if she proceeded with it.

'I suggest it was your wife who wanted the divorce. You on the other hand were opposed to it. And, this, Mr Holborne,' said Wheatley, brandishing the letter, 'was written on a typewriter. Can you see how part of the "a" and the "e" are missing? It's caused by wear on those keys. Before they left your Chambers, my officers asked your clerk to type a short passage on the typewriter in the clerks' room. What would you say if I told you that the typing they produced demonstrated exactly the same defect with those two letters?'

'I would say, if I was going to write such a letter, why on earth would I type it?'

'Are you saying you didn't write this?'

'Yes. That's exactly what I'm saying. I wanted a divorce. She was the one who didn't.'

'Can you think of anyone who might have the slightest motive for writing this and pretending it came from you?'

'Of course I can. The person trying to frame me for Henrietta's murder.'

'Who? Who might have any motive for killing your wife? Or who hates you so much as to kill an innocent woman, just to frame you?'

That, Charles was unable to answer. Wheatley went on: 'You were seen to leave your house last night immediately after a violent row with your wife.'

'Yes, that's right. Although it wasn't violent other than in the sense that she screamed and shouted at me.'

'Well, we agree that much. You were then seen to drive off, in such a hurry as to smash the side of your Jaguar on the garage doorpost. You wife was found dead half an hour later.'

So someone *could* have entered via the garden doors without doing damage, thought Charles. 'Drive off? I didn't drive off. I *walked* back to the station.'

'You did not, Mr Holborne.'

'I did.'

'Why should you do that? You had the car?'

'I didn't have the car. It had broken down and I had to use the train.'

'Where's the ticket?'

Charles sighed. 'I threw it away at Marylebone.'

'How unfortunate. So you say the car isn't working? Your Jaguar motor car?'

'I do.'

'Your Jaguar, registration plate BHA 402, was found this morning by police officers from Snow Hill Police Station outside the Temple. It drove perfectly. It is now sitting in the yard of this police station.'

Charles looked at his interrogator in open-mouthed disbelief.

'Do you wish to make any comment?' asked Wheatley, an unpleasant triumphant smile on his thin lips.

'I…don't understand…that can't be right. You must have made a mistake.'

'Why don't you start telling us the truth, Holborne? Surely, a man with your training can see how hopeless it is? What did you do with the knife?'

'I didn't do anything with any knife. I never had a knife. We argued, I was told to get out. I went across the fields to the station, and got a train to London. I didn't kill her!'

'You were still wearing the muddy shoes when you were brought to the house. I suggest you wore them when throwing the knife away in the fields behind your house before driving off.'

'No! I wore them across the fields, yes, but I never had any knife.'

The superintendent looked at DC Sloane, who shook his head. He continued: 'I propose ending this interview now pending further enquiries. You will have to remain here. One last matter: we have been unable to find a copy of your wife's will. It's supposed to be in safekeeping with a solicitor, but we don't know who. Do you know where we can find a copy?'

Charles frowned. 'Yes. There's one in a safety deposit box at Midland Bank in Fleet Street. I have a key and a combination number.'

'Thank you. Where are they?'

'At the flat in Fetter Lane.'

'Oh, yes, the bachelor pad. We'll need to have a chat about that in due course.'

'It's not a "bachelor pad". It's somewhere I can sleep when working late, that's all.'

'Come on Holborne, it's 1962!'

'No one else has ever slept there except me.'

'Who said anything about sleeping?' interjected Sloane with a smirk.

Wheatley looked across sharply at him, and returned to his earlier theme. 'Where can we find the key to the safety deposit box?'

'I think it's in a little Chinese jar on the windowsill. I'm not sure though, as I haven't used it in a while.'

'And the combination?'

'I can't tell you. I only use the box once in a blue moon,

so I have the number written down.'

'Where?'

Charles thought quickly. 'In the flat somewhere. I'd have to look for it.'

'We're proposing to search your flat this evening. Whereabouts shall we look?'

Charles shrugged. 'I wrote it down somewhere and disguised it as a telephone number.'

Wheatley looked hard at Charles, weighing him up. 'They tell me that people in your profession value integrity more than anything else.'

'What of it?' asked Charles.

Wheatley didn't answer. 'All right,' he said after a moment's consideration. 'There's no time like the present. We'll go now, and you can come with us. Sloane, get him something to eat. We don't want him saying the interrogation was unfair, or that he was so hungry he'd admit to anything.'

Superintendent Wheatley left the room and Charles was taken back to the cell. Once there, for the first time since the day began, Charles permitted himself a small, weary, smile.

Wheatley and Sloane walked back up the stairs from the cells. 'Guv?' asked Sloane.

'Yes?'

'Are you going to ask him about that lump on his head?'

'In due course. I 'spect she got one good thump in before he cut her throat.'

Sloane frowned. 'Maybe. But I spoke to the staff at his

chambers, and they say they found him asleep – or maybe unconscious – on the floor outside his office.'

'So? I'm no doctor, but maybe the Hon Lady Muck gave him a delayed concussion.'

'He was saying he thought he was hit from behind in the corridor at chambers.'

Wheatley turned to the junior officer at the top of the stairs. 'Well he would, wouldn't he? You just listen and learn, Sloane. Don't presume to tell me my job, right?'

'Right, sir.'

CHAPTER TWENTY-ONE

Charles climbed out of the police car onto Fetter Lane, hampered by the handcuffs on his wrist attaching him to a young uniformed officer. The road thronged with people, cars parked on the pavement, vans double-parked – the usual late afternoon clamour. A cold hamburger and soggy chips had arrived in Charles's cell within a half an hour of the interview ending, and Charles had bolted them down as fast as he could, but then nothing happened for over an hour and he'd been pacing his cell. Once on the road his impatience had been almost intolerable. It was essential they reached London while it was still busy. At last, after fifteen minutes of crawling traffic, Wheatley directed DS Bricker to put on the siren, and they completed the rest of the journey in half an hour.

Charles and the young officer waited while Wheatley and Bricker got out of the front of the vehicle.

'Well?' asked Wheatley.

Charles indicated the entrance and the group crossed the road. As they sidled between stationary taxis Charles sized up the two men ahead of him. Wheatley was tall but Charles doubted that he was a fighter, more cerebral and probably past it anyway. Bricker on the other hand, although slightly shorter, probably weighed in at 15 stone. His thick neck and the jacket that pulled taut over his shoulders suggested a sportsman. He was in his mid-30s and he walked lightly on his feet. He can probably handle himself, Charles thought. It was some time since Charles's last amateur boxing match, but he still trained regularly. He'd lost some weight since his prime in the war, and had dropped a weight division, but he was still confident he could handle Bricker. Then Charles glanced to his left at the young copper to whom he was attached. Probably only a couple of years out of the police college at Hendon, and thin as a whip. So, Bricker first.

The porter at the door recognised Charles immediately and was half-way into a salute when he saw the handcuffs. His hand froze in mid-movement, leaving him looking like an uncertain signpost pointing right.

'Mr Holborne?' he asked.

'Not to worry, Dennis. Parking fines,' Charles replied. Dennis nodded and smiled, and then did a classic double-take as his meagre brain cells reconsidered Charles's response, leaving him looking puzzled. The group entered the lobby.

'It's the fourth floor,' said Charles. 'The lift'll take two.' He paused, waiting for the police to make a decision.

'You go in the lift with Holborne,' said Wheatley to the man to whom Charles was attached. 'We'll take the stairs. Wait at the top.'

The lift was a tight fit even with only two in it, and Charles and his escort had to do a little dance before they could arrange themselves for the button to be pressed. They arrived on the fourth floor only just ahead of the others.

'Keys,' demanded Wheatley. Bricker fished in his pocket

for the plastic bag in which Charles's keys had been sealed earlier and handed the bunch to Wheatley.

'Which one?' asked Wheatley.

'The small gold one, and the long Chubb,' Charles replied.

The door was opened and they filed into the small living area. Charles gasped. He barely recognised the place. There were flowers in a pot that he did not own on the table. A huge pink fluffy duck sat in the corner of the couch, an inane grin on its face. The lampshade had been replaced with something frilly, and there were doilies on the arms of the armchair.

'Charming,' said Wheatley, with heavy sarcasm. 'You were telling the truth – at least when you said it's not a bachelor pad.'

'Looks very feminine to me, sir,' said Bricker.

'Maybe the handiwork of this young lady, sir?' said the escort, picking up a photograph from the mantle. It was of a blonde, lots of bright teeth, lots of cleavage.

'"To Charlie, with love and thanks, Melissa",' read Wheatley from the bottom of the photograph. 'I see we've just found another motive. Or maybe even an accomplice, eh, Holborne?' said Wheatley.

Charles shrugged. 'I don't suppose for one minute it'd do any good to say that all this stuff has been planted, would it?'

'Oh, please, surely you can do better than that?' He called to Bricker who had disappeared into the bedroom. 'Bricker: go downstairs and have a word with the porter;

see if Melissa's a figment of someone's imagination.'

'Certainly sir. But look at this!' called back the sergeant. He came out with a very skimpy nightie held aloft in one hand and a pile of women's clothes over his other arm. 'The wardrobe's full of women's clothes. And this lot was on a chair by the bed.'

'I suppose now you'll say you're into women's clothes, eh, Charlie?' Charles noted how the respect had ebbed away as the evidence stacked up against him. At first he had been "Mr Holborne", then "Holborne", now "Charlie". As far as Wheatley was concerned he was now definitely dealing with a murderer, and murderers don't require courtesy.

The final piece of evidence came to light while Wheatley was going through a kitchen drawer: a paying-in book for a Midland Bank account. It was in the names of "C. Holborne and Miss M. Maxwell". Wheatley turned to Charles, wagged his finger at him and tutted slowly, shaking his head.

'Very careless, Charlie. I'm surprised at you. You should have known better than do something official like this. Now I can go to the bank and ask for the correspondence setting up the account. You'll hardly be able to deny an affair then.'

He smiled and shook his head sadly at Charles with an odd expression – an expression which seemed to convey *"I had hoped for a more worthy opponent"* – and it was that expression which caused the cogs inside Charles's head to click into place. He remembered who Wheatley was. He'd been Inspector Wheatley then, but he had faced Charles in the witness box. Charles's instructions had been that his client's confession had been beaten out of him over the space of two days by Inspector Wheatley, then of the notorious Robbery Squad in London. At the trial, with a totally straight face and an almost apologetic air, he had convinced the judge and jury that it had never happened, and Charles's client had gone inside for 15 years. That had been several years before – and this leapt into Charles's consciousness with complete clarity – Detective Inspector Wheatley had been the subject of a complaint of corruption. It had been in the newspapers; Wheatley had been suspended for a while during an investigation, but no convincing evidence had been found and he'd been reinstated. And apparently promoted after his transfer to Buckinghamshire.

'Sir!' called a breathless Bricker, just having climbed the stairs. 'The porter's seen her come and go quite often. Got her own key.'

'That's enough for me,' said Wheatley with satisfaction. 'Get the Scenes of Crimes chaps over. I want the whole place taken apart. Now,' he said, addressing Charles. 'Where's this combination?'

Charles pulled his escort over to the table and began, with obvious difficulty, to go through the papers stacked on it. The other policemen stood watching him as he dropped a sheaf of papers and bent down to collect them, dragging his guard with him. Charles painstakingly tried to reorder the papers.

'How long is this going to take?' asked Wheatley after several minutes.

'A while; I can barely move,' said Charles, continuing his search.

'Unlock him,' said Wheatley wearily. 'He won't get past three of us.'

The young escort reached into his pocket and took out the keys to the handcuffs. Wheatley was standing with his back to the window, watching intently, and Bricker was directly behind Charles in the doorway. The escort undid the cuff on Charles's wrist and was about to unlock himself when Charles whirled round and with all his strength caught Bricker with a perfect right-handed uppercut on the underside of the sergeant's chin. The blow snapped his lower jaw closed with such force that the sound was like a ceramic tile breaking. The policeman's eyes rolled up, his knees buckled and he dropped. Charles recognised the look from many a boxing match; Bricker was out of it. He continued in his spin and grabbed the trailing end of the handcuffs still attached to his escort. He yanked hard, spun the man around, and pulled the officer's own arm round his throat. He heaved with all his might, and the young man gagged, his face suddenly red.

'Don't come anywhere near me,' Charles said to Wheatley, 'or I'll break his neck!'

The superintendent hesitated for a second.

'You'd better believe I can do it,' said Charles, calmly.

'Where d'you think you're going to go?' said Wheatley.

251

'You won't even get out the building. Even if you do, then where? You're no criminal, Charlie. You're just making a fool of yourself.'

Charles backed out of the living room and onto the landing, keeping his grip as tight as he could. The escort's face was turning purple. The lift was there. Charles backed further away to the stairs, Wheatley inching after him cautiously.

'Superintendent,' said Charles. 'Get in that lift, if you'd be so kind.' Wheatley hesitated but did as he was bid. 'Close the gates and press the alarm button,' ordered Charles.

As the button was pressed a bell sounded in the lower reaches of the building. The lift was now immobilised until the alarm was shut off from below, and Charles knew from previous experience that even if Dennis was still in the building, the task would take him at least five minutes.

Charles backed onto the top step of the staircase, took a deep breath, and shoved the escort forward. He then turned and raced down the stairs.

He took them two at a time, hearing footsteps almost immediately behind him. He stumbled, regained his balance, stumbled again, but kept going throughout, his hands on the rails on each side. As he reached the first floor landing he ran headlong into Dennis, on his way up to investigate the alarm bell. He bundled the porter over, leaving him gasping on the landing, hoping that his body would slow up any pursuers for another second.

Charles burst into the street and turned immediately left. He sprinted across Fleet Street, oblivious to the screech of tyres and blaring of horns, and into Sergeant's Inn. He raced down the steps and through the arch into the Temple proper. He could hear footsteps behind, but not as close as they had been. He turned sharp right, ran across the open courtyard, and turned right again by Temple Church.

Charles raced the twenty yards across Hare Court, barged through a group of startled barristers just returning from Inner Temple Hall, and bounded up the steps into number 2. He chanced a look over his shoulder, and saw the young copper about sixty yards back, half way across the courtyard. Charles had been a pupil here and knew the steps led to a landing which also served Chambers in Middle Temple. On the far side of the landing was another short staircase, leading back down into Middle Temple Lane. This was his one advantage – he knew the Temple like the back of his hand whereas these officers did not. He jumped down the steps into Middle Temple Lane and turned left, effectively turning back on himself. He felt the beginning of a stitch in his chest but pressed on, his breath coming in short ragged gasps. He reckoned he had about ten seconds to round the next corner. If he made it without pursuers emerging from Hare Court, they would have three potential routes to choose from. He counted as he sprinted. 5…6…7…8… made it! Hugging the wall, he ran through Fountain Court and out of the night gate, leaving the Temple, and passing the Devereux

Public House where he had spent so many Friday evenings standing in the sun, chatting to other barristers. That last turn, he thought, would give them three further options.

Charles emerged, sweat streaming down his forehead, onto Essex Street and ran straight into a taxi pointing towards the Embankment and pulling away from the kerb. He leapt in.

'Waterloo East!' he shouted. 'I've got four minutes to make a train!'

'Right you are, guv,' replied the cabbie, and away they sailed.

He was free.

PART FOUR

ON THE RUN

CHAPTER TWENTY-TWO

'What time d'yer make it, mate?' asked Charles through the screen. He deliberately softened his accent, slipping into the Cockney he had tried so hard to eradicate, in case the cabbie was asked about a posh fare.

'4.58,' replied the cabbie over his shoulder. They were going over Waterloo Bridge. 'When's the train?'

'Five,' replied Charles.

'Then you've 'ad it, aincha? It's gonna take more than that from 'ere. There's always a jam at the other end of the bridge.'

'Yeh – you're right. Tell you what: turn left at the end of the bridge, and try London Bridge Station. I might just catch it there.'

'Righto.'

Charles hoped that even if anyone had been near enough to hear him ask for Waterloo, the change of direction would finally throw them off the scent.

They made good time to London Bridge.

'Don't bovver wiv goin' inter the station,' said Charles to the back of the cabbie's head. 'Go right inter Tooley Street. If I've missed it, we can go on to New Cross, the next stop.'

The cabbie regarded him with narrowed eyes through the rear-view mirror. He was being dragged further and further south of the river, somewhere London cabbies never venture voluntarily. And now the geezer wanted to get out and check the platform before paying. Charles held his breath for the answer.

'Fair enough,' said the cabbie, eventually. 'At this rate, I might as well take yer all the way 'ome!'

The cabbie turned right, and pulled up by the steps that ran up to the station.

'Won't be a sec,' called Charles, and ran off up the stairs. For a man who prided himself on his honesty and integrity he realised with a shock that he was lying and cheating as well as any of his clients; probably better than most. He didn't like to bilk the innocent cabbie out of his fare but he was penniless and he couldn't afford a wrangle.

He walked swiftly onto the station concourse, crossed the front of the platforms and left the station by the far exit that took him out onto St Thomas Street. He walked off down the road and onto the High Street.

His first problem was money, or the total lack of it. He stopped in a doorway and went carefully through his pockets. He always used to lose tickets in this jacket because there were so many little hidden pockets. Maybe…just maybe…Yes! He felt a coin in a tiny pocket inside one of the others. He took it out. Half a crown. Enough for a bus fare and a sandwich, maybe a cup of tea.

He caught sight of a bus approaching. He decided to change direction again, and he crossed the road, ran to the next stop, flagged it down, and got on. It was going towards Aldgate.

•

Rachel stepped out of the door of the Whitechapel Gallery followed by another young woman. Charles watched from the shelter of a closed shop doorway on the other side of the street. Rachel and the other woman chatted for a moment, waved, and separated. Rachel walked towards the station. Charles crossed the road swiftly and approached her from behind. He grabbed her elbow.

'Rachel.'

She turned and smiled. 'Hello. What're you doing here?'

Charles leaned forward, speaking quickly. 'I'm in trouble. I need your help.'

She heard the urgency in his voice and searched his face. 'Let's go to my place. You can explain there.'

She turned round and led the way to a bus stop. A bus was coming. 'Quickly!' she urged.

They got on and without asking Rachel paid for both of them. She led the way upstairs to the front of the bus where there was an empty seat. Charles sat on the aisle, looking frequently at the pavements as they flashed by. After a few minutes he seemed to relax a little, but Rachel saw him wipe away beads of sweat trickling from his temples.

Fifteen minutes later they were walking along a quiet residential street in Hackney as dusk fell. Entire families of Hasidic Jews passed them. Charles realised that it was Friday night, the start of the Sabbath. They're all off to synagogue, he thought. Rachel led the way up the steps to a narrow terraced house, and opened the door.

'Come in,' she said. She led Charles up a carpeted staircase. He caught a glimpse of a lighted kitchen at the back of the house and a woman stirring something on a stove. He followed Rachel up two narrow flights to the next floor where she unlocked another door and led the way into a large bedsit. There was a double bed with a cheap plywood bedside table, a sink in the corner of the room, and a heavy oak sideboard which once belonged in a Victorian dining room. A single wooden chair, once part of a different dining set, was piled with books. There was no wardrobe, but a rack of clothes on hangers.

'You can sit on the bed,' she said. She hung her coat and bag on the back of the door, shut it behind Charles, and started filling a kettle. She placed it on a small two-burner electric hob on the sideboard. 'I've only got tea.'

'Tea's fine.'

'OK. What on earth is the matter? Is someone *chasing* you?' she asked in disbelief.

'Can you leave that alone for a minute? I need you to sit down.'

Rachel glanced sharply at him, but she turned off the hob, lifted the books from the single chair onto the floor, and drew it up two feet from Charles. She sat down.

'I'll tell you what the headlines will say tomorrow,' started Charles. He took a deep breath. 'They'll say "Leading Barrister Murders Wife – Escapes from Police".' He heard her sharp intake of breath and he forged on. 'Underneath it will explain how I viciously cut her throat; how I did it for the money; how I was having an affair with some blonde floozie; how I killed her to stop her divorcing me; how the evidence against me is overwhelming. And how I am very dangerous and any member of the public seeing me should immediately call the police.'

There was a long silence.

'And will any of it be true?' Rachel asked in a small voice.

Charles did not answer immediately. Rachel shrank back as he leaned forward towards her. He reached out to hold her shoulders at arm's length, felt her freeze with fear, and looked straight into her eyes. He measured every word carefully, pouring sincerity into each one as he spoke.

'Henrietta is dead. I had to identify her body. That's true. Beyond that, not a single word of it, Rachel. I swear on everything I hold dear, not a single word.'

Rachel stared deep into Charles's eyes, and he tried not to look away.

'Tell me,' she demanded. 'Everything.'

Charles did – the problems with his marriage, the row at the house, his arrest, the trip back to Thame with the police, and his escape. She sat on the chair, occasionally asking questions but for the most part listening intently as darkness filled the room. Her face didn't betray any emotion and Charles couldn't tell if she believed him or not. When he had finished she stared out of the black curtainless window over the rooftops, and said nothing. Charles sat on the edge of the bed, waiting.

'Well?' he asked finally.

'Can I see the bump on the back of your head?' she asked.

'Yes, if you want.'

He stood and turned his back to her. 'There,' he said, probing carefully, and parting the hair.

She stood and explored gently with her fingers.

'OK. Sit down again,' she commanded.

'Do you believe me?'

She paused before replying. 'I did wonder if you had concussion and were having hallucinations or something. But… yes, I do believe you. If you take my advice, you'll hand yourself in. By running off like that you've confirmed your guilt in their eyes.'

Charles sat back on the bed, and rubbed his eyes. He was exhausted, but there would little chance of sleep that night. 'I know. But someone's gone to a lot of trouble to set me up, and all the evidence points to my guilt. The police are not going to listen to me. Especially the man leading the investigation.'

'Why? Who is he?'

Charles told her about Wheatley's methods, the investigation and his exoneration.

'But was your client guilty?' she asked.

'Well, the jury said he was. But I do know this: he was beaten black and blue by Wheatley before he confessed. Maybe he *was* guilty, but Wheatley's methods stink. He sets himself up as the jury, makes his decision, and then creates the evidence to support it. There's no way I'll get a fair hearing from him. If he thinks he's got a watertight case he won't let it unravel it by looking elsewhere. He likes things neat and simple. If anyone's going to prove my innocence, it has to be me.'

'I think you'll just make things worse.'

'How can it be worse? I'm facing the hangman in any case. And that's the thing so far as you're concerned.' Charles paused. So far he'd banked on her not turning him in, but this was the crunch. 'If you help me, you'll be an accessory.'

'Which means?'

'Prison, probably – if I'm convicted. We only have tonight before you're at risk. My escape was too late for the last evening editions, but it'll be all over the papers by morning. After that, you can't be seen to assist me.'

'And if I help you right now?'

'You'd have to lie. Say you knew nothing about it – you just bumped into me.'

She thought for a long time. 'What do you want me to do?'

'I need some money. But the tricky thing is, I have to get into Chambers. I need my notebooks.'

Rachel frowned, puzzled. Charles explained. 'Barristers all use these blue notebooks – you must've seen them. No? Well, perhaps not. Foolscap light blue notebooks. Anyway, every case I've ever done is recorded in them. I date and number them. I've got the names, addresses, and *modus operandi* of hundreds of active criminals, most of whom I've defended. It's a directory of crime. And most of them have cause to thank me. So I need the notebooks, but I don't know if the building's being watched. But…'

Charles hesitated. 'But… if you decided to go for a walk through the Temple, you could find out for me. If not, I'll try to break in. I doubt they'll be looking for me there – they'll think I'll try to get as far away as possible – but I can't take the risk of just walking in.'

•

Rachel and Charles entered the Temple from the Embankment entrance by the new Queen Elizabeth Buildings. It was a more open access than the Victorian alleys off Fleet Street and Charles would be able to see if it was being watched. The sky was overcast and the Temple was darker even than usual. The only person they passed was the lamp lighter in Fountain Square. Charles pointed Rachel in the right direction and she left him at the corner of Essex Court and Middle Temple Lane. Charles backed into a nearby doorway to wait. He would have been completely invisible to anyone passing, but in fact no one passed him at all. Rachel only had to walk 200 yards or so to the door of 2 Chancery Court, and Charles expected her to return within a couple of minutes.

Two minutes turned into five, and five into ten. By fifteen minutes Charles's anxiety had reached breaking point and he was certain that Rachel had been arrested. He was on the point of emerging from the shadows and walking the remaining distance to Chancery Court when he heard muffled footsteps approaching. He backed into the shadows and watched a figure emerge, almost bent double with a heavy burden. The figure approached, passed Charles, and hesitated, looking around the dimly lit square. Charles stepped out, and Rachel whirled round.

'Oh, there you are. It was all clear, the lights were on and the doors were wide open. Here,' and she unslung from her shoulder a red robes bag. 'I think I got them all.'

'But how on earth did you – '

'The cleaner was at the back, empting the bins. Your room was obvious – there was police tape across the door. So I ducked in. Your blue notebooks were on the shelf behind your desk, right?'

'Yes!' responded Charles, astonished.

'I think I got them all. They're bloody heavy, aren't they?'

'Yes, let me take that. We need to get out of here.' Charles took the bag, pulled the cord tight, and hoisted it onto his shoulder. They set off back the way they had come.

'What took so long was finding something to carry them in, but I found the bag hanging on the back of the door. It's got your initials on it.'

'I think you're amazing,' said Charles. 'But that was really dangerous. Are you sure you weren't seen?'

'There were definitely no police, and the cleaning lady was vacuuming in the basement when I slipped out. I don't think anyone saw me at all.'

'Amazing,' repeated Charles, and he put his arm round Rachel's shoulder and pulled her towards him. It had been intended as a friendly squeeze, but she turned her face to his, put a hand behind his head, and pulled it down to her.

It was awkward because they were still walking, but her lips touched his and they stopped. The kiss was short, but their faces remained inches from one another.

'My heart was pounding so hard I thought it would burst through my ribs,' she whispered. 'And it's the most exciting thing I've ever done in my life!'

CHAPTER TWENTY-THREE

Rachel put a plate bearing a sardine sandwich on the chair next to what had been Charles's third cup of instant coffee and sat on the edge of the bed. Charles lay on his front on the bed, poring over the notebooks, making notes on a sheaf of blank pages torn from the current one. Rachel's glance lingered on his broad shoulders and the curly hair at the nape of his neck. Every time he finished a notebook he reached over and put it in a growing pile on the floor beside the bed, and Rachel studied the muscles under his white shirt as they rippled, like the uncoiling of a large snake.

Charles picked up the next notebook and checked the date and number. Then he reached over to the remaining pile and fanned them out, running his finger across the neat numbers written in black ink in the top right hand corner of each cover.

'There's a gap,' he concluded. 'At the end of 1960. Is there any chance you missed one or two?'

Rachel shook her head. 'No. The shelf was empty when I left.'

Charles checked the numbers again. 'Well, there's definitely … one…maybe two missing.'

'Could it be anywhere else?'

'Not that far back. November 1960…' Charles swung his leg round and sat upright. 'What was I doing at the end of 1960?' He shrugged. 'Never mind, there's plenty here.'

Rachel stood. 'I know you've a lot to do, Charlie, and nowhere else to do it. But I have to go to sleep. It's almost 2.'

Charles looked up from his notes. 'Is it really? I'd not realised the time.'

'I don't know how you can concentrate when you're so tired.'

'I'm used to it. "Burning the midnight oil" as they say at the Bar. I do it once or twice a week.'

He rolled over and looked up at her, and then at the bed littered with notebooks. 'Ah, I see.'

'Yes. It poses a problem. Would you be able to work on the floor just using the bedside lamp?'

'I should think so.'

'Then I'm going to get changed in the bathroom and go to bed.'

Charles looked around and realised there was nowhere else he could sleep but the floor. 'Right. I'll be fine on the floor,' he offered, standing.

'I have no spare bedding.'

'I'll manage. It's not that cold.'

'Well… Charlie, look… it's a big bed, and I'm only little. Once you finish, I have no problem with you getting in… but…'

'Of course. On my honour.'

'I know what lots of people are getting up to nowadays, but… I'm not one of them.'

'Understood.'

•

Charles finished at almost 4.00 am. He got undressed, looked across at Rachel in the bed, and put his underpants back on. Then he slipped into bed beside her. She had started on one side of the bed but had migrated to the centre, so Charles moved as far as he could to the edge and curled round her so they wouldn't accidentally touch. His face was only inches from the back of her head, her short dark hair fanned out over the pillow, and the moonlight from the un-curtained window struck the skin of her slim white shoulder as it protruded from the blanket. Charles watched as it rose and fell with her regular breathing. He was suddenly conscious of the fact that, for the first time in years, he was sharing a bed with someone other than Henrietta. Rachel was a stranger – lovely, desirable and astonishingly kind – but a stranger nonetheless, and Charles was suddenly overwhelmed by a wave of loss. His breath caught painfully in his throat as a sob rose in his chest. He slid his legs back out from under the covers and he sat on the edge of the bed, his feet hard against the cold lino and his body rigid as he tried not to disturb the sleeping woman behind him.

Hot silent tears spilled down his cheeks as, for the first time, he was overborne by loss, fear and dislocation. He cried silently, his huge shoulders shaking uncontrollably. He felt a cool hand on the back of his neck.

'Lie down,' said Rachel softly. Charles shook his head

vigorously but couldn't trust himself to speak. 'Lie down,' she commanded again.

Charles did as he was bid, facing away from her, knees drawn up to his chest. He felt Rachel's body as she curled into his and stroked his hair.

'Hush,' she whispered.

As Rachel stroked, Charles's sobs gradually became less frequent and his breathing more regular. Rachel watched as he became still. After a few minutes she began to allow longer pauses between each movement of her hand and then, slowly, she stopped. She moved away slightly from the sleeping man and propped herself up on her hand, staring at the stranger in her bed. Charles turned over in his sleep, now lying on his back, his muscled arm hanging out of the bed. Rachel noticed for the first time how long were his dark curly eyelashes, almost as long as a girl's. Her eye travelled down his neck to the rise and fall of his enormous barrel chest with its central patch of black curls. Rachel had had boyfriends in the past – she was no virgin – but they had been boys compared to this powerful, very masculine man. She was tempted lean over and kiss his full lips as he slept, but she resisted. She knew how exhausted he was and, despite his apparent confidence, how frightened. She divined that the one relationship in which this man had placed all of his trust – his relationship with the law – had failed him, and it was that as much as losing his wife that had left him completely disorientated. She also knew what might follow if she succumbed to the temptation to place a kiss on those lips. And, as she reminded herself, within days he'd probably be in prison, maybe even sentenced to hang. She did believe Charles was innocent – she trusted her own judgment on people – but even she could see how the case against him seemed impregnable. It was plain foolish to become romantically involved with someone in his position. She lay down again and settled herself once more to sleep.

Some hours later Charles's eyes opened and he was suddenly and completely awake. It was still night, but there was now a blue tinge to the dark rectangle of the window which heralded the dawn. He reached over gently and felt for his watch on the floor beside the bed. Rachel stirred, turned towards him sleepily and jumped, her eyes also now wide open.

'Sorry!' she said, 'I'd forgotten you were here.'

Charles smiled. 'It must be really weird waking up to find a hunted man in your bed. I'd do the same if our roles were reversed. What time is it?'

Rachel turned away from him and leaned over the edge of the bed to look at an alarm clock also on the floor. Charles watched her nightie ride up and expose most of her buttocks.

'Just gone 6,' she replied, laying on her back and pulling the bedclothes up under her chin.

'OK. I'll get out of your way,' said Charles, swinging his legs down and sitting up. 'Can I use the bathroom?'

'Yes – it's directly opposite. I share with Nina – in the attic room above – but she's on nights this week. She won't be back for an hour. Use the towels on the left.'

Charles turned to Rachel. 'You've been wonderful, Rachel. Whatever happens... thank you. From the bottom of my heart, thank you.'

She smiled. Then: 'Oh, I've just remembered: you asked for some money. I haven't got much, but there's £15 in the sideboard drawer. I needed another seven and six for next month's rent anyway, but I'm never going to find it, so you might as well have what I've saved.'

'Thanks. I promise I'll repay it.'

Their eyes locked again, and this time Rachel sat up and took Charles's head in her hands and kissed him hard on the lips. Then she shoved him away with a grin.

'That's all for now Charlie. If you get out of this mess... then we'll see.'

CHAPTER TWENTY-FOUR

Superintendent Wheatley was still seething at Holborne's escape. But escaped he had. Despite managing to persuade the Met and the City police to set up roadblocks at both half a mile and one mile radii from Fetter Lane within 20 minutes, somehow Charles had slipped through. It was extremely frustrating but Wheatley was confident it was no more than a temporary setback. An almost unrecognisable photograph of Holborne had appeared on the television news that night, but the morning papers had something more recent splashed across the front pages, and it was only a matter of time before someone recognised him. How long could a man like that survive on the run, with no money and no passport? Especially in such a high-profile case involving a barrister and a Viscount's daughter. It would be in the news for weeks, months probably.

So Wheatley had returned to the scene of the crime with seven officers who were in the process of going through every scrap of paper in the place to build a picture of Holborne's life. Usually within 24 hours they would have a list of friends, acquaintances and contacts where he might have sought shelter. But – and this was odd – it was if Holborne was almost completely unconnected. Enquiries with his parents and brother revealed reliably that he had not been in touch with any member of family for almost a decade, and all the contacts turned up at Putt Green were those of the deceased. Wheatley began to get the flavour of the Holbornes' marriage and was not at all surprised it had been failing. Holborne was a loner and, as Wheatley assured himself, possessed of just the sociopathic profile he'd have expected of a cold-blooded murderer.

It was Wheatley himself who happened to be at the foot of the stairs when the doorbell rang. He opened the front door to find a man in oily overalls on the doorstep.

'Where's the car, mate?' asked the man cheerfully.

'What car?' asked Wheatley.

'The Jag. I was told it would be in the garage, but it ain't.'

'Who told you it would be in the garage?'

'My guvnor. I've come to collect it.'

'Can you explain please sir? Who are you?'

'Roger, from Breck & Co.'

'Well, Roger from Breck & Co., who exactly asked you to collect the Jag?'

'Look,' said Roger, very patiently, because he was clearly dealing with an idiot, 'Mrs Holborne rings us up on Tuesday or Wednesday, or whenever it was, and says that the Jag won't go and would we book it in for work, right?'

Wheatley glanced swiftly over his shoulder and escorted the mechanic away from the front door. He walked him to the end of the drive, where a tow truck was parked next to one of the police vehicles, engine idling.

'Go on,' he said.

'Well, we were so busy that we couldn't do it till today.

My foreman asks me to come and collect the car and leave a courtesy car, which I have. Over there.'

Wheatley looked across the road where another man stood by the open door of a grubby Ford Anglia.

'But the Jag isn't there,' continued Roger.

'OK,' replied Wheatley. 'We have the Jaguar and it's now important evidence in an investigation. So it won't need repairing.'

'What about the Anglia?'

'Didn't you watch TV last night?'

Roger looked puzzled, but shrugged. 'We had a darts match.'

Wheatley nodded. 'Well Mrs Holborne won't be requiring the Anglia, thank you very much.'

'I can go then?'

'Yes. One thing less for you to do today.'

'Suits me.'

And Roger walked across the road to tell his colleague, who got back in the Anglia, and started up. Roger climbed back in the tow truck and the two vehicles departed. Wheatley watched them disappear. It might mean nothing – cars, especially Jags, did develop intermittent faults – but Wheatley wasn't going to waste police resources investigating a peripheral issue. Even if – most especially if – it might confirm Holborne's story that he couldn't have driven off after the murder.

•

Charles stepped out of Covent Garden Tailors, having

275

spent over half of Rachel's loan. He wore narrow Hepworth trousers, a white cotton shirt with a narrow black tie, a boxy black leather jacket, and a trilby. With his new Mod haircut and his big-framed glasses containing clear glass he looked like a darker version of Michael Caine. He paused to look at his reflection in the window. People who knew him well would have no difficulty recognising him on a second look, but he looked sufficiently different from the photograph splashed across the front pages of the newspapers that he should be able to move undetected around London as long as he was careful. He pulled his collar up and lowered the hat over his brow, and walked towards the Strand.

It took Charles 15 minutes to reach the corner of Fetter Lane and Fleet Street. He entered Oyez, the legal stationers on the corner, and while pretending to read one of the law books watched the entrance to his apartments for a few minutes. A single bored police officer stood by the door. He wore the dark blue uniform of the City of London Police, which probably meant he knew little about the case, but Charles wasn't going to take any chances. He waited.

After ten minutes Charles realised he'd have to move. The shop assistants had been glancing in his direction for a while and he couldn't afford to raise suspicions. He put the book back but, as he was about to leave the shop, the front door of the apartments opened and Dennis came out. Charles turned his back slightly as Dennis crossed the road and walked past on the other side of the window.

Charles called "Thank you" to the shop assistants, opened the door, and followed.

Dennis had a small paper bag in his hand and a newspaper under his arm. He dodged the traffic on Fleet Street and went into the Temple through Sergeant's Inn gate. Charles followed him past the Clachan pub, along Kings Bench Walk and out of the Tudor Street exit. Dennis jogged through the traffic on the Embankment, reached a bench overlooking the Thames, and sat down. He opened the newspaper on his lap and took out a sandwich from the paper bag. He took a bite, following the progress of a large launch as it cruised past him on its way downstream. Charles crossed the road behind the concierge, put his hand in his jacket pocket and walked up silently behind the bench. He placed his leather covered finger on the back of Dennis's neck.

'If you move a single inch Dennis I'm going to blow your head off. Do you recognise my voice?'

Dennis choked on cheese and pickle and it took him a few seconds to answer.

'Yes Mr Holborne, sir.'

'Don't turn round. Just carry on watching the boats and listen carefully. I have a few questions. That blonde woman who you saw coming in and going out of my flat.'

'Miss Maxwell?'

'Yes, her. Did you ever see her arrive?' Dennis nodded, the sandwich clutched tight in his right hand. 'Did you notice a car?' asked Charles.

'Yeh. A big gold Mercedes.'

Charles raised his voice to be heard above two buses thundering past behind them. 'Did she arrive alone?'

'Yes.'

'Did you ever speak to her?'

'Only the time I helped with her shopping.'

'Explain.'

'She had stuff for the flat, you know, lampshades an' all. And that enormous teddy or whatever it was. I kept an eye on the car while she went up and down cos otherwise she'd've gotta ticket.'

'I don't suppose you remember the registration number, do you?'

'I do actually. NF 777.'

'Do you know anything else about her?' demanded Charles.

'No, honest, Mr Holborne, not a thing. I'd tell you if I did.'

'OK Dennis. Now listen to me very carefully indeed.' Charles waited for a lorry to go past before continuing. 'You know they say I killed my wife, don't you?'

Dennis nodded.

'The police reports don't say how I'm supposed to have done it.' Charles paused for effect. 'My wife's throat was cut from ear to ear. Her head was hanging by a shred of skin.'

Charles could see the man's hands trembling in his lap.

'If you say one word, I will come back and do to you *exactly* what I did to her. Do you understand?'

Dennis nodded again, vigorously.

'Your Brenda lives in Westcliffe, doesn't she? So as soon as you finish your lunch, you're going to take a two-week holiday to visit her and the baby. If anyone asks, the stress of what's happened has been a bit much. Don't go back to Fetter Lane. Go home and pack a bag and get the next train to Westcliffe. Make it a nice surprise, and don't tell her anything either. Do you completely understand what I've said?'

'Yeh, sir, really I do!'

'Tell me.'

'I'm gonna finish me sandwich and go back to Poplar, pack a bag and go visit my girl in Westcliffe. I'm gonna say nothing to no one about this conversation or seein' you. If I do, you'll… you'll come back and…'

'…exactly. Yes. Remember, Dennis, I'm facing the rope for one murder anyway. They can't hang me twice. So I've nothing to lose.'

'Yeh, I geddit.'

'Right. I'm going to go now. I want you to wait there without moving for five minutes. I'll be watching. You just finish your lunch and read the football results.'

'Got it.'

'Oh, and while I'm here, did the Hammers win?'

'No. They lost two nil.'

'Bad day all round,' said Charles quietly, and he looked behind him and ran back across the road, leaving Dennis still talking through the match to himself.

•

Charles walked swiftly into the basement car park at Shoe Lane and found the Austin Healey. Other than Simon Ellison no one in the world knew that he owned it, and Ellison was out of town on a case. It would take the council at least a month to register it in his name.

Breaking in was no difficulty – he just lifted the corner of the soft top and opened the driver's door from the inside – but how to start it? The keys had been at Fetter Lane and were now in the custody of the police. Charles sat in the driver's seat, took his sheaf of notes from his jacket pocket and leafed through them until he found a passage of cross-examination. One of his early clients had been charged with hot wiring six cars in twenty minutes so his mates could each have one to race along Southend seafront. Part of the Crown's case had been to prove that it was possible and Charles had notes of his cross-examination of a police vehicle engineer.

Charles flattened the sheets of paper on the passenger seat, took a pair of scissors borrowed from Rachel from his pocket, and put on his new leather gloves. He popped and lifted the bonnet, disconnected the battery cable and located the power wires running up the steering column through the bulkhead. He went back into the car, and lay on the seat with his head under the steering column. Taking a deep breath he started to cut the power cables. The scissors were too small, and it took some time, but eventually he got through them, and twisted the ends together to complete the circuit. There were two other brown wires going to the ignition. He cut them both and made sure they weren't touching. He got out of the car and reconnected the battery. The radio started crackling. So far, so good. Charles got back in the car and read some more of his notes. He pulled the choke and bent down into the foot well and, using his hand, he pumped the accelerator pedal twice.

'Moment of truth, Charlie,' he said softly to himself. He twisted round and, with his torso and legs hanging over the sill and half lying on the seat, he touched the two bare wires together. The engine started first time.

Charles leapt out and shut the bonnet. He got back into the car and manoeuvred it slowly up the exit ramp. It was a lovely day, with white clouds scudding across a blue sky, a perfect day for driving with the hood down, especially as the interior of the car smelt unpleasantly damp, but with reluctance Charles decided against it. Better not to be seen. He turned left onto Fleet Street, and headed east.

•

Charles slowed to 15 mph, moved the gear lever into third, let the clutch out sharply, and allowed the car to stall. He then disengaged the clutch and coasted gently into the kerb. He was outside a shop on Leytonstone High Road. He checked the numbers of the shops and looked again at the notes. Right number, wrong place.

'Bugger,' he swore quietly. What he had expected to be a car showroom was now a kitchen and bathroom centre. He got out of the car and went through the door. The place smelt new, of freshly-sawn timber and plastic.

'Can I help you, sir?' asked a young kitchen salesman. Charles judged that he was about 22 years old, also evidently a Mod, with a face that was a mass of pink and yellow pimples. Less Brylcreem might help, Charles observed to himself.

'Aye, meybe,' he answered, adopting a Scottish accent. Ever since the days when he acted in school plays he had always found accents easy. He and David, his brother – also a good mimic – would adopt foreign personas for days, driving their parents to distraction.

'What happened tae the car dealership that used tae be here?'

The boy shrugged, uninterested. 'Was there a car dealership? I dunno. I only started last week. Mr Wilson!' he called.

An older man's head appeared above a bathroom cabinet in the process of being assembled.

'What?' he answered irritably.

'This geezer wants to know what happened to the car showroom.'

'Well it ain't here, is it? He sold up, the Arab.'

The youngster turned to Charles, and shrugged. 'Sorry, can't help you.'

Charles reached into his pocket and came out with a pound note. 'Would you look in the office and see if there's anything that says where I might find him. His name was Kharadli.'

The lad looked at the pound. He whisked it from Charles's fingers and it disappeared into his jacket pocket.

'Wait there,' he said quietly, and he walked swiftly to the office at the rear of the showroom.

He emerged a couple of minutes later with a scrap of paper.

'That's the forwarding address for 'is post. Should still be good, we only started fitting out the place last month.'

'Thank you,' said Charles, and he returned to his car.

The address was only half a mile away, a breaker's yard. Outside the yard was an old blue Rolls Royce. Charles parked just round the corner where he could watch the yard unobserved. The gates were open but there was no movement inside, and no customers Charles could see. The difficulty was that anyone might emerge from behind the piles of rusting car chassis or vans with flat tyres and collapsed axles. A large dog was tied by a rope to a hook on the wall of a prefabricated office. It gnawed at a bone between its paws and seemed unconcerned.

After fifteen minutes Charles made a decision, and he got out of the Healey and walked across the road towards the gates. The dog looked up but made no sound or movement. Charles stepped carefully into the yard, trying to avoid oily puddles, and the dog leapt to its feet, barking and straining at the rope. A slim, handsome dark-skinned man in his 50s emerged from the office, stepping out onto a small metal landing but not descending the steps. Charles noted his expensive leather shoes and mauve silk socks, and wondered how long the shoes would last in this environment.

Charles skirted round the dog and approached the office,

his right hand held stiffly in his jacket pocket. Kharadli was no fool and had plenty of experience dealing with members of the criminal fraternity. He had been one of London's major suppliers of ringed vehicles for both criminal enterprises and onward sale to unsuspecting punters. Charles didn't expect for one minute to frighten him with a stiff finger in his jacket, but he held no other cards.

'Mr Kharadli?'

The Arab looked down at him suspiciously. 'Who asks?' He looked down at Charles's jacket pocket, and then up again at Charles's face, amusement in his eyes.

'You don't remember me? I'm Charles Holborne. I represented you in court some years ago now. Two cases, at the end of 1958? Remember?'

Recognition gradually dawned, and Kharadli's face broke into a smile.

'Yes, I remember! How are you?' He frowned suddenly. 'Wait one minute,' he said. 'You're in big trouble with police, yes? You killed your wife?'

Charles moved closer to him. 'Can I talk to you, just for a minute?'

Kharadli backed off, shaking his head. 'I don't know…'

'Mr Kharadli, when I represented you, the police were saying you'd done all sorts of things, but I didn't believe them,' lied Charles. 'We both know that the police say many things which are not true.'

Kharadli's retreat halted while he thought about this. 'That is true, my friend,' he replied, brightening immediately. 'Anyway, what do I care that you killed your wife?' and he laughed loudly. 'Come in!'

Charles followed him into the office, a smell of strong coffee greeting him.

Kharadli poured a tiny amount of coffee from a metal jug into two plastic cups and handed one to Charles. He sat behind his desk.

'Take a seat. You like my new business?' he waved his arm expansively, indicating the muddy yard and piles of rusting metal. 'No money in ringed cars, always hassle, hassle, hassle. This is better. No one asks for money back! Now, how can I help you?'

Charles sipped the coffee. It was good, sweet and strong. 'You used to have a policeman friend who could look up car registration numbers. I need to know who owns a particular vehicle, very urgently. It's to do with…well… you've obviously read the papers.'

'Yes. This should be possible. But why should I help you? You paying me?'

Charles shook his head. 'I have no money to pay you.'

Kharadli leaned back in his chair and sipped his coffee, his handsome face still smiling slightly. There was a long pause.

'I like this situation, Mr Brief. You've never been on the wrong side of the law before, yes?'

'No,' replied Charles. 'Never.' Which was a lie. A big fat lie.

'It is different, is it not? Maybe this does you some good; to see life on the other side.' He paused again. 'OK, I shall help you. Just once for… how you say… old time sake.'

He reached for a telephone on the desk, dialled a number, and waited.

'Is PC Compton on duty today? Tell him it's Mohammed.' There was a short pause. 'So, it's Sergeant now, is it?' Kharadli gave the thumbs up sign, and continued talking. 'Congratulations my friend! Have you time to look one up for me?' He snapped his finger at Charles and shoved a piece of scrap paper across the desk to him. Charles quickly scribbled the number on it, and pushed it back.

'NF 777.'

Kharadli snapped his fingers again, and made writing signs, and Charles handed over his pen.

'Yes,' he said as he wrote. 'Yes…got it. Thank you Steve, much appreciated. You must come round to the house soon…yes, it's been too long. Bring the children too…Okay. 'Bye.'

He hung up, and handed the paper over.

Charles read the scribble. 'Starline Model Agency, D'Arblay Street, W1.' He sighed. 'A company,' he said. Any number of people might have been driving the vehicle.

'I am sorry,' said Kharadli with a shrug. 'That's all I can do. Now, Mr Holborne, I must get back to work.'

He stood and held out his hand. 'I do sincerely hope that everything works out for you, but please do not contact me again. One cannot be too careful who one is seen with.' He was completely serious.

Charles shook his hand and returned to the Austin

Healey. He looked at his watch. With luck, he would get to Companies House before it closed.

CHAPTER TWENTY-FIVE

Peter Bateman, pupil barrister, and his flatmate, a trainee doctor at Guys, were just settling down to their grilled lamb chops when they heard the landlady's call from the foot of the stairs. Peter went down and found himself summoned by Stanley to Chambers where he was to prepare an overnight return for Middlesex Assizes. One of the other barristers had been stuck on the Western Circuit and couldn't get back in time. Peter didn't relish working through the night, but a brief – any brief – was a Godsend for a young man just starting at the Bar.

When he got to Chancery Court Peter found the brief as predicted in Charles's pigeonhole with a note from Stanley: "Court 2 Middlesex Assizes, NB 12 noon" – not to be listed before noon. That at least was good news. If Peter got finished by the early hours he might manage to snatch a few hours' sleep.

He opened the door to Charles's room where he usually sat waiting for the pearls of wisdom to drop from his pupilmaster's lips. The City of London police tape that had formerly barred entry had been removed, and Peter had been told it was safe to use the room. He sat at the desk facing Charles's, wondering where his murderous pupil master was. Peter was convinced there must have been some mistake. Six months of sharing a room with a man – travelling on trains with him up and down the country, burning the midnight oil – and you got to know him pretty well. And Peter found it difficult to believe that Charles was guilty of the offence, whatever the newspapers said. And a cut throat razor? Not Charles's style at all; too theatrical. Someone was making a statement.

He turned on the desk lamp and almost immediately noticed something wrong. The day before, when he'd had to work in an adjoining room, he had distinctly seen from the threshold the shelf behind Charles's desk lined as usual with its series of annotated blue notebooks. They had been gathering dust there from the day he'd joined chambers. Now they were gone. Perhaps the police took them? he wondered, but what on earth for? He looked at the back of the door where Charles's robes bag usually hung. It was bare. It was not unheard of for a barrister to borrow another's robes – if he had an unexpected court hearing for example – but the absence of the bag and the notebooks taken together was puzzling.

Peter picked up the telephone and dialled Stanley's number.

'Stanley, it's Peter Bateman. I'm in Chambers now. Have the police removed any property from Mr Holborne's room?'

'Not as far as I know. An officer came yesterday with the scenes of crime man, and when they finished they simply took down the tape. Why?'

'Mr Holborne's robes bag and all his notebooks are missing.'

There was silence at the other end of the line. Then: 'If you go to my desk you'll find a piece of paper on the blotter from the City of London Police. It's got the name of the officer who came yesterday. I'd like you to give Snow Hill a call just to make sure.' There was another pause. 'You don't think Mr Holborne might have broken in and taken them do you?'

'The thought did cross my mind,' replied Peter. 'But I wouldn't want to get him into more trouble.'

'I understand your loyalty, sir, but I don't see how he could be in any more trouble. And this has caused very bad publicity for Chambers – I've been fielding press calls all day – so we need to distance ourselves from it. We have to be seen to be helping in every way possible. Give Snow Hill a call, and keep me informed of developments.'

'Alright. Will do.'

Peter hung up and went through the darkened building to fetch the officer's name and telephone number. He hesitated, but then smiled and sat in Stanley's chair while he dialled the number. The officer was off duty, but the duty sergeant gave Peter the phone number of someone at Buckinghamshire Constabulary, DC Sloane, who might be able to help. Peter dialled again.

'DC Sloane.'

'Hello Detective Constable. My name's Peter Bateman. I'm Charles Holborne's pupil. I've just come into Chambers, and there's something odd which I think you should know.'

'What's that?'

'All his old notebooks from his criminal cases have disappeared, together with his red barrister's bag, you know, the one he used to carry his robes. I may be making a mistake, but did one of you or the other officers remove them?'

'I'll need to make enquiries sir about the notebooks, but I think you're mistaken about the robes bag. That was last seen at Mr Holborne's property. And it's blue, not red.'

'No, that's not right. He's never had a blue one, not since I've known him. I've seen him with his red one almost every day for the last six months. And he wouldn't be seen with a blue one anyway.'

'Why not?' asked Sloane, puzzled.

'The blue ones you buy yourself. The red ones are given by a leader to a junior as a gift, to mark good work done on a case. Charles was very proud of his red bag. He wouldn't use a blue one.'

Peter waited, listening to the scratch of Sloane's pen at the other end of the line.

'You don't know what case it was for, do you?'

'Yes.' Peter smiled. 'You don't have to spend long in Charles's company to find out. It was his first murder case. The Queen versus Sands and Plumber.'

'Has anyone taken a statement from you, Mr Bateman?'

'No. You're the first.'

'Well, it may be unimportant, but I'll send an officer over in the course of the next couple of days to take down what you've told me, and get a signature. You're not planning on holidays in the near future are you?'

'No. You can get me through Chambers.'

•

At almost exactly the same time as Peter was hanging up and starting his late-night work, Charles was standing in the dark, in the back garden of the house where Rachel had her bedsit. Her room was in darkness. He was undecided. The idea of sleeping in the Austin Healey was distinctly unappealing, but he had nowhere else to go. He had had to put petrol in the car and had bought two meals. And when the car radio had refused to tune to any radio stations, he'd been forced to buy a small transistor radio so he could pick up news reports of the investigation. It was more expensive than buying newspapers, but meant that he didn't continually risk being recognised by newsagents or paper vendors – all of whom had hundreds of copies of his photograph right in front of them. But it meant that he had less than £3 of the money Rachel had lent him, enough for the cheapest of hotel rooms, but little else thereafter. In any case, he couldn't risk being asked to produce a passport.

Charles picked up a pebble from a flower bed and threw it at Rachel's window just in case she'd gone to bed early. It was a good shot, and the clack made by the impact would certainly have disturbed her, had she been there. The room remained in darkness and there was no sound.

Immediately beneath Rachel's window was the sloping ceiling of the kitchen at the back of the house which Charles had glimpsed the night before. The window of the kitchen was illuminated and every now and then a middle-aged woman in a dressing gown passed to and fro. Charles could hear laughter from a radio or television inside. On the flank wall of the property, around the corner from the window, was a garden bench.

Charles took off his fake spectacles and stowed them carefully in his breast pocket. He climbed onto the bench, reached up to the overhanging tiles, and tested their strength. They creaked dangerously and he desisted, but underneath there was a gap under the line of the roof and the soffit, and a very slight overhang of the roof beam. He got a good grip on the beam and pulled. It held firm. He reached up again and hauled himself onto the edge of the kitchen roof, making sure he didn't stand right on the edge where his weight risked snapping the tiles. He tiptoed his way up the gradient to the top of the roof where it joined the wall. Rachel's bedroom window was now at waist height, an old wooden sash window with no lock. He put his hands under the lower sash and heaved upwards. The window opened and Charles rolled into the room.

It was empty and smelt enticingly of Rachel's perfume. Charles didn't want to move further than necessary in case his footsteps were heard from below. He slipped off his shoes, took one pace to the bed, and carefully lay down, fully dressed.

Rachel arrived two hours later. Charles was half asleep but he heard her voice at the front door and her steps coming closer to the door. He reached to the floor and turned on the bedside lamp, and Rachel saw him the moment she opened the door. She stopped, but smiled, and immediately closed the door quietly behind her.

'I wondered if I'd see you. In fact I almost left the

window open for you.' She took her coat off and hung it on the back of the door. 'How did you get in?'

He nodded towards the window. 'You should have it looked at. If I can get in, anyone can.' He stood and approached her. 'I'm really sorry,' he continued, 'but I'm almost out of money, and I had nowhere else to go. I know I said I didn't want to put you in any danger, so just say if you want me to leave.'

'No, it's fine. You can stay, although you have to be very quiet as the house is full. You'll need to leave by, say, 6?'

'No, I need to leave before then. I've got somewhere to be at about 4.00 am.'

'Really? Well, you can explain in a moment. We need to talk about your family.'

'My family? What about them?'

'Charles! They're frantic with worry!'

'I doubt it,' he replied, bitterly. 'They said *Kaddish* for me years ago.'

Rachel stepped closer to him, examining his face carefully, her eyes narrowed. She shook her head sadly. 'And you think that means they don't care?'

Charles shrugged and shook his head sharply, an awkward movement, as if trying to throw something off. 'They made their position absolutely clear,' he said, breaking eye contact with Rachel. She reached up and gently turned his face back towards hers.

'You're wrong, Charles. They love you. Your father in particular misses you terribly. I see him in synagogue every week. You know he's never let anyone sit in your seat?'

'No,' replied Charles. He sighed. 'I didn't know that.'

'If you saw him, Charles, you'd know. He looks so forlorn. Anyway, newspapermen have been camping on their doorstep since the news broke this morning, and they can't even go out. Your brother thinks your parents' line is tapped.'

'They'd need a warrant, but it is possible I guess.'

'For heaven's sake, will you stop being a lawyer for a moment?'

'Sorry. So you've spoken to them?'

'I thought someone should tell them you were okay. And that you're innocent! That's where I've been. I didn't want to risk calling – so I went round.'

'And?'

'They're relieved. To know you're okay, and that I'm … well, that I can do something to help.'

'Does dad think I did it then?' asked Charles.

'How can you say that? Of course he doesn't.'

Charles nodded introspectively, turned, and sat on Rachel's bed.

'So,' said Rachel, after a moment. Charles looked up. She was standing next to the open door of a tiny refrigerator that he hadn't noticed before. 'I have four eggs and some cheese. Your choices appear to be scrambled eggs or omelette. Any preference?'

'No, either would be wonderful.'

'Ok. Tell me what you've been doing. Oh, by the way – I like the new look.'

CHAPTER TWENTY-SIX

Charles woke at 3:30 am. Rachel lay on her front, her left arm across his chest and her head snuggled into his side. He inhaled her smell and watched the creamy bumps of her vertebrae rise and fall with her breathing, and found himself becoming aroused. He slipped out of bed quickly, his feet hitting the cold unheated lino.

He dressed hurriedly in the dark, opened the door a couple of inches, and listened for a few seconds. Satisfied that the household was asleep, he crept silently downstairs. The front door was unlocked and he stepped into the cold night, closing the door gently behind him. He had managed to sleep for almost four hours and felt refreshed and alert.

The street was deserted. He got into the Austin Healey, started it up by touching the ignition wires together again, and headed towards the West End.

The streets of Hackney were silent and almost devoid of traffic, but as he headed west it became slightly busier. There was still a fair bit of action in Soho. The less successful toms still prowled the pavements looking for clientele, competing for the few late or desperate kerb-crawlers. Several of the clubs were closing, and Charles had to swerve as a drunk ejected by two bouncers almost fell under his wheels. The men laughed, and Charles watched in his rear view mirror as one took a half-hearted kick at the prostrate punter as he tried to crawl out of the gutter.

Charles found a space to park off Wardour Street and walked back towards D'Arblay Street. Fitting snugly in the palm of his right hand was the final purchase he had made that day, a shilling's worth of pennies in a cardboard tube, fresh from Lloyds Bank on Chancery Lane.

Two young women in costume and tall golden headdresses emerged in a gale of laughter, trailing cigarette smoke and cheap perfume from the back door of a club and got straight into a waiting taxi. The bouncer on the door watched Charles carefully as he passed, and then shut the steel door with a clang. Charles heard shoot bolts being fastened behind him.

Charles rounded the corner and turned into D'Arblay Street, looking for the Starline Model Agency. Parked right in front of him outside a strip club was the gold Mercedes, NF 777. A flashing pink neon sign over the club's facade told Charles that inside he could find "Live Naked Acts" and a big yellow poster over the blacked out windows further informed him that although this was a private members club, membership could be purchased in the foyer for only ten shillings. Photographs of scantily-clad women in improbable poses were displayed on a board on the pavement.

Two large men stood by the front entrance. Charles noticed that they were unusually alert for that time in the morning, constantly checking up and down the street.

Charles continued slowly past the club, feigning interest in the photographs of the strippers. As he walked past the door he saw, to the right of the foyer, a staircase leading to the first floor and a sign for the Star Line Model Agency, with an arrow pointing upwards.

Charles's presence seemed to make the two men on the door even more nervous. One, a giant of a black man with a gold ring on each of his 10 fingers, took a step towards Charles. Charles assessed him. At over six feet four and 18 stones he was almost six inches taller and four stones heavier than Charles. Charles wondered what would happen if he had to force his way in. I'll just bounce off him, he concluded.

'We're closing,' the giant said in a Jamaican accent, looking down on Charles. He leaned even closer to Charles's face, and Charles smelt aftershave, lots of it. 'Move on, man.'

'I'm not going to the club,' replied Charles, stepping back slightly, and smiling. 'I need to speak to Mr Fylde.'

'Who's asking?' asked the other man from behind Charles, an extremely fat white man with an improbable quiff and an earring in each ear.

Charles turned. 'Tell him it's Charles Holborne.'

The two men looked at one another.

'Put your hands against the window,' ordered the white man. Charles did as he was told and allowed himself to be frisked expertly. 'He's clean,' the man concluded, and stepped back. The roll of pennies remained undetected.

'You sure pick your time,' commented the Jamaican, but he went inside. Through the door Charles watched him lift a telephone on the ticket booth counter and press a button. A second later ringing could be heard from the first floor offices above the club and Charles looked up at the window which cast a rhomboid of yellow light on the pavement.

Charles watched the conversation and after a moment the Jamaican hung up and returned to the street. 'You can go up.'

The two bouncers watched Charles carefully as he went through the door and entered a small lobby smelling of cigarette smoke. At the far end was a black curtain from which emanated the sound of muffled recorded music. A tired hat check girl wearing tight golden shorts, bustier and goosebumps watched from behind the counter as Charles climbed the stairs opposite.

Charles found his eyes travelling up the shapely legs of a female walking down the stairs towards him. Good legs, he thought, though not as toned and muscular as Rachel's. His eyes travelled further up the girl as the steps between them narrowed and Charles found himself staring at bouncing brown nipples. The bare-breasted dancer paused in her attempt to pull on a gold lamé waistcoat and stopped a couple of steps above Charles. Charles eyes travelled further north to be met by a grimace which might, earlier in the evening, have been a reasonable facsimile of a smile.

'Piss off, pervert,' she said in a weary voice, and pushed past him, tucking a heavy breast into place through an armhole.

At the top of the flight was a wooden door with a brass plaque on it saying "Starline Model Agency" and, underneath that in smaller writing, "Mr N Fylde, Managing Director". That was the name of the director listed at Companies House and presumably the user of the gold Mercedes, NF 777.

Charles knocked on the door. Another Jamaican accented voice from inside said: 'It's open.'

Charles went in. He was surprised to find the office well appointed. Light grey carpet covered the floor and the walls were hung with classy black-and-white photographs showing scenes from the race track. In front of him was a large mahogany desk behind which sat a short but powerful black man with a shaved head. He wore a light brown three-piece suit the jacket of which was hung behind him from the back of his leather chair. A gold watch chain pulled tight across his waistcoated belly, and he wore a gold coloured silk tie which Charles rather coveted. A heavy gold chain hung from his neck and his fingers flashed and sparkled with rings. He was evidently counting the night's takings because as Charles entered he snapped a rubber band around a thick wad of notes, turned, and threw the wad into an open safe on the floor behind him.

'I thought you said we'd never meet,' said Fylde rising from his chair, and studying Charles. 'Anytin' wrong?'

'No,' said Charles. 'But there's a loose end or two, and I need a word with Melissa.'

'That's not possible,' replied Fylde, kneeling to the safe. Charles thought he was locking it but a second later Fylde stood up with a pistol in his hand, and pointed it at Charles's chest.

'OK. Who da fuck are you, man?'

'Charles Holborne,' replied Charles.

'No you ain't. De man I deal with talk different.'

Charles nodded. 'That's because I *am* Charles Holborne. Look at your newspaper.'

Charles indicated the Evening Standard at the end of Fylde's desk. His photo took up the top half of the front page. 'Whoever you dealt with set me up. And used you and Melissa to do it.'

Fylde looked across and then back at Charles, who had taken off his glasses and put them in his pocket. Fylde shrugged. 'That ain't – '

There was a sudden explosion from downstairs, a woman's scream, and the sound of glass shattering. Footsteps thundered up the staircase and Charles backed behind the office door at the same instant as it crashed open. From behind the door, through the narrow gap afforded by the hinged edge, he saw on the threshold a short man in a black suit, dark overcoat and a trilby hat, pointing a sawn off shotgun at Fylde.

'Put that peashooter down,' he ordered, 'or I'll put daylight through you.'

Fylde hesitated for a moment and slowly lowered his right hand, placing his pistol on the desk.

'Now move to the side.' Fylde did as he was told. A crash echoed up the staircase from the foyer. The man in the black suit called over his shoulder, his eyes not wavering from Fylde.

'You okay, Jackie?'

There was no response.

The man in the suit took half a step into the office. Charles nodded at Fylde, who raised his eyebrows almost imperceptibly. Charles launched his considerable weight with all his force into the door and, at the same instant, Fylde ducked. The shotgun exploded, bringing a shower of plaster and dust from the ceiling, but the force of Charles's unexpected charge knocked the intruder to one side. Charles rammed the door again with his shoulder, hearing a whoosh of air from the chest on the other side of the door as it was compressed between the door and the door jamb. Charles spun around the leading edge of the door but he wasn't fast enough and the gunman had regained his balance and stepped back half a pace to give himself room to fire again. Charles had no time. He threw a left jab and a straight right with the roll of pennies, using all the weight he could command. The right landed just under the intruders left eye, the blow snapping his head sideways. His eyes rolled up and his knees sagged. He folded vertically onto the grey carpet like a marionette with its strings cut. Charles caught the shotgun before it hit the ground.

The fat doorman appeared at the head of the steps, wheezing, blood trickling from his scalp. He held a pistol in his hand. Fylde had regained his feet and his pistol.

'You okay, boss?' asked the doorman.

Fylde crossed the room with surprisingly light steps and rolled the unconscious man onto his back. He turned slowly to look at Charles with surprise.

'I am now. How many were dere?'

'Three. Kimani got one outside – but he's been hurt – knife wound in his side. The third did a runner when he heard the gunshots.'

'Okay. Drag dis one out and lock him in the van. Then take Kimani to hospital,' ordered Fylde.

'What about this geezer?' he asked, pointing at Charles, who was brushing dust and ceiling plaster off his new jacket.

Fylde looked Charles up and down. 'I tink we okay, yes, Mr Holborne?' He held out his hand for the shotgun. Charles turned the weapon over once, shrugged, and handed it over.

'Too noisy for my taste,' he said.

'Yeh,' said Fylde to the doorman. 'We okay.'

The doorman started dragging the unconscious man feet first towards the stairs.

'Hold on a second, please,' said Charles. Charles patted the man's inside pockets and from one breast pocket took out a pistol. He searched again and from the other pocket he withdrew a black leather wallet. Charles opened it and found ten crisp brand-new £20 notes. He took two and pocketed them. 'Cleaning expenses,' he explained, and he tossed the wallet onto Fylde's desk. 'No objections?' he asked.

This time Fylde shrugged and shook his head. He nodded at his employee and the unconscious man's head disappeared out of the door and could be heard thumping on each step as he was dragged by his feet to the ground floor.

'What was that all about?' asked Charles. 'It looked as if you were expecting it.'

'Turf war,' replied Fylde shortly. 'The Krays want my business.' Fylde brushed dust off the edge of his desk and leaned against it, assessing Charles. 'You really dat steppa? The one all over de papers?'

'"Steppa?"'

'Escapee.'

'Yes.'

Fylde regarded Charles carefully. He shook his head slowly and sniffed. 'OK. I's very busy, as you can see. So, here's the story.' He spoke swiftly as he busied himself with clearing his desk and locking the safe. 'A geezer phone. He say he want a girl to fake adultery, you know? So de wife can get a divorce?'

Charles nodded. There was a thriving market in providing the evidence necessary for grounds for divorce, hired co-respondents, photographers and hotels that looked the other way.

'If me agree, a courier will come in twenty minutes with a monkey. All me have to do is supply one classy tom to pose as de mistress a few time. Got to be white, drive a flash car, speak well and dat. Just go in and out dis flat a few times, you know, be noticed? And another monkey tomorrow, if it all go well.'

'And access to the flat?'

'Same courier, next day, brings a key and a timetable, when to go, when not to go.'

'Who was the man?'

'Me never see him, but, he was white, spoke like you. But not your voice. I can leave a message at an answering service if I need to… for Mr Holborne.'

'And the girl's real name?'

Fylde focussed all his attention on Charles again. 'I ain't lettin' you hurt her. Girl just doing a job.'

'I'm not going to hurt her. Not my style.'

Fylde considered. 'Shirley Lovesay.'

'Is she here?' demanded Charles.

Fylde shook his head. 'On de Costa. Geezer pays her to lay low. I 'spect her back in de club on Monday.'

'Did she ever meet him?'

'I don't know man, maybe. He give her a few tings to take to your place. Now, I got to attend to business.'

'Last question: where does she live?'

'Las' house on Grafton Road, Kentish Town. Next to de pub.'

'Thank you. I'll leave you to clear up.' Charles turned to leave, but Fylde called after him.

'Maybe you need a change of career, Mr Brief Man! I can use someone like you.'

Charles turned. 'I'll let you know.'

CHAPTER TWENTY-SEVEN

Charles sat in the Austin Healey checking out his newly acquired pistol and considering his next move. The pistol was American, a stainless steel AMT Backup made in California. The serial number had been filed off but it had been well maintained. Charles checked the magazine: full – six gold-coloured rounds of 0.38 calibre. It was small and Charles found it fitted snugly in the breast pocket of his jacket without any obvious bulge. He took it out again, turning it over. Not much use at a distance, but as a concealed backup, it was perfect. He wished he had time to find somewhere to test fire it.

Charles turned his attention to Fylde's story. Wheatley wasn't the sort to be interested in loose ends when he already had a nicely packaged prosecution, but even he couldn't ignore the pimp's evidence of another man posing as Charles, especially when added to the evidence of Dennis. But that meant Charles first needed a description of whoever was using his name, and *that* meant waiting until Shirley returned from the Costa Del Sol. Charles doubted he'd have another four days at large before the police caught up with him.

The only thing of which Charles was sure was that he was famished. He looked at his watch. Where to get a decent cheap meal in London at quarter to six in the morning? He smiled to himself, started the engine, and drove back east towards the city.

The streets were getting busier but it took Charles only 15 minutes to reach Smithfield's meat market. He turned off Farringdon Road and parked in West Smithfield. Under the dome of the new market there was a jam of unloading lorries, porters and men with bloodied overalls and carcasses hefted across their shoulders. Charles had to sidestep swiftly as he was almost run down by a man trotting across the cobbles carrying half a cow. Charles crossed the central courtyard to The Fox and pushed his way through the heavy doors. The pub was half-full of market traders and drivers. The smell of frying steak and beer made Charles's mouth water immediately.

The Fox was one of half a dozen pubs that opened at 4.00 am specifically for the market trade. Charles had discovered it shortly after the rebuilding of Smithfield finished the previous year on one of his insomniac walks around the city's deserted streets, and had loved the slice of London underbelly it revealed.

He pushed his way to the long wooden bar, attracting a few glances as he did so. A huge bear of a man took his order for a rare steak sandwich and chips, and served Charles with a pint of mild. Charles threaded his way through the butchers and porters to a small wrought iron table in the corner of the bar. He sat facing into the corner of the room, pulled up his collar and tried to focus on his next step.

He was stuck. He could think of nothing to do but lay low until Monday and hope he could then find Melissa – or Shirley. A harassed waitress brought over his steak and a large pot of mustard, and handed him some cutlery rolled in a paper serviette.

Charles was working his way through his wonderfully bloody steak sandwich when he looked up. In the mirror facing out onto the bar he saw a man staring at him. He was middle-aged, with a few strands of sandy hair combed across a mottled pale scalp and a day's growth of stubble on a doughy chin. A rollup stuck to his lower lip bobbed up and down like a conductor's baton as he spoke out of the corner of his mouth to another man at his elbow. He wore a donkey jacket over a blood and fat-streaked white knee-length apron and heavy wellington boots.

Charles considered reaching for the pistol in his inside pocket, but decided against: it would bring things to a head too quickly, and if there was any chance, he wanted to finish his breakfast. Instead he altered his grip on the steak knife, ready to use it as a weapon if necessary. He managed to eat a couple more mouthfuls before he felt a hand touch his shoulder.

'Alright if I sit down, mate?'

It didn't look as if he was to be grabbed immediately so Charles muttered 'Free country,' through a mouthful of cow, and indicated the chair opposite with the knife. The man pushed past the table and lowered himself onto the seat opposite Charles.

'We've met before,' said the other, keeping his voice low and not making direct eye contact with Charles.

'We have?'

'You represented me brother at the Bailey. Derek

Plumber.' He spoke through lips that barely moved and Charles had to concentrate to catch the words over the hubbub in the bar. It was years since he'd last seen Derek Plumber, but Charles thought he detected some resemblance in the man opposite him; something about his build, and the heavy jaw.

Charles tensed. There was no denying now that he'd been recognised.

'You won't remember me,' said the man. 'We only met the once, just before sentencing, and you was busy. But I remember you. And I know you're in a spot of bother.'

'I'm tooled,' warned Charles. 'And not just the knife.'

The man looked Charles in the face for the first time. 'Easy...easy. If I was gonna grass you, why'd I come over?'

'What then?'

'Derek's in trouble –'

Charles interrupted him. 'Well, perhaps you've clocked it, but I've got problems of my own right now.'

'I know that. But I wonder if they're not connected. You hear about Robbie Sands?'

'Sands? Derek's co-defendant? No. Why?'

'He's out. 10 days ago. Got hisself into a fight with a nonce and did a runner on the way to the hospital.'

'What makes you think he's connected to my... troubles?'

'He's been bothering Derek. And your name was mentioned.'

Charles studied the other man's open face, and decided that he was telling the truth. He tried to remember the details of Plumber's case and realised he had not seen reference to it when going through his notebooks. So, that accounted for the the missing books. And then, like a sudden flash of light, he remembered: a cut throat defence. A cut throat.

'I need to go,' said Charles, urgently. 'Where does that leave us? What are you going to do?'

'About seeing you? Nuffink. Not my business. I've never had form, but I still don't talk to rozzers. The family'd never forgive me. But go and see Del, eh? He's in a right state. He wants to get away, but there's no way.'

'Why not?' asked Charles, but the other didn't reply. He was pulling a Rizla cigarette paper from a packet and writing on it with stub of pencil taken from behind his ear. He slid it across the table.

'That's the address. Have a shufti.'

Without another word he got up and brushed past Charles, causing the table to wobble and some of Charles's beer to slop over the edge of the glass. Charles watched him in the mirror as he rejoined the man he'd been talking to, laughed and slapped him on the back, and then disappeared through the throng. Over the heads of the traders and butchers Charles saw the door of the pub open and close again. He looked at the wafer of paper in his hand. The address, in Limehouse, was only a mile or two to the east. Charles slipped it into his pocket and resumed his breakfast.

•

Charles brought the Austin Healey to a halt outside a Georgian house in Narrow Street, Limehouse. He could smell the river on the other side of the houses – less than 100 yards to his right – and two seagulls screeched, flapped and squabbled over something dead in the gutter opposite him. The smell reminded him instantly of the war and his time working on the Thames. He put the thought firmly out of his mind.

The pavements were quite full as people hurried to work and more than one person noted the Austin Healey and looked into its windows as they passed. Charles realised that he needed to move. The house he was looking for was two doors down from The Grapes public house, a well-known dockers' watering hole. Charles got out of the car and approached a faded blue door. Tacked to the door post was a dog-eared index card with a message in block capitals: "PLEASE KNOCK AND WALK UP." Charles knocked, flakes of peeling blue paint falling to his feet as he did so, then turned the handle and opened the door. A narrow wooden staircase faced him. He climbed to a small landing at the top from which another half-glazed door opened. A radio could be heard through the door. He knocked on the glass and waited. There was no answer so he pushed the door open. He was assailed by the sharp odour of urine and he wrinkled his nose. He was in a large kitchen. This was a poor household, but despite the smell it was immaculately clean and tidy. The room had once been elegant, with tall ceilings, a large intact plaster ceiling rose and an imposing fireplace which now housed an electric two-bar radiator. The floor was covered in lino and there was a scrubbed pine kitchen table. The previous night's dishes were dry on a metal drainer.

Charles followed the sound of the radio which came from another room leading off the kitchen. He knocked on the door, twice, with no response. He opened the door slowly.

The room beyond was in darkness and here the smell of urine was stronger still. Charles paused to allow his eyes to become accustomed to the gloom. There was an unusually high narrow bed against the far wall and a hoist attached to the ceiling hanging over the bed. The room's curtains were closed. Then Charles saw two dark shapes on the floor. He took a couple of steps to the window and pulled the curtain nearest him. Light entered the bedroom. Derek Plumber lay on the floor, unconscious, face down with his knees drawn up under him. His pyjama trousers were saturated with urine, and his right arm was outstretched, as if reaching for something on the dressing table. Beside him, on its side, was a wheelchair. Charles righted the wheelchair and bent to lift Plumber back into it. As he did so Plumber's pyjama legs flapped emptily and Charles realised with a shock deep to the pit of his stomach that the man had no legs below the knees. He held Plumber under the armpits, a deadweight. He changed his mind and instead of putting him into the wheelchair from which he might simply slide back onto the floor, Charles managed to swing him partially onto the bed. He then turned and rolled the unconscious man into a more secure position.

It was only as he was straightening Plumber that Charles realised there was another strong odour in the room. It took him a moment to recognise it so incongruous did it seem, and then he remembered the smell from Henrietta's dressing room: nail varnish remover.

Charles looked round at the dressing table against the wall; it was almost completely covered with bottles and boxes of medications, and Charles's eye was immediately caught by half a dozen ampoules of clear liquid and an open box of disposable syringes. Charles picked up one of the ampoules: insulin. He looked back at Plumber.

'You poor bastard,' he said softly. 'You couldn't reach.'

Charles returned to the bedside and tried to rouse Plumber, shaking him and slapping his face once or twice, but he knew he was wasting his time. Plumber was in a coma from diabetic ketoacidosis, which explained the nail varnish remover smell on his breath, and he needed an ambulance, and fast. His breathing was fast and shallow and his face the colour of wet concrete.

Charles raced to the door, across the kitchen, and down the stairs. He scanned the road – no phone boxes – and turned around to the shut door of The Grapes. He hammered on the door with increasing urgency. Eventually a sash window on the second floor was thrown up.

'We're closed!' shouted a man in pyjamas.

'I know. Call an ambulance, quickly! The man two doors up needs help.'

'What, Derek?'

'Yes!'

'Righto!' said the man, and his head disappeared back inside.

Charles retraced his steps to Plumber's bedroom. He only had a few minutes. For the first time he looked around at the otherwise very tidy home and saw that the bedroom was the exception. All the drawers and cupboards were open, some of their contents strewn on the floor. Someone's gone through the room before me, thought Charles. But what for?

A sudden noise startled Charles and he whirled round to see a short young woman in nurse's uniform enter the bedroom. She halted in surprise.

'Who are you? What's going on?' she demanded. Then she saw Plumber. 'What have you done to Derek?' she demanded, brushing past Charles and going to the bedside. 'Oh, Jesus!'

'I found him on the floor with the wheelchair turned over. I got him back into bed and asked the landlord of The Grapes to call an ambulance.'

The district nurse was taking Plumber's pulse. 'Oh Jesus!' she repeated. She whirled on Charles. 'He's got DKA. Was it you on the phone last night?'

'Me? No.'

'One of his friends said he'd stay with him and that I needn't come. Said he was a doctor and he could do the insulin.'

'Not me. Was he a Scotsman?'

The nurse frowned at him. 'How did you know that?'

'Educated guess. That Scotsman was no doctor, believe

me. Did Derek have anything of value here?'

'I doubt it – though he keeps his rent and housekeeping for the carers in the bottom drawer over there.'

Charles followed her gaze and opened the bottom drawer of a small chest behind the door. He found assorted underwear and two spare pairs of glasses, but no money. 'Not any more, he doesn't.'

The bell of an ambulance could be heard approaching.

'I'll go and direct them up,' offered Charles. He went back through the kitchen. As he was stepping through the door onto the landing, he registered a notepad by the telephone fixed to the wall and a pen hanging from a piece of string next to it. He broke his stride and stepped back into the room. On the notepad were the initials "CS", a telephone number and an address in west London. Charles ripped off the top page with the details and raced downstairs. As he emerged onto the pavement an ambulance was approaching from the far end of the street. He got into the sportscar and drove off in the opposite direction.

CHAPTER TWENTY-EIGHT

Detective Constable Sloane knocked on the door of Superintendent Wheatley's office, and was told to enter. The room was neat and tidy to the point of obsession. The desk had two files on it, positioned perfectly parallel to the desk edge. Four sharpened pencils were placed in a line, like a musical stave, at the top of one of the files. The Superintendent's coat was folded on a small table as if just unpacked from the cleaners, but Sloane knew that an hour ago Wheatley had been wearing it when he came in. He folded it that way every time he took it off.

'I thought you ought to know immediately, sir,' he said, standing to attention in the doorway. He had once been deemed to be slouching in the same doorway and had been bawled out for ten minutes.

'Now what?'

'We've just had a phone call from PC Blake, the local bobby at Putt Green. He's been away on honeymoon. The police house was supposed to be monitored by someone from the adjoining village but....'

'And?'

'He just got back and found a note from Mrs Holborne, saying that her husband's Jag had been stolen.'

'Stolen? When?'

'The note's not dated – but probably early last week. And the note said something about the car not running.'

Wheatley leaned back in his chair and folded his hands

across his stomach, staring at the ceiling. He shook his head and opened his eyes. 'Forget it.'

'But it corroborates Holborne's story.'

'No, it doesn't. There's no reason he couldn't have taken the car to fix it – if he wanted it as a getaway after the murder.'

Sloane frowned. 'But it doesn't make sense. Are we saying he snuck up in the night, rolled a broken down car out of a garage, somehow got it to somewhere he could fix it, and then silently put it back? Why? All that effort – why did it have to be *that* car? Surely he'd want to use a car that was *not* immediately linked to him. Someone *wanted* everyone to think it was Holborne.'

'I said forget it,' repeated Wheatley. 'We're stretched enough as it is without running round chasing loose ends. We've a cast iron case; leave it that way,' he ordered.

Sloane stared at his boss for a moment and then nodded. 'As you like, sir.'

The DC closed the door behind him and walked thoughtfully back down the corridor to his desk. He sat for a moment, staring out of the window, ignoring the ringing phones and banter going on around him. Then he reached over and lifted the phone.

'Ross? It's Sean. What was the name of that garage in Putt Green? On the other side of the green to the Holbornes' place?'

•

Charles pulled up at a telephone box and got out of the

car. He opened the telephone box door – urine again, he noticed – cleared a space to stand amongst the cigarette ends, crumpled chip bags and other detritus on the floor, and dialled the number torn from Plumber's pad. After a couple of rings an Irish woman's voice announced that he had reached the Oaks Lodge Boarding House and Charles hung up, satisfied. He got back into the car and drove the remaining couple of miles to the address, making a stop at a supermarket on the way.

He parked the Austin Healey in a space on the suburban road, shifted down in his seat and pulled his hat over his eyes. From his vantage spot he could see the stone steps leading up to the "Oak Lodge Boarding House." A sign swung gently in the front window informing the world that there were still vacancies.

The weather had turned cold and blustery, and within an hour Charles had identified the half a dozen or so gaps in the roof of the Austin Healey where the wind whistled in. Sips from the half-pint of whisky snuggling in his jacket pocket – courtesy of the Krays' shooter's donation – and two cheese sandwiches apparently made of cardboard kept him tolerably warm for the next few hours.

Dusk gathered over the Edwardian houses and the pavements became busier as people returned home from work. The Irish landlady closed the curtains on her ground floor sitting room, and smoke began to emerge from the chimney, but no there was still no sign of Sands.

By 7:30 pm all the children had returned from school and people from work, and the streets were again emptying. Most of the houses now had lights in their rooms, some curtained, some shuttered and a few revealing the movements of their occupants as they went about their cooking, homework and other domestic dramas.

Charles's legs were stiff and, despite the whisky, his hands and feet were cold. He got out of the car, closed the door quietly, and crossed the road toward the boarding house. He climbed the steps and rang the bell.

The outline of a woman could be seen approaching down the corridor and the door opened a couple of inches.

'Yes?'

'I'm looking for a room. Just for a week.'

The woman looked Charles up and down. She had sharp, dark eyes, and straggly black hair streaked with grey. 'No luggage?'

Charles nodded across the road. 'In the car,' he explained.

'Just you?' she asked. 'This is a respectable house,' she added.

'Just me. And I can pay a week in advance, right now.'

'I've only got a single room left.'

'That's fine. Although I'd like to see it first, please.'

The woman sized Charles up for a few moments longer and then opened the door fully to admit him. Charles entered the hallway and stood waiting on the polished tiles for the woman to shut the door behind him.

'Follow me,' she said, and she led Charles past a closed door from which emanated the sound of a radio, and up the stairs. Charles played a hunch.

'A colleague of mine told me about your boarding house. A Scotsman. I think he might be here now. His name's Robbie?'

'Mr Smith? That's his room,' and she indicated a door on the first landing as she went past it. Charles glanced down. A thin band of yellow light escaped from underneath the door.

They reached the head of the stairs and the landlady opened a door and stood back. Charles cast his eye around a small attic room with a single bed, a sink in the corner and a tiny wardrobe large enough to accommodate two or three hangers at most. Charles sat on the bed experimentally, bounced once and rose.

'This'll be perfect,' he announced cheerfully. 'I'll get my bag from the car, and pay you. Where can I find you?'

'Downstairs in the front sitting room. Just knock on the door. You'll need to register, Mr ....'

'Collins,' replied Charles.

'Well Mr Collins, the rent's six shillings for the week, with a further one and six security deposit. No food allowed in the room, no guests allowed after 9 o'clock, and no female guests allowed at any time. Understood?'

'Perfectly.'

The landlady gave him one last searching look and returned downstairs, leaving the bedroom door open. Charles waited until he heard the footsteps reach the hall and the sitting room door close. He crept back down two flights and stood outside the room below, putting on his gloves. He took the pistol out of his inside pocket and leaned with his ear against the door. At first he could hear nothing except the occasional car passing outside and the ticking of a large clock from somewhere downstairs but, then, there was a new sound. It was like the noise of a kettle before it boiled – a steady bubbling – but, as Charles concentrated on the noise, it paused. There was a gurgling noise for a second, and then the bubbling sound resumed. Charles gently took the door handle and tested it. It turned silently, and the door moved inward slightly; not locked. Charles held his breath, turned the knob fully, and launched himself into the room.

There had been no need for surprise. Facing the door was a small couch on which Robbie Sands sat, wearing an overcoat and a hat. He looked comfortable, his hands in his lap and his chin resting on his chest, as if he had just come in from a walk and was taking a rest. His chest rose and fell regularly. But where his weight created a depression in the couch seat there was a pool of dark shiny liquid. Sands's overcoat was open and the top of his torso was a slowly expanding circle of dark red in the centre of which was a black hole. It was just at the top of his sternum, slightly off centre and immediately below his left clavicle. With every gurgling breath another small gobbet of blood pulsed out of the hole, ran down his saturated shirt, and joined the growing puddle in which he sat.

Charles took a further step into the room and noted the dark drips of blood leading from the door to the couch. So, he wasn't shot here, thought Charles. Another thought occurred to him, and he put his head back out into the corridor. He bent down and looked carefully at the carpet. It was dark brown in colour but looking carefully Charles could see the drips of blood heading not towards the front of the house, but towards another door Charles hadn't noticed on the way up. A fire escape?

He stepped back into the room and closed the door quietly. The gurgling suddenly stopped as the dying man coughed gently. Blood suddenly appeared between Sands's lips, and his head lifted. He looked straight at Charles, and his mouth widened into a black grimace. He tried to speak but the effort simply brought more blood from the hole in his chest and through his teeth.

Charles cast about looking for a weapon by Sands's hands but, finding none, stepped closer.

'Too late,' said Sands softly. He mouthed the words rather than spoke them.

'Why?' demanded Charles, but Sands's head was slowly dropping to his chest again. The breath whistling through the hole in his trachea was less regular, with longer pauses between each one. Charles grabbed Sands's bloody chin and lifted his head. The Scotsman's eyes were half-closed but for a second they focused, and he reached up with a bloodied hand and grabbed the sleeve of Charles's leather jacket. He seemed about to say something, but the light died from his eyes and with a final bubbling wheeze, his arm and head fell in unison.

Charles returned to the door and locked it and then sat at the small table that looked down onto the dark street below. He regarded the dead man thoughtfully.

One step behind, yet again. And a growing body count. Until less than a week ago Charles had rarely seen a body – one of the advantages of the RAF over the other armed services. Now they were turning up everywhere he went.

He stood and surveyed the room. There was a massive old wardrobe, its mirror blotched with age, but it contained only a coat with nothing in the pockets and a small pile of clothes, a change of shirt and underwear, none of it clean. A spare blue blanket was folded on the floor of the wardrobe. On a shelf by the door was a bathroom bag contained shaving gear, toothpaste and so on, but nothing of interest. Charles balked at searching Sands's body, but he was about to start when he glimpsed something dark by the end of the bed. Partly hidden under the trailing edge of the counterpane was a small brown leather attaché case. It looked like a narrow school satchel with two buckles fastening it. Charles pulled it out and sat on the bed. Inside was a sheaf of papers, including a simple sketch of Putt Green with his own home marked with a large red asterisk, the layout of the house, and a blurry photograph of Henrietta. Charles's heart thundered in his chest; here, at last, was real proof.

He stood up and took the photograph to the light hanging from the central ceiling rose. It looked as if it had been a section from a larger photograph, but blown up. It was a grainy photograph of Henrietta standing in a line with other young women, all wearing summer dresses. Some wore hats and others were shading their eyes against the sun, which appeared to be low and shining directly in their faces. Behind them was a section of a single storey wooden building with a veranda, behind which were tall trees in leaf. Charles had a vague recollection of the scene, but couldn't immediately place where the photograph had been taken.

A lightning bolt of illumination suddenly struck Charles, and he whirled round and reopened the wardrobe door. He lifted out what he had supposed was a blanket and turned it over. It wasn't a blanket; it was a barrister's robes bag, blue, and brand-new. It still had the Ede & Ravenscourt price label hanging from the cord which pulled the mouth of the bag closed. Charles felt around inside it, but it was empty. His scrutiny was suddenly cut short by a shout from downstairs. He threw the bag back into the wardrobe.

'Mr Collins? Mr Collins!'

Charles hurriedly slid the documents back into the leather case and replaced it half-hidden at the foot of the bed. He tiptoed across to the door, unlocked it, and put his head out onto the landing. The landlady was calling from the bottom of the staircase. Charles closed the door behind him, and went downstairs.

'I'm awfully sorry,' he said, 'but on reflection, I think I'll find somewhere closer to the centre of town. I've business in the City, and this is a bit far out for me. I'm really sorry to have troubled you.'

Without waiting for a response, Charles strode past her and out of the front door, closing it behind him. The woman watched him go and then ran upstairs as fast as her arthritic knees would allow to reassure herself that Charles hadn't stolen the furniture from her top room.

PART FIVE

THE REVEAL

CHAPTER TWENTY-NINE

'Is that Buckinghamshire Police?'

'Yes. How can I direct your call?'

'I need to speak to Detective Constable Sloane. I think he's based at Aylesbury Police Station. It's very urgent.'

'Please may I have your name?'

'Charles Holborne. I'm wanted for the murder of my wife. And I have another murder to report, perhaps two.'

There was no sharp intake of breath from the young telephone operator at the other end of the line. 'Please hold the line, sir,' she said calmly, 'and I'll put you through.'

Remarkable sang froid, thought Charles. It took five minutes before Sloane was located.

'Holborne?' he asked, without precursor, his voice echoing down the line.

'Yes. Listen carefully. I'm going to have to trust you, Detective Constable.'

'You're going to have to trust me? And why would you be doing that?' asked Sloane. Charles thought he detected a very faint Irish accent.

'Because I can't trust your Superintendent. I have proof of my innocence, but if I give it to him, it'll disappear.'

'What proof is that?' asked Sloane in a neutral tone.

'If you get your men quickly to Oak Lodge Boarding House, Ormiston Grove, Shepherd's Bush, in the front bedroom on the first floor you will find Robbie Sands, recently of HM Prison Long Lartin. He escaped 10 days ago. He's dead – shot – and before you ask, no, I didn't kill him either. At the end of his bed you'll find a briefcase with the instructions he was given prior to killing Henrietta. It should have his fingerprints all over it. And with a little luck, if you check under the bonnet of my Jag, you might find some more there.'

'Where are you Mr Holborne?'

'I'm in a call box in West London.'

'Don't you think it's time you handed yourself in?'

Charles laughed sardonically. 'Are you serious? I may have been a yard behind the murderer throughout, but at least I've been looking. I know how this works, Sloane, and I know your bastard of a Superintendent. If anyone's going to break the seal on his "watertight case", it's going to have to be me.'

'We're not all as stupid as you think, Mr Holborne. We already know the Jag wasn't running, so it had to be fixed before you could make your supposed getaway. And we've also traced the owner of the girl's Mercedes, Neville Fylde – who I gather you've already visited – and we know he was paid to make it look like you had a mistress. Was it you who put the hole in his ceiling?'

'Ceiling? Don't know what you're taking about.'

'What colour's your robes bag?'

'What?' asked Charles, incredulous.

'You heard. What colour?'

'Red.'

'Your wife's murderer was seen to run off with a *blue* bag.'

Sloane was, after all, no fool. 'Which you will find in the wardrobe of Sands's room,' confirmed Charles. 'It's brand-new – the price label's still on it – and it has no barrister's initials on it.'

'I'm telling you all this Mr Holborne to persuade you to come in. I assure you I have more than just an open mind, and my guvnor is… coming round. But you must realise the danger you're in. You've done well so far, but you've been lucky. You're not trained for this; we are.'

'I've a got a few things to do first. But I promise I'll hand myself in when they're done.'

There was something about the way Sloane referred to his guvnor which made Charles suspicious.

'Are you recording this?' he asked.

'Of course I am.'

'And how many others are in the room with you, Sloane?'

There was a pause. 'Most of the team.'

Another dry voice added: 'Including DC Sloane's bastard Superintendent.'

It was Wheatley. He continued: 'You told the switchboard you wanted to report one murder, perhaps two? Do you want to tell us anything about the other one? Or are you keeping that one as a surprise?'

'Hello, Superintendent. Sands's accomplice on the Express Dairies robbery was a man named Derek Plumber. When I left Plumber's house in Limehouse this morning he was in a diabetic coma. I organised an ambulance and left him with the district nurse. I'm not 100% certain about this, but I think Sands deliberately kept him from his insulin. I'm not sure of the motive yet, maybe simply for money. And I have one further lead to – '

And at that, Charles's money ran out. He fished in his pockets for more change, but then stopped and let the beeps finish. The line was cut.

At Aylesbury police station DC Sloane hung up and turned off the tape recorder. He turned to face the room. Behind him sat or stood all the members of team who he could round up in response to Holborne's call. He'd made sure they were all in the room before he called Wheatley down. Only then did he have Holborne's call put through.

Superintendent Wheatley pulled another chair out from the desk and sat down heavily. 24 hours after the murder he'd had enough evidence to convict Holborne. Now what had looked like a simple collar was falling apart in his hands. And half the team had heard it, so he had no choice; he had to follow through on Holborne's information. What galled him most was that that arrogant Jew-boy had more or less demolished the case against him by a combination of dumb luck and brute force.

'Bricker,' said Wheatley.

'Sir?' replied the detective sergeant from the other end of the long table.

'Have we got all the elimination prints from Chancery Court yet?'

'All except three. One's confirmed as being in the British Caymans for the last month, so he's ruled out. Two others are here, but out of town on cases.' He fished in

his pocket for his notebook and flicked over some pages.
'Erm...Jonathan Beardsley and Simon Ellison.'

'Where are they?'

'According to their diaries, Beardsley is in York on
a three-week civil trial and Ellison is at the assizes in
Wiltshire.'

Wheatley turned to Sloane. 'I assume you've had the
Jag looked at? Seeing as you ignored my earlier orders
about it?'

Sloane smiled cheerily at his Superintendent, trying
to look fresh-faced and not too clever. 'Yes. There were
prints all over it belonging to Holborne and his wife, a
couple from two of the mechanics at the local garage, and
some half-prints from someone presently unidentified.'

'You think Sands was working with someone in
Holborne's Chambers.'

'Well, sir, we know someone set him up to make it look
as if Holborne had a mistress. They had to have access to
the Chambers diary, to know where Holborne would be –
they couldn't risk running into him at Fetter Lane. And
they had to have his keys copied. Both of which would be
easy if they worked in the same office. There's no security
of any sort and the barristers wander into one another's
rooms all the time. So, yes, I'm thinking that it was one
of the other barristers. Several witnesses say that Mrs
Holborne was, if you don't mind my language, a right tart.
I'm pretty sure we'll turn up any number of motives.'

Wheatley sighed. 'Alright. I'm not saying I'm buying
it, but we'd better get down to the Temple. Get one of

the SOCOs to bring the prints from the Jag. If it is one of the barristers we need to identify him before Holborne gets himself killed. Not that I'd shed any tears, mind, but still…Bricker, get on the radio. Get the City of London boys to bring in the clerk, Stanley Wigglesworth. Sloane – you and PC Redaway go to Shepherds Bush and see about Sands. Come on. Let's get on with this.'

CHAPTER THIRTY

Stanley arrived at Chancery Court just before 11.00 pm. He had still to get over the shock of having one of his guvnors on the run, charged with the murder of his wife. Rita had never known him to get home so early, so assiduously had he been avoiding all his usual haunts for the last week. He couldn't bear the looks he received whenever he met other clerks. But then, to be called out of his bed just as he was settling to sleep, raced to London in a speeding police car while still in pyjamas, and required to open up Chambers for more investigations, this time into *another* member of Chambers, well that was the final straw. 'I'm going to retire at the end of term,' he'd announced to Rita, as he pulled a coat on over his pyjamas.

Superintendent Wheatley, DS Bricker and a third man got out of the car in which they had been waiting for Stanley's arrival. Bricker introduced Stanley to Wheatley and to the third man, Reeves.

'Mr Reeves is a Scenes of Crime Officer,' explained Wheatley.

'Who should have been off duty four hours ago,' added Reeves, pointedly.

'Now, Mr Wigglesworth,' said Wheatley, 'can you let us in, please?'

Stanley led the men upstairs to the first floor and opened the main door.

'We need to see the rooms of Mr Beardsley and Mr Ellison.'

'They're both on the other side of the landing,' replied the clerk. 'I'll show you.'

Stanley unlocked the other door on the landing and led the way inside to the far room. He pointed to the desk facing the door. 'That's Mr Ellison's, superintendent,' he said.

'And which is Mr Holborne's?' Stanley pointed to the room next door, and Wheatley and Bricker shared a glance. 'Does anyone else use Mr Ellison's room?'

'Not usually, no.'

'Okay,' said Wheatley to Reeves. 'Off you go.'

'Nobody touch the light switch, please,' requested Reeves.

Reeves took a torch from his pocket and entered Ellison's room. He went over to the desk. He prowled round it, bending over, looking closely at the surfaces without touching anything.

'Hmm,' he said, turning on the desk lamp and extinguishing his torch. 'The phone might be the best place to start.'

He stood upright again and walked back to the other men who were watching him. He examined the door frame and then the light switch. 'And then the light switch,' he concluded.

He went back to the desk and opened his briefcase. He took out a small pot and unscrewed the lid to reveal a brush inserted into it, rather like those used by photographers to blow dust from their camera lenses. He lifted the telephone handset off its cradle by the cable and placed it carefully on the desk blotter. The others standing at the threshold watched him silently. Reeves dusted a tiny amount of silver dust over the inside of the handset and looked carefully at the result.

'Lovely,' he said. 'There's a couple of quite decent ones.'

He reached down into his case and took out a roll of tape. He cut a small piece off with a pair of scissors and pressed it firmly over the handset. He repeated the procedure twice more and then gently lifted the prints off. He immediately attached them to pieces of plastic card obtained from his case, and initialled the cards with a pen. He then moved to the light switch, and started again.

Wheatley's foot tapped impatiently. 'Well?' he asked.

'What do you want me to compare them with?' asked Reeves. Bricker opened his briefcase and handed Reeves an envelope from which Reeves took a further set of plastic cards. 'Is there another room I can use?' Reeves asked Stanley.

'Next door?' suggested the clerk.

'Fine,' said Reeves. He went to the adjoining room, taking the plastic cards with him, sat at the desk, and turned on the desk lamp. He took a magnifying glass from his breast pocket and looked closely at the fingerprints Bricker had provided. Then he turned to the lifts he had just taken. Wheatley peered over his shoulder like a vulture.

'You realise this is not supposed to be my job, don't you?' asked Reeves.

'I know. But didn't you used to be – '

'Used to be, yes. But that was almost eight years ago. Would you mind, Superintendent? You're distracting me, hovering behind me like that.'

Wheatley moved away and Reeves continued his perusal. Every now and then he would make a jotting on the pad next to him. After about ten minutes, he switched off the lamp, and sat back.

'I'm not a fingerprint expert any more, you understand, and these are hardly the best conditions to work under… but…'

'But?' demanded Wheatley.

Reeves was not to be hurried. 'This wouldn't stand up in court, Superintendent. You have to have a minimum number of identical features, and the prints marked "bonnet" aren't complete and they're not of the best quality – '

'Yes, yes, yes! I know all that!' shouted Wheatley. 'But what is your opinion?"

'Okay. There are no clearly inconsistent features between the prints here and those lifted from the car. As to common features, I can see six or seven in the thumb print on the phone, and ten on the forefinger by the door. Yes. If you have to have an answer, I'd say that in all probability – no higher than that, understand? – they were made by the same man. Not enough to convict, though.'

'And they're definitely not Holborne's?'

'Definitely not.'

'That's enough for me, especially if a rather high-profile barrister is about to be murdered!'

'What?' demanded Stanley. 'Is Mr Ellison about be murdered?'

Wheatley turned to Stanley. 'I'm sorry sir, I shouldn't have said that in your presence. No, he's not. But I need to know where he lives, right now.'

'Er… er…Chelsea somewhere…I've got the address in my room…'

'Bricker, go with Mr Wigglesworth and get the address. Then make him a cuppa and sit with him till you hear from me. He's not to contact anyone.'

'But – ' protested Stanley.

'Sorry, sir, but I'm not taking any chances.'

CHAPTER THIRTY-ONE

Almost as soon as he had left the boarding house in Shepherd's Bush Charles had remembered when that grainy summer photograph had been taken, and by whom. Simon Ellison was the captain of the Chambers cricket team, and every year Chancery Court barristers used to play a motley group of clerks and ringers gathered together by Stanley. Two years before Charles had been persuaded to play and, to his surprise, Henrietta had asked to watch and help with the tea. The photograph of all the wives and girlfriends had been taken by Jenny Ellison during the tea interval. Charles had seen the original on several occasions on the wall of Ellison's study.

As soon as he had finished speaking to DC Sloane, Charles drove to The Boltons, Chelsea. The home of Simon and Jennie Ellison was just around the corner in Gilston Road. Charles had found Ellison's car without difficulty, parked 100 yards further up the road, its bonnet still warm. So much for the trial in Wiltshire, he thought.

Whoever had employed Sands to kill Henrietta had had access to the photograph. Just to make sure, Charles had sneaked in through the wrought iron gate at the front of the Ellisons' house and peered into the study window to see if the photograph was still there. It was. He then retreated round the corner to pace up and down under the dark trees in The Boltons, and to think. All his best jury speeches and cross-examination had been developed like this, pacing up and down.

It all fitted: detailed knowledge of Charles's movements, access to his keys for Fetter Lane – even down to Ellison's ability with cars; he had the skills to repair the Jaguar and replace it into the garage at Putt Green. But why? What was the motive? Charles had considered the possibility that Henrietta and Ellison were having an affair – in fact he remembered Michael Rhodes Thomas once saying something about Henrietta being seen at the Ellisons' home, which had puzzled him briefly at the time – but even if that were right, it still didn't suggest a motive. A lovers' tiff? Possible, but unlikely.

So, with no obvious motive Charles needed incontro-vertible proof – proof sufficient to convince even the sceptical Wheatley. And it was that which kept him pacing up and down The Boltons for half an hour. But the beginning of a plan was starting to take form. He jogged back to the Austin Healey and drove back to the Kings Road, stopping first at a tobacconist to get some change, and then at the next telephone box he saw. Again he dialled Buckinghamshire Police.

'DC Sloane please.'

There was a delay. Then: 'I'm afraid DC Sloane is unavailable at the moment.'

'Is there anyone else from the Holborne murder enquiry team I could talk to?'

'I'm afraid they're all out of the moment, sir. Can I take a message?'

'No,' replied Charles, irritably. 'Forget it.'

He hung up without waiting for an answer and was about to leave the phone box when he had another idea. He reached into his jacket pocket and pulled out the piece of notepaper from Plumber's kitchen. He dialled again.

'Is that the Oak Lodge Boarding House?'

There was a catch of breath and sobbing at the other end of the line. It sounded like crying. Perhaps Oak Lodge was no longer quite as respectable as it had been before bodies starting turning up in its bedrooms, Charles thought.

'If there's a policeman just arrived, I need to talk to him,' said Charles.

That promoted crying in earnest at the other end of the line but Charles heard the phone being handed to someone else.

'Yes?' said DC Sloane's voice.

'It's me, Holborne,' said Charles. 'How long till you can get to the Temple?'

'Why?'

'I know who killed Sands, and I'm going to try to get a confession out of him that you can hear.'

'Now, Holborne, don't interfere. It's all under control, and you'll just get yourself hurt.'

'Be at Chancery Court by quarter past midnight, OK? Not earlier and not later. Don't use the lights, go straight to my room and keep out of sight.'

'Holborne, don't be so fucking stupid! You're unarmed, and so am I!'

'Just be there. If you can get some backup, so much the better.'

Charles broke the connection, got back in the car and drove to the Temple. As he passed Charing Cross station he saw the Wimpy on the corner and realised how tired and hungry he felt. Perhaps the whisky – on top of almost no sleep for three days – had been a poor idea, he thought. He stopped and went into the deserted burger bar to pick up another lukewarm burger and soggy chips, and bolted them down in the car. Then he completed his journey to the Temple. Rather than driving up Middle Temple Lane he parked on the Embankment. He hoped it was far enough away from the Temple that, even if Ellison saw the car, he wouldn't be suspicious. Having immobilised the Austin Healey, he opened the boot to look for some tools, and came up with a tyre lever. Perfect. He slipped it inside his belt and strode off towards the Temple. Then, on an afterthought, he retraced his steps for 100 yards to the telephone box at the corner of Temple Place. Better to call from a payphone, rather than from Chambers. He delved into his pockets and came up with enough change to make one last call. He dialled and while the phone rang Charles checked the time: twenty-five to midnight. It took a while for the phone at the other end to be picked up.

'Yes?' said Jenny Ellison in a sleepy voice.

Charles pressed the button to speak and the coins dropped. 'Simon Ellison, please,' he said in a Scottish accent.

'May I say who's speaking?'

Charles effected a wheeze, and panted: 'Say it's Robbie

343

Smith.' He heard Jenny speaking to someone else. It's a Scottish man…Robbie Smith? In a callbox.'

Ellison came on the line. 'Who is this?' he demanded.

'It's me, Sands,' croaked Charles.

'You…you're…'

'No, I'm not. You winged me, but I'll live. I'm back at my digs. I want tae talk.'

There was no reply at first. Then, in a low whisper: 'I can't talk now…Sorry, darling, go back to sleep; it's work.'

'Not on the phone. Meet me in your room at Chancery Court…one hour.' Charles inhaled deeply as if fighting for breath. 'And bring money. I'll need at least a grand if you want me tae disappear. Can you do that?'

He waited for Ellison to find a phrase which wouldn't give him away to his wife. 'Not quite, but close perhaps.'

'Bring what you can, then. I'll give you back the photo of Holborne's missus and the plan of the house…. And if you don't come, I'll post them to the polis – oh, and bring Holborne's notebook. I want it back on the shelf with the rest. It's go' my name all over it. Have you go' all that?'

'Yes,' whispered Ellison.

'And no tricks, Ellison. You'll no' catch me unawares again…. I've got a gun too, and it's a lot bigger than that wee peashooter o' yours. I'll be watchin' you all the way in. Just go straight to your room, and wait for me.' Charles gave one last cough for effect, and hung up.

Charles ran up Middle Temple Lane. He reckoned he had at least half an hour's start on Ellison, but he had to find a way in without keys. He'd need every second.

2 Chancery Court backed onto 3 Pump Buildings, another set of chambers, with a narrow light well between them. Charles had often wondered why the architect had placed a window on the first floor landing of Chancery Court when its sole function appeared not to admit light but a howling draft in the winter. He hoped that the draft meant that the window wasn't secure.

A few lights shone from the upper storeys of some of the old buildings, but the courtyards of the Temple were completely deserted. Charles ran under the plane trees through the yellow gaslight. A thin mist was drifting up from the Thames and carpeted the courtyards in wisps of white. Charles slowed his footsteps as he realised that the sound of his running was making too much noise; he didn't want the echoes disturbing any of the judges in their cosy flats on the top floors. He skirted round the back of Pump Buildings, trying to orientate himself and find the window that overlooked Chancery Court's landing. There was a locked ironwork gate behind which there was a service door for the other chambers. The gate was set in a wall which extended to first floor level, where there was a ledge, and there was a bicycle chained to the gate. If Charles could make his way along the ledge without falling he would be in the light well at the same height as the window.

Charles took off his fake spectacles and put them in an inside pocket. He moved the tyre lever to the back of his belt so it wouldn't get in his way and, gripping the top of the gate, heaved himself up by standing on the bicycle seat. Within seconds he was on top of the wall, hugging the side of the building. He inched his way around the ledge for ten feet, turned a corner, and found himself outside the window. Feeling behind him for the tyre lever, he pulled it out of his belt and inserted it into the base of the sash window. It slid up without any effort and he rolled in. I really would make a decent criminal, he thought. He closed the window behind him, tucked the tyre lever back in his belt and ran up to the landing above. The outer door leading to the rooms he and Ellison occupied was closed and locked. He had expected it to be locked, but he was nonetheless disappointed. His choice was to force the door, which if seen by Ellison would certainly arouse suspicions, or hide, perhaps on the stairs above. The second option was not attractive; he would be in plain view if Ellison happened to look further up the stairs. He decided on the former. Ellison might assume that Sands had already arrived and broken in. It would also clear the way for Sloane to get in and take up position.

The outer door was solid oak, seasoned over the centuries, with enormous studs and strap hinges covered in layer upon layer of paint. It also formed a very flush fit with the door frame. Charles attacked the door with the tyre lever with all his strength for 15 minutes, and was almost ready to give up when one final shove produced a loud cracking noise as the lock housing splintered. Charles opened the door fully flat against the wall, just as it would be during office hours, and picked up the larger splinters of wood from the floor. The inner door was simpler, and he forced the Yale lock at the first attempt. He stood back and surveyed his handiwork in the dark. He doubted anything would look unusual to a cursory glance.

He went into Ellison's room. There was absolutely nowhere to hide there, and he realised that there was no chance of him surprising the other barrister. He looked into his own room briefly, but discounted that. If he showed himself to Sloane he might get himself arrested before he could put his plan into operation. He tried the door opposite. This was the room of Gwyneth Price-Hopkins. Charles was surprised to find his entrance to the room partially blocked by upended desks, a table and stacks of chairs. The party! This was the furniture cleared from Sir Geffrey's room. Charles also saw several bouquets of flowers in assorted receptacles dotted around the room, and the desk and one of the shelves had a large display of greetings cards. Charles picked up one of the cards. It congratulated Gwyneth and her husband on the birth of their child. The baby must have arrived early, thought Charles, and in the knowledge that she would be away for the next few weeks at least, the clerks hadn't got round to moving all the furniture back into what had been Sir Geoffrey's room.

Charles moved one of the desks slightly so that it impeded the door opening fully, and then returned to the corridor separating this room from Ellison's. From a position standing at the threshold of Ellison's room it wasn't possible to see into Gwyneth's room even though her door remained open. On the other hand, Charles would have a view of Ellison's desk.

It was the best that could be managed. Charles ran to the ground floor and opened both main doors to Chambers from the inside, leaving them ajar. He took the opportunity offered by the moonlight to take out his pistol and check it. Then he returned to Gwyneth's room to wait.

As the minutes ticked away Charles's nervousness grew. The smell of flowers, trapped for a couple of days in the closed room, was cloying, and seemed to increase his agitation. He waited twenty minutes before he heard soft footsteps on the stairs. He checked his watch, angling it toward the little light coming through the window. 00:15 a.m. exactly. The sound stopped, but no one came past his position. The silence lengthened for so long that Charles began to wonder if he'd imagined it, but eventually the footfalls continued. A shape went past Gwyneth's door. Sloane – not tall enough to be Ellison. Then a second man, bulkier, almost bald, went past. Good – reinforcements. Charles heard the floorboards creak and the sound of his room's door opening against carpet, and then silence.

The building settled into complete stillness again. Charles strained his ears, but he could hear only the sound of the wind in the trees from the courtyard outside and, once, a lonely ship's horn drifting up from the Thames.

When he did next hear a noise from inside the building it was so close it made him jump. A floorboard creaked right outside Gwyneth's room and Charles realised that

Ellison had made it all the way into the building a good deal more quietly than the police. Now I know why they're called "the Plod" he thought. Through the crack in the door Charles watched Ellison's shape approach the half-open door of his room cautiously. Ellison held his right hand out and although Charles couldn't see a gun he knew what the pose signified. Ellison prodded the door gently with his free hand and it swung inward silently until its brass handle bumped gently on the adjoining wall. He waited, listening intently, and then entered the room. Evidently satisfied that it was unoccupied, Ellison strode to his desk and sat at it, his gun hand pointed towards the door.

Curtain time, thought Charles.

'Are ye there, Ellison?' called Charles hoarsely from across the corridor. He watched Ellison start and stand up, but the man remained behind the desk.

'Sands?' Ellison called back.

Charles gasped for breath as if he were a drowning man, pausing between breaths for dramatic effect. If Ellison thought he was seriously injured, he'd be less suspicious about a change in voice.

'Got ma money?' called Charles.

'Where are you?' demanded Ellison. 'Come out so I can see you.' Ellison took a couple of steps round the desk towards the door.

'Stay put!' said Charles, coughing loudly. 'I can put…a hole right though you… from where I am,' he gasped.

Ellison came to a halt, but he was looking hard at the

door to Gwyneth's room; he knew now where Charles was hiding.

'Throw the money intae the corridor,' ordered Charles.

'No. Not without the documents.'

'They're here…dinnae fret yoursel'. But first, explain something…. I ken you think that Jew-boy stole your practice … but why kill his wife? She was harmless.'

Ellison began inching towards the door, speaking to distract and cover his movement. 'Harmless? The woman was a fucking landmine! It was only a matter of time before it all went public. With my name splashed all over the papers!'

'Stay where ye are!' croaked Charles, but Ellison had almost reached the door of his room, and he didn't stop. Charles backed away from the door shielding him, his pistol arm raised. His bluff was being called and he knew the only way to stop Ellison was to shoot, but he needed him to carry on talking.

'But the worst thing? She threw me over – and for Corbett! – an arrogant oaf who treated her like a whore!'

The speech had covered Ellison all the way to the threshold and as he uttered the last word he launched himself through Gwyneth's door and fired at the same time. The bullet smashed the window behind Charles. Charles stood and pulled the trigger of his borrowed pistol at the advancing man. The trigger clicked and jammed, leaving Charles unarmed and silhouetted against the window, a sitting duck.

Ellison paused in his advance, his gun held in both

hands, pointing directly at Charles's chest. 'Now,' said Ellison conversationally. 'Where are the documents?'

Only then did Ellison realise that something was wrong. 'Just a minute...' he said, and he reached out with his left hand to feel for the light switch behind him. For a fraction of a second his gun arm wavered, and Charles leapt at the desk standing on its end to Ellison's right, colliding heavily with it and causing it to topple over. Ellison was a big man, and although the weight of the desk knocked him off balance, he didn't fall. The desk rolled off his shoulder and fell with a crash, knocking the door further closed as it fell. Ellison stepped sideways and fired again, and Charles felt as if he had been struck in the left shoulder by a sprinting prop forward. Charles knew he'd been hit, but also that if he backed away the next shot would finish him, so he rolled with the blow, allowed it to spin him round and brought his right fist in an arc up to Ellison's head. He felt it connect with the other man's temple and both men went down in a tangle of limbs. At the same moment the door swung violently open and smashed into Charles's head.

He saw stars, and then nothing.

CHAPTER THIRTY-TWO

The first of Charles's senses to start operating again was his sense of smell: antiseptic, washed linoleum and cabbage. This doesn't smell like the afterlife, he thought, so that's a good start. He opened his eyes. He was in a darkened room but he appeared still to have vision. Another hopeful sign. Then he tried to sit up and pain raged all down the right side of his body from his neck to his lower ribs causing him to groan involuntarily. He closed his eyes again and tried to stay still. He reopened them after a moment or two and saw a plastic cord trailing from a bedside table on his left. Gingerly he tested the ability of his left arm to move and found that, although stiff, it didn't hurt. He reached out, grabbed the cord, and pressed the red button at its end.

The door opened almost immediately, spilling bright light across Charles's bed from the corridor.

'Hi,' croaked Charles. 'Sorry to trouble you, nurse, but can I have some water?'

The silhouetted shape in the door came round to Charles's bedside. 'Charlie, it's me,' said Rachel's voice. 'Did you press the buzzer?'

'Yes. Where am I?'

'University College. Don't move. You've had surgery on your shoulder.'

Another shape briefly obscured the light from the corridor and a nurse entered. 'Good, Mr Holborne, you're awake. We were beginning to get a little worried.'

Rachel stepped back and allowed the nurse to stand beside Charles's bed from where she took his pulse and blood pressure. 'Fine,' she concluded, rolling up the pressure cuff. 'Would you like to sit up?'

'Yes please.'

The nurse went to the head of the bed and rotated a wheel, and the top third of the bed lifted up slowly. Even that movement hurt like hell. Charles gasped.

'Pain?' asked the nurse.

'Yeh.'

'I'll have a word with the doctors and see what we can do about that. Your friend can get you some water in the meantime. Small sips to start, please; you've had a general anaesthetic.'

She bustled out of the room and Rachel took her place. She poured Charles some water and held the glass while he took a few sips.

'What happened?' asked Charles when he had finished.

'You were shot in the shoulder.'

'Got that bit,' said Charles wryly.

'As far as I can understand from the surgeon – he was a bit vague cos I'm not a member of family – it more or less destroyed your clavicle and scapula, in and out, so they've had to pin you. But it missed all the important arteries and nerves, so apparently you were lucky. Oh, and you were knocked out by the police officers when they charged into the room. So the medics were a bit worried about the anaesthetic on top of a concussion.'

'Clever chaps, those policemen.'

'Don't be too hard on them, Charlie. One of them took a bullet in the hand trying to disarm Ellison. He's in the room next door.'

'Oh,' said Charles, feeling bad. 'And Ellison?'

'In custody, charged with two murders and attempting to kill you. You had a policeman on the door for a few hours, but he's gone now you're no longer a danger to the public.'

Charles smiled, but even that hurt. 'What's with my face?' he managed.

'You're very swollen all down the left side, to your jaw. Maybe where the door hit you?'

'Great. How long have you been here?'

'Since the early hours. The police called your parents, and they called me. We came together.'

'Where are they?'

Rachel took his left hand and held it in hers. It felt good. 'They went home to get some sleep when you went down for surgery. Your mum's been in a bad way since you went on the run. She's not slept for days. I said I'd wait and call them when you woke. I'll go and do it now.' She made to leave, but Charles called her back.

'Rachel.'

'Yes.'

Charles lifted his left hand and Rachel took it again. 'You've been… so kind… so …'

'Stow it, Charlie – '

'No I mean it. I'd never have managed without you. My guardian angel.'

'Oh, please! Let me go and make that call. Then I'll push off.'

'Why?'

'I don't want to be in the way when your parents arrive. I think you should be on your own with them – at least the first time. I'll be back at the end of visiting time.'

'I don't want to see them.'

'Oh, Charlie, surely now – '

'No. I'm not ready. Maybe I won't ever be.'

'But – ' started Rachel.

'No. I mean it. Maybe later, on my own terms, but not now. I haven't got the energy for it.'

Rachel stared hard at him, her eyes narrowed in the way that Charles now recognised as disappointment in him, and shook her head. 'You took on an armed murderer and, according to the nice policeman next door, a Yardie boss,' she said quietly. 'Not to mention one of the Kray twins' thugs. But you haven't got the courage to apologise to your own parents.'

'Courage? What are you talking about?'

'Just think about it, Charlie. I know how much they hurt you by cutting you out of their lives. But how do you suppose *they* felt when you changed your name and married Henrietta without a word to them?' She turned on her heel and left.

CHAPTER THIRTY-THREE

Charles showed his cards. 'Twenty-one,' he announced, and with his good hand collected the pennies on the table. DC Sloane shook his head and scowled good-naturedly. 'I played a lot as a kid,' explained Charles.

To prove it, he placed the discards on top of the pile and, with one hand cut the deck and shuffled it.

'So, you're a card sharp on top of everything else,' said Sloane. 'Is there no end to your criminal talents?'

Charles looked across at the police officer. He and DC Sloane had taken to having their afternoon teas in Charles's private room and would play a few hands of cards while chatting. Charles had been moved out to a general ward after a couple of days, but the press attention had made the nursing staff's lives a misery and he had swiftly been moved back and his name removed from the board on the door.

The two men had become celebrities in the hospital, known by some of the younger staff as the "one-armed bandits." Their photographs were still on all the front pages. Charles's recovery was proceeding rather better than that of his saviour. Sloane had had two operations on his hand, but the blood supply to his index finger had been destroyed by the bullet, and eventually the finger had been amputated.

DC Sloane had a triangular, impish face, unruly light brown hair, intelligent blue eyes, and a small but well-shaped cleft chin. Definitely Irish, Charles thought. They got on well.

'What time are you being collected?' asked Charles.

Sloane checked his watch. 'Any minute now.'

'And then what?'

'What do you mean?'

'Will they take you back, even missing a finger?'

Sloane laughed. 'Sergeant Bricker seemed to think so. They can't decorate me and fire me the same week.'

There was a knock on the door and DS Bricker appeared.

'Really to go?' asked Bricker. He addressed Sloane directly and didn't look at Charles at all.

'For Christ's sake, Sarge, say hello to the man,' said Sloane as he stood. 'He's still sore that you decked him at Fetter Lane,' he explained to Charles.

'Fucking sucker punch,' muttered Bricker.

Charles held out his good hand. 'Come on, sergeant. No hard feelings, eh?'

Bricker paused and reluctantly took Charles's hand. 'No, I guess not. I can't say I'd have done any different in your circumstances. I've got these for you.'

Charles saw that Bricker was carrying a large clear plastic bag in which he could see his keys, his watch and some of his clothing. Bricker put it on Charles's bed and handed Charles a pad of forms with his belongings listed on the top page. 'Do you want to go through all of it?' he asked.

'No, just give me a pen. Any news of Ellison?' asked Charles as he signed. 'Wasn't it his first remand this morning?'

'Yup. And he applied for bail.'

'He never had much judgment, in my professional opinion. And?' asked Charles.

'What do you think? One conspiracy to murder, one actual murder and two attempted murders in the space of a week. And an overheard confession? "Risk of further offences and of absconding."'

'Very right and proper too,' said Charles.

Bricker turned to Sloane. 'I need to be back at the station.'

'Yes, sure.' Sloane held out his hand. 'Take care, Charles. See you at Ellison's trial.'

Charles took the other's hand and the two men regarded one another silently for a moment with mutual respect. 'Thanks again, Sean,' said Charles. 'Obviously, for saving my life, but also for keeping an open mind.'

Sloane nodded and smiled. 'Do you mind if I ask you a question?' he asked.

'Shoot.'

'What're *you* going to do now? You can't go back to Chambers, can you? We all know you didn't do it but… well, she was still the daughter of the ex-head of Chambers, wasn't she? Isn't it going to be…?'

'Embarrassing? Yes. I'm not sure, to be honest. Neville Fylde offered me a job, you know? I think I'd make quite a good career criminal.'

'Don't joke about that, sir,' said Bricker. 'I've always said it. Barristers think things through, work logically; they can assess evidence; and they know how to avoid the mistakes that get their clients caught. You proved me right.'

'Did you find my notebook, the one with the details of the Sands and Plumber trial?' asked Charles.

'Yes,' answered Bricker. 'Ellison had it. But it's now an exhibit in the case against him, so you'll have to wait for it. But why do you want it back? If you want my opinion, sir, you shouldn't be allowed to keep any of them. They're a directory of crime.'

'That's why I want them. They'd be useful if I pursue the other option.'

'Other option?' asked Sloane as he picked up his bag.

'Private detective.'

The two policemen stared at him, unable to decide if he was serious.

'Now, what sort of job is *that* for a nice Jewish boy?' asked Sloane with a smile.

'But as I've demonstrated, I'm definitely not nice. And as for Jewish, well, the jury's out on that one.'

The two police officers left and Charles returned to sit on his bed. He realised that he was still holding Bricker's pen. They'll have to add theft to the list, he thought. He gazed out of the window over the grey slate rooftops of Bloomsbury. There was still an hour until visiting time. He hoped Rachel would come. Somehow she'd slipped into his life so completely that the thought of her not being there made Charles uncomfortable.

The door opened behind him and for a second, lost in thought, Charles didn't turn.

'Turn and face me!' said a familiar voice.

Charles whirled round, causing the pain in his shoulder

to start again. Standing with his back to the closed door was Ivor Kellett-Brown. He held a large bouquet of flowers in one hand and an old army revolver in the other. The second of these was unwelcome.

'I want to see the look on your face as I pull the trigger,' said Kellett-Brown.

Charles was too surprised to reply. After all he had been through – all the narrow escapes – his mind refused to accept that he was actually going to be shot by a crackpot ex-barrister wearing pinstriped trousers and a black jacket which had gone out of fashion in the 1930s.

He knew there was no chance of his getting across the room fast enough to prevent Kellett-Brown firing, so he leaned back on his pillows, put his feet up, and smiled.

'What a lovely surprise, Ivor. Nice flowers; are they for me?'

'I'm quite serious about this, Holborne. If Ellison's not up to it then I certainly am. I'm going to shoot you. It's nothing less than you deserve. Get on your knees.'

Charles laughed as if the request were a joke. 'Fancy a cup of tea old chap?' he asked, indicating the pot. 'There's plenty left. What news of the Temple?'

Kellett-Brown took a step further into the room. 'Get on your knees!' he demanded, his cracked voice rising by an octave.

'Oh, come on Ivor. A joke's a joke, but you'll disturb the other patients.'

'This is no joke! I swear, I'm going to kill you. But first I shall humiliate you the way you did me!'

Kellett-Brown was shouting now. Someone must have heard that, thought Charles. And they had. The door burst inwards and Kellett-Brown was sent flying. The flowers and gun fell from his grasp as he tottered over, trying to catch the end of the bed. The gun skidded half-way under the bed, and Charles hopped off and kicked it into the corner of the room. DS Bricker grabbed the falling Kellett-Brown in a rugby tackle, and Charles heard the air whoosh out of his would-be assassin's lungs. Bricker sat on his back and pulled his arms behind him.

'I'm arresting you on suspicion of attempted murder!' he shouted.

Sloane entered the room ahead of several members of nursing staff.

Charles went to the corner of the room and, using Bricker's pen, picked up the revolver by its trigger guard. 'Got a bag?' he asked Sloane.

'Dear God, Charles, you don't half push your luck! If we'd left five minutes earlier we'd never have seen him coming in.'

'How did you know who he was?'

'We didn't. But he was making a scene – demanding your room number – and he looked a bit odd. He kept putting his hand into his jacket pocket and you could see the outline of that – ' he pointed at the revolver. 'So we followed him up.'

Bricker had attached handcuffs to Kellett-Brown and was hauling him to his feet. 'Come on, you,' he said. He turned to Charles. 'Does he always smell this bad?'

''Fraid so.'

Bricker turned to one of the nurses. 'Anywhere we can keep this bloke until the Met arrive? He's not really our concern.'

'Yes. Follow me. Shall we call 999?'

'Yes, please.'

Bricker dragged Kellett-Brown out of the room. Sloane turned to leave, his good hand on the door handle. 'I'll get one of the Met boys to take your statement. Any more of your former colleagues want to kill you, do you suppose?'

'I hope not,' replied Charles, lightly. But then, with greater gravity: 'No. I don't think so.'

'You might want to think about that, Charles, when considering your career options. See you.'

The door closed. Charles resumed his place on the bed. He closed his eyes and waited until his thudding heartbeat slowed to normal. He suddenly felt profoundly tired and wondered if he might be able to sleep, but he could not calm his seething mind. DC Sloane's final comment was something he had been turning over incessantly for several days. Every part of his life seemed shattered, like the shards of a smashed mirror, and he had no idea how to put them back together again. Could he really go back to Chancery Court after two of his colleagues had tried to kill him? And then there were the tattered remnants of his private life. He was single now; where was he going to live? He'd have to go back to Putt Green and sort out Henrietta's affairs and, he supposed, eventually get the house sold, but he wasn't sure he could face it.

And then there was Rachel's parting shot. He opened his eyes and gingerly reached over to the bedside table where a slip of paper protruded from underneath the fruit bowl. Written on it in Rachel's firm angular hand was a telephone number, the number of his parents' home somewhere in north London.

Charles turned the scrap of paper over and over in his hands, contemplating the ever-shifting grey clouds as they scudded past his bedroom window. Then he reached for the telephone. First things first.

Simon Michael was called to the Bar by the Honourable Society of the Middle Temple in 1978. In his many years of prosecuting and defending criminal cases he has dealt with a wide selection of murderers, armed robbers, con artists and other assorted villainy.

A storyteller all his life, Simon started writing short stories at school. His first novel (co-written) was published by Grafton in 1988 and was followed in 1989 by his first solo novel, *The Cut Throat*, the first of the Charles Holborne series, based on Simon's own experiences at the criminal Bar. *The Cut Throat* was successful in the UK (WH Allen) and in the USA (St Martin's Press) and the next in the series, *The Long Lie*, was published in 1992. Between the two, in 1991, Simon's short story "Split" was shortlisted for the Cosmopolitan/Perrier Short Story Award. He was also commissioned to write two feature screenplays.

Simon then put writing aside to concentrate on his career at the Bar. After a further 25 years' experience he now has sufficient plots based on real cases for another dozen legal thrillers.

Simon still practises law countrywide but now works only part-time. He lives with his wife and youngest child in Bedfordshire. He is a founder member of the Ampthill Literary Festival.

ISBN 9781911129394, £8.99, paperback

'**An Honest Man** drops you into the murky depths of gangland
London when the Krays and Richardsons were in their prime.
The criminal trial at the Old Bailey is gripping and utterly
compelling, as well as thought provoking. The author keeps
us guessing with clever, authentic twists and turns as Charles
Holborne seeks justice for his client. Brilliant! ... a must read ...
a rare treat of an insight into a trial.' – RC Bridgestock, author of
the bestselling DI Dylan series, story consultant to BBC's *Happy
Valley* and ITV's *Scott & Bailey*.

The thrilling sequel to **The Brief** is out now and is available
from Amazon and all good bookshops.